Late Night Show

T.J. Alexian

*To Rose —
all the best
+ TJ Alexian*

Late Night Show

Copyright 2018 T.J. Alexian

Acknowledgements

This book took a while to get out into the world. And perhaps as a result, it's probably impossible to name everyone who had some say in the matter. If I've left you out, please accept my apologies.

A very special thanks to Mary Ann and Jackie, who both provided editorial insight and numerous helpful suggestions, each in their own distinct style. This story is truly stronger for your insights, suggestions, and in some cases, brutal honesty (some of which it took me weeks to absorb).

Thank you to my terrific cover artist, Renee Barratt.

To my kids, Krista, Kayla, Alex and T.J. for your love and support. All of you have added something to this story. And to Josie, who I was separating from at the time I started writing this. Yes, it began that long ago!

To Caryn, for being there at a certain point in time. And to Mary-Beth, Mig, Carol, Diana, Jim and so many others for your review and suggestions of previous drafts through the years.

To Mom and Dad, for all your support through the years. I have such vivid memories of writing some of these chapters at the beach house.

To Corb, who will be my married mate, come this July.

Thank you, all of you, for all that you've done, to make this book..and my life...that much better.

CHAPTER ONE

Hey, baby, do you know who I am?

It's addictive I know it and kind of thrilling too, which is why I guess most addictions exist. It makes me feel like I'm Queen of the Night, which is saying a lot given the life I lead.

Yeah, that's it. Queen of the Night, I like that. I control the vertical. I control the horizontal. Which brings us back to . . . this person I'm supposed to know.

NIGHTQUEEN22: No, baby, who are you?

I glance at his screen name. I mean, it has to be a he. Undertaker_16. Tall, dark, and six feet under, eh?

His response is rapid.

UNDERTAKER_16: I'm the one who's going to make you scream tonight.

Make me scream, eh? That sounds a little stalkerish. Oh, and by the way, I seriously doubt it. One of my golden rules is I don't get digitally horizontal with anyone who hits on me in the first five seconds. Not ever. You never know who the person really is on the receiving end, no matter how hot they look. And that reminds me, how hot is the screaming Undertaker anyway?

Let's take a look. I'll drag my mouse over to his name, check out his profile, and . . .

Oh, ick.

He's at least 40 and balding with straggly dishwater hair and a disgusting leer. What, he didn't think I'd notice? How stupid does he think I am? I'm Queen of the Night, buddy. I don't get fooled by anyone.

UNDERTAKER_16: Skype?

Go back to ChatRoulette I want to type. But you never know when I might need a little extra in my pathetic checking account. Instead I type:

NIGHTQUEEN22: Maybe if you treat me right.

There. Vague. Noncommittal. He doesn't need to know it's never going to happen.

UNDERTAKER_16: Cha ching.

Cha-ching this, creep. I'm not in a Girls Gone Wild kind of mood right now. I'd rather talk to normal people who aren't obsessed with show-and-tell. Emphasis on the show.

By the way, in case you haven't guessed, my addiction? It's not exactly crack; it's webcams. I'm part of a webcam community called PeoplesCam.com. Have been for about six months and I have all of 142 loyal followers, thank you very much.

Not that those numbers mean much. Most of the time you'll find me hanging in a certain special video chatroom on PeoplesCam. It's called GroundUnder and it's hosted by the lovely Nautical Ninja. She's a gamer from Wellington, New Zealand, with green eyes and an opinion on everything. One day, for no particular reason, I entered her room and I've been there ever since.

I should expand my horizons. Sometimes I actually do. PeoplesCam has hundreds of different chatrooms broken down by interests and hobbies. If I were a proper queen, I'd spend my time whoring myself out to each and every one of them, ordering them to curtsy.

If I were smart, I'd spend some time in the Late Night section every now and then. It's probably where the Undertaker belongs.

Anyway, it's a slow night in GroundUnder-land. I don't even have my mike on, I'm in message only mode listening to the Ninja talk to JadeMermaid (from Calgary) about this badass cat she named after some character in Harry Potter. Hey, I'm not judging.

Occasionally they throw some of the conversation my way. Right now for example. Like, the Ninja just said, with her cute Australian accent, "Wyke up, Jeannette! How was your day at Julliard, my pretty ballerina?"

Oh, yeah. About that. They think I'm a dancer living in New York City and going to Julliard. This is the internet, guys. Sometimes you get creative.

NIGHTQUEEN22: It was okay.

KTDid: Going all silent on us, NightQueen?

KTDid is about my age and lives on a ranch in California. She raises horses. Compared to her, I'm a super underachiever in real life. That might be why my life on camera is such a lie. I smile and nod.

NIGHTQUEEN22: Trying to study for a big test tomorrow.

That much is true.

A new screen pops up in the chat room.

WIREHANGER: Hey, babyfish :)

WIREHANGER: How do you keep a blonde busy all day?

I scan the screen name and smile. Josh, my best friend in the whole wide world. King of the dumb blonde jokes. We've been friends since my Mom first moved me to the boondocks from New York City. (See, the NYC part isn't a complete lie.)

He's the only person in the Godforsaken town I live in who knows about my obsession. No one else would understand; he does. We let him hang around GroundUnder. Token white male.

Bored with my lame attempt at studying, I push Biology 101 off the blue and white checkered spread that covers my bed. It bounces off my white metal bedframe and falls onto the messy floor, crashing on top of my favorite stuffed pet, Mrs. Tibbs. She stares up at me with lifeless eyes. I blow her a kiss and unwrap the stick of gum that's been trapped underneath the most boring textbook in the world.

Biology 101. This test is not going to turn out well. I might seriously have to drop the class.

Anyway, back to Josh's dumb blonde joke.

NIGHTQUEEN22: Dunno. How?

WIREHANGER: Put her in a round room and tell her to go sit in the corner

NIGHTQUEEN22: Ha.

"Hey, NightQueen," KTDid says on camera. "Is that a private conversation or can anyone join in?"

I smile and wave and switch to private chat mode.

NIGHTQUEEN22: How's it going?

WIREHANGER: Busy doing nothing

NIGHTQUEEN22: Same here. I almost flattened my kitty. :(

WIREHANGER: Don't worry. Your kitty's stuffed.

NIGHTQUEEN22: She's such a pig.

WIREHANGER: LOL I'm trying to talk to a REAL kitty, but she doesn't talk back either

I smile. Poor Josh. Nice guy, but not exactly the lady's choice. He's hopeless around girls even on a site like this. In fact, he attracts more guys, which amuses me to no end. I've tried to show him the ropes—what not to say, what not to wear—Josh lets his hormones rule. He's a guy. Worse. He's too obvious. Way too obvious and too anxious. And the blonde jokes. Don't get me started on his dumb blonde jokes. He's a rejection waiting to happen.

Josh is like the brother I never wanted. He's never once tried to make a move on me. I'm not sure whether I should be upset or grateful.

NIGHTQUEEN22: What does kitty call herself?

I'm bored. I don't want to do any studying. It's getting late. I want to paint my toenails and hit the sack. Mom's coming home from work any time now and I'd like to see her for a minute or two before the week ends.

WIREHANGER: Tulip2

Okay, Tulip2, let's see why Josh thinks you're all that and a saucer of milk.

I type in her screen name and her image appears. WTF? Black spiky hair. Five piercings per body part—at least those parts I can see on the screen. Is that a Rottweiler tattoo? I have to laugh.

NIGHTQUEEN22: She looks like a spider!

WIREHANGER: I know. She's very dark and scary. My kinda kitty.

NIGHTQUEEN22: She's spiky. She isn't much of a tulip. Not even a dead one.

WIREHANGER: Who wants a tulip? I wanna talk 2 a spider!

NIGHTQUEEN22: Try not to get trapped in her webcam.

See? That's what I mean. Josh has no taste, and he's bound to get burned trying to snag tough venomous little spiders like Tulip2. She's going to take one look at his scrawny body, bushy red hair and freckle explosion, laugh until she drops, and then freeze him out.

NIGHTQUEEN22: You're better off letting me choose your girlfriends.

WIREHANGER: Very funny. So who WOULD be a good pick?

For Josh? I sit back a bit. A site like PeoplesCam wouldn't exactly be the first place to go looking for romance. Still, I've gone through all my friends at school and even considered frenemies, trying to find him a love slave. Every single time: Disaster.

Well, why not this site? Although it might be nice to see him talk to someone who didn't look like they escaped from a Fang Bangers convention.

NIGHTQUEEN22: Give me a minute.

I glance back at GroundUnder:

NIGHTQUEEN22: gtg, ladies. It's been lovely chatting with you. I need to find Wirehanger a mate!

NAUTICALNINJA: Tell him to ring me if he's ever in Wellington!

She shakes her head and her ruby red hair bobs up and down. She blows me a kiss. I give her two thumbs up and exit.

Okay, so where should I start my search?

The problem with a site like PeoplesCam is it's not meant to be a dating site. It has too many private sites with only a dozen or so people in each. It wouldn't be right to barge into one and ask if they want to flirt with my best friend. They might find it annoying.

Hmmm. Except in the Late Night section.

Of course! Why didn't I think of it sooner? I can rent him out!

Late Night is where you find all the more grown up things, like BDSM or the 420 friendly crowds. Yeah, I've been on it a little.

There has to be someone slightly venomous for him there.

Sold.

I click to the home page and navigate to Late Night. I scroll down the list of active rooms for the perfect one. The greatest congregation of eligible venomous females for my hormone riddled friend.

World of Freaks? Maybe.

StonersUnited? Maybe not.

Hmmm. The RabbitHole.

That sounds like it might have possibilities! Okay. Time to take a trip down the RabbitHole for Josh.

The room has 18 watchers and only 10 people with live broadcast. There must be someone cool Josh can . . .

Ugh. This RabbitHole may not have the right bunnies after all. The Widowmaker? She's at least 60. Brrrr.

Maybe I should send Josh to the Widowmaker to be a pain. No, he'd like that too much. And might ask to see her wrinkles.

I scroll down some more.

Hmmm. Okay.

I sit back in my chair. This one looks interesting.

GOASKALICE. Pretty fitting for a RabbitHole.

I click on her webcam. I size up the girl on the screen. Looks to be my age. Dirty blonde hair cut to her shoulders. Wide brown eyes. Full lips. Shiny white skin. She might be related to elves. She's wearing a black tee and her skin seems to glow in the light of the camera.

My eyes glance past her to look into her room. She's sitting on a black leather chair. Behind her I can make out red wallpaper. That's about it.

NIGHTQUEEN22: Try this one. GoAskAlice. She's in the Late Night section, RabbitHole room.

WIREHANGER: k

I sit there, watching Alice watch the camera. She has a nice face. She looks sweet, even if she hasn't smiled once. She reminds me of someone. No, something. But what?

It takes me a few seconds to notice something's off. Then it dawns on me. She hasn't moved. Not even to blink her eyes. Is her webcam frozen? No, wait, she just changed position, then froze again.

Oh, I get it. Her camera isn't in real time. How old school! I didn't know webcams could still work like that.

One . . . two . . . her image changes every three seconds. I let the clock tick away waiting for the next shot to come up then freeze again.

She lifts her head. Her attention has shifted. Josh?

Her soft lips are parted. She's very pretty. I've picked well.

A wounded bird. That's it. She looks like a wounded bird.

Next moment, her head is back up staring at the screen. She has a blank look in her eye and her teeth appear to be clenched. No smiles. That's not good . . .

NIGHTQUEEN22: Okay, what happened?

WIREHANGER: Ummmm

NIGHTQUEEN22: So?

WIREHANGER: I sent her a PM

NIGHTQUEEN22: And?

WIREHANGER: She told me to go somewhere super-hot AND THEN she told me what to do with myself while I was down there

NIGHTQUEEN22: WHAT?

> My laughter echoes through my empty house.
> Is the wounded bird a tiger in disguise? Nah, it has to be Josh.

NIGHTQUEEN22: What'd you say?

WIREHANGER: Nothing! I asked her how's it hanging.

NIGHTQUEEN22: JOSHHH! She doesn't have an IT to hang, you moron.

WIREHANGER: I told you it wouldn't work.

NIGHTQUEEN22: Do I have to write your lines for you, too?

WIREHANGER: g2g Later!

Josh is off. I shake my head and stare at the screen, defeated. Absolutely hopeless. Well, maybe it's time for me to leave and end my reign. At least for tonight.

My stomach starts to rumble, because I haven't eaten since four. It might be nice to get some chips and salsa and wait in the kitchen for Mom.

But for some reason, I can't leave my seat. All I can do is sit there, staring at Alice.

It's dark in her room. I can't see the red wallpaper any more, only shadows. I can only make out her face and shoulders.

She stares at the screen, motionless. Did her webcam freeze? But no, the background light on the monitor changes with the next frame, so it's clear everything's still working.

I bend down to pick up Mrs. Tibbs. Once she's on my lap, I push up her floppy white head and twist her nose affectionately. I stroke her soft stuffed animal body and glance back at Alice.

What is Alice's world like? These tiny screens are like entrances into someone else's world. You can easily get drawn in if you're not careful.

I want to talk to her.

There's a little wiggle in my stomach. Should I? Nonsense. I'm royalty. I can talk to whoever I want. Ignoring the parental voice inside my head I decide to go for it.

NIGHTQUEEN22: Hey, there.

Why am I so insecure all of a sudden? Most people I don't give two shits about, but something's different about her. Will she turn me down the way she did Josh? Maybe she isn't looking to talk to anyone. Maybe she had a fight with her boyfriend and that's why she looks so sad. Like, she returned home from a night out and things ended badly. Maybe he said it was over.

I hear a leopard purr.

My heart starts to race. She's answered.

GOASKALICE: Hi.

Hi. Well, it's a start.

"Is everything all right?" Then, feeling bold: "You look sad."

I sit there, waiting with Mrs. Tibbs. No response. No way am I going to let it end there. I need to keep the conversation going.

GOASKALICE: My name's Jeannette. I call myself the Queen of the Night—big laff

I watch her. She actually smiles for a second! Her smile seems to transform her, fills everything out, completing the sweetness I imagined in her face.

Three seconds later, it's replaced by a frown. How disappointing. I wish I'd saved the image.

GOASKALICE: I'm

GOASKALICE: That's funny

GOASKALICE: I'm lost in the night.

Lost? I straighten my shoulders and push kitty to the floor. Lost. I wasn't expecting that one.

NIGHTQUEEN22: What do you mean?

She lowers her head. All I can see is a crown of gold hair. What's she talking about? Why is she lost?

She stares straight at the camera, straight at me, and the look on her face makes me believe she really has been eaten up by the darkness. The sweetness from a few seconds ago is completely gone, as if never existed.

I hear the leopard purr again. A return message.

GOASKALICE: Help me.

Her message hits me like a fork in a toaster.

NIGHTQUEEN22: Help you?

NIGHTQUEEN22: How?

NIGHTQUEEN22: What can I do?

I lean forward, as if I could reach out a hand to save her. Seconds tick away. Time runs out. A new image springs up.

This one is a fuzzy blur. I can't make out much, save for a swirl of yellow in the center of the screen. It must be her dirty blonde hair, as if she lunged forward.

Lunged? Or been pushed?

Then the picture goes black. It's too late.

I sit there staring at the flickering words on the screen.

GOASKALICE: Help me

CHAPTER TWO

"Kami Corley!"

They like to play the music loud at the Fandango Café, but even the blast of Calypso music coming from the speakers is no match for Daphne's bellow, which carries clear over from the other side of the room.

Yes, Kami Corley is my real name. It's not Jeannette, NightQueen22 or even babyfish. Those are convenient covers.

I decide to ignore her sonic boom and pretend I'm adding up a bill. Daphne was one of the first people I met when we moved here. I didn't get warm vibes from her then, and they've grown even colder since.

Maybe she'll forget about me. I can hope. Maybe one of the exotic plants hanging from the watermelon-colored walls will turn into a man-eater and gobble her up.

No such luck.

Daphne makes her way to the counter and pushes the bill aside. She's wearing a fluffy fake furry hooded coat as protection from the cold, rainy afternoon. A splotch of rain lands on my clean counter, and I fight the urge to wipe it dry.

My manager, Robyn, is busy helping a customer but looking my way. I shake my head. I can handle Daphne all by myself.

"Kami Corley!" Daphne loves to make a big show of my name. "Have YOU seen IT yet?" Like, OMG. Daphne seems so super excited. Her dark, bushy hair keeps bobbing up and down wildly, and her smile takes up half of her face, revealing two rows of picture-perfect white teeth, the best money can buy. Of course, this is Daphne's 'after' shot. Her father spent a fortune on those teeth. Before that, Daphne had a smile only a rabbit would love.

"See what, Daphne?"

"THE gift, of course!" Daphne reaches out and dangles a key under my nose. I'm tempted to sneeze. "Daddy bought me the most FABULOUS little yellow car!"

Oh. The car. Yeah, I heard about that. Who hadn't? Daphne got a yellow Bug for her eighteenth birthday but was oh-so-upset because it wasn't "yellow enough." It was a matter of time before daddy gave in. But then, he can afford it. He has more money than the man who invented underwear. At least, more money than anyone else in

Farnham. In fact, he owns the Fandango Café, which is another reason I don't want to call Robyn over.

I can't resist. I look straight at Daphne and bat my eyes dumber than a supermodel. "Fabulous! So when are you taking me for a ride, Daphne?"

Daphne wrinkles her nose as if I said something smelly. "Well, maybe SOMEday." She pockets the keys. Then again, probably not. She takes a mirror from her other pocket to check her face for damage. As if I had nothing better to do than to stand there and watch Daphne preen. Natural beauty my unwaxed eyebrows.

Just for kicks, I take a look at my reflection in the stainless steel surface of the napkin container.

Yep, that's me. Dark hair, although mine's a softer shade of brown than Daphne's. Oh, and I could use a haircut; it's moving below my shoulders. Ugh. Same too-long forehead, same blue eyes Daddy always said were his grandmother's. When I was a little kid, I was afraid I had stolen them from her.

"Oh!" Daphne's face brightens. "I saw your Mom last night at that donut place. What a DUMP, girlfriend! Isn't she AFRAID to work all alone at night?"

I grit my teeth. Daphne can say what she wants to me, but bring up Mom and I see red. Calm down. Laugh and lie, girl. Laugh and lie.

"Mom said the night person called in sick." As if you need to know that Nancy the night girl called in sick.

"Then your mother should STAND UP to her boss and say 'If she doesn't work, NEITHER DO I!'" Daphne hands are on her hips, and she's doing her best Elizabeth Warren.

I suppose that's easy to say when you work for your daddy, Daphne. Oh, did I say work?

There are so many things I'd like to say.

Some of us don't have it so easy, Daphne. Some of us don't have a daddy any more. We have a mommy who does her best, which means holding down two jobs and taking accounting courses in her spare time so we can afford to live in a house that's about the size of the garage you store that cute little Bug in.

When I get angry, the tips of my ears turn red. I can feel them changing now. "Listen, Daphne—"

"Hey, babyfish!"

And like that, Josh is here to save me before I say anything stupid.

He walks over, fumbling around, trying to tie the strings of his apron together. It's clear he just got to work, to assume his glamorous role as fry cook for the not-so-rich or famous.

"You're late." I smile sweetly. "Robyn's gonna have you for lunch."

"I'm so good I bet she makes me the daily special." With a groan, he finally manages to tie the string behind his back.

"DAPHNE!" He calls her name loudly and I watch her face grow red. If anyone can get to her, it's Josh. One more reason I like the guy. "How's life? Run anyone over in your itty bitty bananamobile?"

It takes her a minute to recover, but she bounces back. "Not if you're still alive."

"Oh, come on, Daphne," he whispers, using his deepest, sexiest voice, which for Josh isn't deep or sexy. "You know you'd rather have me in the back seat of your car, not underneath it."

"Think what you want," she snaps. "But don't try thinking too hard or you'll hurt yourself." Without saying goodbye, she spins around and leaves us in the dust.

"Feisty. I like it!" Then, dead serious. "Oh. Robyn's looking at me. I am gonna be the daily special."

I grab his arm before he gets away. "About last night . . ."

"What about it?" He shrugs. "Boy meets girl, boy asks how it's hanging, boy gets burned. Happens to me all the time."

"That's not what I'm talking about. That girl last night. The one I picked for you. Something's wrong with her."

"Sure is," Josh laughs. "She said no, right?"

"Listen!" I have to talk fast, because I can see Robyn's getting ready to pounce. "I spoke to her after you signed off."

"You did?" Josh's bright blue eyes twinkle. "Babyfish, is this a side of you I've never seen? You were really impressed with her, huh?"

I know he's teasing, but I can feel those ears burning again. "Please. She looked sad so I tried to talk to her. And I did."

Josh whistled. "You got farther than I did. Ever think about becoming a vagitarian?"

"Josh! Listen! I asked what was wrong and she said some strange things. She asked for my help, Josh. Why would she need help? Then the screen went blank."

"You didn't read her profile last night, did you?"

I frown. "No. Why? What does it say?"

Josh winks and smiles so wide his freckled nose dips down. "Here comes Robyn. Read it yourself next time you become the Duchess of

Darkness or whatever you call yourself." With that, he's off to the kitchen, trying to avoid the wrath of Robyn.

Her profile. Okay, fine. I'll see what it has to say.

CHAPTER THREE

I sit at my desk and try to concentrate on chapter four of Western Civ II, but I know in my heart I'm not going to be able to pay much attention to the adventures of some dead white guys for very long. I try my best though and stare at the book for all of five minutes before I give up and go back to my laptop.

The screen makes an angry hiss that cuts through the silence of the room. Mom is at work again, although after tonight she's promised to take it easy and only work one full-time job for at least three days.

I place my fingers on the keyboard. A small tickle of anticipation creeps up from the base of my spine.

Okay, Alice, let's see what you have to say.

www.PeoplesCam.com

The gee-you're-ugly purple and blue screen with the registered PeoplesCam logo appears. "PeoplesCam—connecting your world to the rest of the universe." I slide my cursor over the user profile field to type in Alice's screen name.

GoAskAlice. Why can't I stop thinking about her? Her smile keeps haunting me. Was Josh right? Do I have a girl crush on her? What made her look so sad? Why had she asked for help?

I have to see if she's around.

It takes a while for her webcam to come up, but finally I'm connected. Instead of a glimpse into her universe, I'm staring into the black void from the end of last night.

She isn't around. The tickle along my spine is replaced by a strange empty feeling in the pit of my stomach. I wonder, not for the first time, what happened after she signed off.

I admit it. I'm disappointed. But not defeated. It's time to take a look at that profile.

GoAskAlice. Okay Alice, I'm asking.

PeoplesCam ID: GoAskAlice
Real Name: What is reality, anyway?
Location: Out there
Age: 17
Relationship status: Please (that's NOT an invitation)

Gender: Female
Occupation: Personal dreamer
More About Me:
Interests: cupcakes, Narnia, superheros, steampunk, bad tattoos, diet Coke, chick flicks, pink hair, computers, Joe Manganiello, Princess Daisy, turbo jam. AFab rules!
Famous Last Words: We're all going down into the dark. Only some of us are gonna go sooner than others. How far down am I? Only the GKS knows
If youve got a key, don't vote for me.
Links: www.gks.com

Shit.

How aggravating. Her vital stats aren't that vital at all. In fact, they don't tell me anything, except that she likes Narnia. Which is pretty cool because I've always had a warm spot in my heart for C. S. Lewis, too.

But what are her famous last words about? We're all going down into the darkness. There's that talk of darkness again. Why is her life so dark?

And that last line: "Only the GKS knows for sure." What does GKS mean? Is it a band?

I grab my Android and do a quick search for GKS. Nothing.

Well, duh. There's a web site at the bottom of the page, so it has to stand for something. Her blog maybe? Nah, she doesn't seem like the blogging kind.

Curious, I click on the link.

My screen turns black. Even the web address is washed away. The empty feeling in my stomach is replaced with cold hard lead. Have I overloaded the delicate circuitry of my ancient three-year-old laptop? Again?

But slowly, in the bottom right hand corner of the screen, three letters form. Three little white letters.

GKS

I shake my mouse around trying to figure out whether I'm frozen or not. I'm not. I slide the arrow to the GKS logo. A small hand appears, the only link on the page.

I click. A window opens up.

"WELCOME TO GKS, YOUR DOORWAY TO ANOTHER SIDE OF ENTERTAINMENT. ENTER YOUR GKS ID AND PASSWORD."

Another side of entertainment? What does that mean?
Too strange. I hit the escape key and exit.
What the hell is Alice into?

CHAPTER FOUR

Alice isn't on until after midnight.

I don't sit around waiting. I finish Western Civ, work on some English. Spend an hour or two with the ladies of GroundUnder. Tonight, JadeMermaid is going on and on about some lame English actress who wants to make like Godzilla and take over the world. I play with Mrs. Tibbs, who doesn't play back, and I catnap a bit. Oh, I even visit Mom when she finally gets home at 11:15. That's early for her.

She's tired. We don't talk for long. She stands by the refrigerator, guzzling a glass of orange juice.

I tell her the Daphne story. "I have a friend who thinks you should tell your boss if Nancy can't work nights, you can't either."

Mom puts down her glass, wipes her mouth with the sleeve of her shirt, and gives me the stink eye. "Is this a good friend of yours?"

"Not good at all." I can't help but smile. I love getting a reaction out of her. "Not even a friend."

She opens her mouth to speak then stops. Shakes her head. "I have a message for her, but I'm too grumpy and tired and it wouldn't be nice." A quick kiss on the top of my head. "I'm going to bed, sweetie. I love you."

Grumpy. Honestly, I don't think I've seen her smile since forever. She looks so old lately. She let her hair go gray. She says it's been gray for almost ten years and she simply stopped dyeing it. I wish she hadn't given up the fight.

Right after she leaves, I run to the bathroom and stare in the mirror. I give my face a hard look, trying to imagine myself with gray hair. No way I'm going to let that happen until I'm ninety at least. No way.

And I send Josh a text message: Don't go gray.

He texts me back: Stay gold, Pony Boy.

So around 12:15 I'm in bed trying to sleep, but really staring at the ceiling. Then, with a jerk, I throw Mrs. Tibbs to the floor, roll over in bed, and open my laptop. I keep it on a TV table I stole from downstairs. It's right by my bed and set up in a way that gives me my best look for the webcam.

It's time to go on cam again. Time to pay a visit to Alice.

My eyes are so heavy. I sit up and fumble around in the darkness, searching for the keys on the keyboard and only getting every other one right. I should go back to sleep, but I'm pretty sure that's not going to happen.

In a flash, I'm on PeoplesCam. The Wi-Fi is actually behaving. Wow. I nibble at the edges of my cuticles, nervously. Will I find her in the RabbitHole again? I click and . . . there she is.

Everything is alive again.

She has the same sad look, is sitting in the same room with the red wallpaper. Only her clothes are different. This time she has on a sleeveless gray and white cardigan with silver buttons going up the front. She's staring at the screen with dead eyes.

I take in a deep breath and hold it in for a moment, my fingers hovering over the keyboard. Finally, I type.

NIGHTQUEEN22: Hey Alice.

It's about two frames before I get a response. It's what I hoped for, too. She flashes her Cheshire smile.

GOASKALICE: Hi

Contact. Perfect.

In the next frame, she has a finger to her lips. She looks like she's considering her next words carefully. What? Does she regret what she typed last night? Afraid I might dig deeper?

Well, I plan to. I'm dying to ask her more, even if it might scare her away.

I wrack my brain trying to think. What can I say to get her to open up? Working at it can be awfully hard, especially with so much to say. And when you're so tired. Should I talk about the weather? Lame. Narnia, maybe? What can I say about that? Think, think . . .

She beats me to the punch.

GOASKALICE: I shouldnt have said what I did. I didnt mean it. It was stupid of me

NIGHTQUEEN22: Why did you?

There's a huge lag before she says anything. I watch her brush her hair back with her fingers and close her eyes. I see a black mark on her upper arm, but can't make out what it is. A tattoo? A bruise?

Her arm goes down. The mark disappears.

GOASKALICE: I dont know

NIGHTQUEEN22: I know I could use help practically every day.

NIGHTQUEEN22: My Dad had his brains blown away two years ago. My Mom's a mess and she stuck me away in some stupid little town. All I want is to get back to NYC and slurp an espresso in Central Park.

GOASKALICE: Your dad had his brains blown away?

Wait. Why had I typed that?

NIGHTQUEEN22: Don't want to talk about it.

GOASKALICE: Id do anything to be AWAY from the city

NIGHTQUEEN22: You live in New York City?

GOASKALICE: No. Its a city just the same

NIGHTQUEEN22: I'd take any city over this place. It's so flat and so boring and so freaking cold right now. NYC can be way colder in February, but I'd do anything to breathe in some sweet smog. To be crammed into a booth at Gils. Walk down Times Square at night.

GOASKALICE: It's freaking cold here too.

GOASKALICE: Ive never been to NYC but I could go for a burger from a little tin diner

NIGHTQUEEN22: Mmmm, sounds good. Can we switch places?

I glance at the screen. Sometimes when you're typing, you forget to look at the person you're talking to. Her head is tilted back, mouth open, and she's pushing back against the leather chair. She's laughing. Laughing?

Finally, three seconds later, she's looking serious again.

GOASKALICE: Believe me

GOASKALICE: You wouldnt

Okay, now it's time to get serious back.

NIGHTQUEEN22: Why not?

No answer. But I can't stop there.

NIGHTQUEEN22: Alice, why aren't you in real time? Is your web cam broken?

GOASKALICE: Something like that

GOASKALICE: Im lucky it works on here at all

NIGHTQUEEN22: I want to talk to you real time

GOASKALICE: I wish you could

GOASKALICE: Believe me

I take another deep breath.

NIGHTQUEEN22: What do U need help with?

GOASKALICE: I think

The cursor blinks.
And blinks.
And blinks.
The words hang there. Think what? It's all I can do not to type back, to ask more. But I'm afraid if I push too hard Alice will hop right back into her rabbit hole.

GOASKALICE: It would be nice to have someone 2 talk 2

NIGHTQUEEN22: Talk 2 me.

I want to know so badly what's going on in her head. I feel like we're making a connection, even if she's holding back. It's like I have this tunnel into her room, that her eyes staring out from this box are looking into mine. Even with the delay. But next image she's turned away.

GOASKALICE: I dont know who you are Ur just a goldfish staring out from another bowl. Dont you have any other friends 2 talk to, Jeannette?

Well, that's harsh. And by the way, no, I don't.
Oh, and then there's the Jeannette thing. Well, if I want her to trust me, I might as well start there.

NIGHTQUEEN22: My real name's Kami.

NIGHTQUEEN22: I don't let every1 know who I really am.

NIGHTQUEEN22: Only people I trust.

Her gaze on the screen softens. She almost smiles again.

GOASKALICE: Thank you.

NIGHTQUEEN22: I have one person I can talk to about anything. He's a guy, believe it or not. He tried to hit on you last night. His screen name is Wirehanger.

GOASKALICE: You mean the hows it hanging guy?

NIGHTQUEEN22: That's the one. I told him I should write his lines for him.

GOASKALICE: He needs your help!!!

New screen. My image laughs the same time hers does. She lets her teeth show, breaks out into a wide smile.

It feels nice, almost like girl talk. I don't have any girl friends in Farnham, Ohio. Most girls treat me like a stranger, even though I've been around for two years now. Even though I graduated from their high school and I'm going to their community college. Doesn't matter. None of the girls here would know what it's like to taste a burger from a tin diner and they treat me like a freak because I know. I wish—

NIGHTQUEEN22: I wish you could trust me.

She lowers her head.

GOASKALICE: I cant. I do and Im dead.

I consider my next words carefully.

NIGHTQUEEN22: Isn't there anyone you CAN talk to?

The cursor blinks. And blinks.

GOASKALICE: I can talk to Jeremy

NIGHTQUEEN22: Is Jeremy your boyfriend?

Nothing. I measure the silence in terms of frame changes. At least a dozen. It's time to try again.

NIGHTQUEEN22: Do you trust him?

More dead space. This time I lose track of the frame changes.

What time is it? 1:30. My arm is starting to fall asleep. I should fall asleep too, but I'm determined to see this through.

GOASKALICE: Im not sure who to trust any more

I look around the room, out into the hallway. Toward mom's room. I have to say this, have to get it off my chest.

NIGHTQUEEN22: I haven't known who to trust since Dad died. Even Josh doesn't get everything. You never know when they're going to be yanked away from you. Keep your mouth shut and keep it to yourself. That how U feel?

GOASKALICE: Kind of

I uncross my legs, feeling almost intoxicated. I can't believe I typed what I did. I've never said that to anyone else. Mom's tried to get me to talk to all sorts of therapists. Yet here, in front of a stranger . . .
She stares at the screen with curiosity in her eyes.

GOASKALICE: Kami can I ask you something

NIGHTQUEEN22: Sure.

GOASKALICE: Whats it like to be normal?

NIGHTQUEEN22: After what I said, you call me NORMAL?

GOASKALICE: Youre in a world thats safe, Kami You may not be able to trust but you have people U can turn to

What do I say to that?

GOASKALICE: Whats school like

GOASKALICE: I havent been for so long. I kinda miss it

NIGHTQUEEN22: Why haven't you been to school?

No answer. For a long time.

GOASKALICE: Just stopped going

NIGHTQUEEN22: It's okay. The college I go to sucks. I'm barely passing half my classes. Lunch with Josh is the best part.

GOASKALICE: Do U have a lot of friends?

NIGHTQUEEN22: I have Josh.

NIGHTQUEEN22: Can I ask U something?

GOASKALICE: You can ask

NIGHTQUEEN22: Is there anything in the world that could save you from the darkness?

GOASKALICE: Jeremy has what I need

NIGHTQUEEN22: What's that?

GOASKALICE: Hey wanna see something?

She has a smile on her face, although it's more of a twisted grin. The next image I see from her rabbit hole is a blur. Oh. The camera's being repositioned.

When things refocus, the camera is close to the wall. I can make out the white spots on the wallpaper.

The camera moves in closer. No, not white spots. They form a pattern. Little people?

The camera's even closer with the next frame. No, not people. Cherubs. With puckered lips and tiny feathered wings.

The next image I can see part of Alice's face, her wide smile, and a finger outstretched pointing to a cherub.

GOASKALICE: I like to fly with the angels

I'm not sure what to say.

NIGHTQUEEN22: It's better than the alternative.

GOASKALICE: I know, right? Thats where I am right now. Flying. At least they let me fly every now and then.

The picture changes. She's stretched out her arms as if to fly. I'm able to catch another look at the black mark on her upper arm. I still can't make it out.

NIGHTQUEEN22: Alice, what does GKS stand for?

I wait breathlessly for the next image. She looks upset. She's holding the arm with the black mark.

NIGHTQUEEN22: I saw it in your profile. What does it mean?

GOASKALICE: It doesn't mean anything Its a saying

NIGHTQUEEN22: But what does it mean?

GOASKALICE: Will tell you next time G2G Have an appointment

NIGHTQUEEN22: An appointment?

NIGHTQUEEN22: But when's the next time?

GOASKALICE: Ive G2G Kami

NIGHTQUEEN22: Alice!

GOASKALICE: My names Barbara

NIGHTQUEEN22: Barbara?

GOASKALICE: 11:00 Friday night See you then.

The last shot Jeanette/Kami has of Alice/Barbara is a glance to her right. As if someone's entered the room. Then the screen goes blank.

CHAPTER FIVE

"Seriously, babyfish. Tell me the truth. Are you ever going to learn to drive?"

"That depends. When are you going to hand me the keys to your silver shitbox?"

"Oh, no. No no no. I like the silver shitbox and I like staying alive even better." He sits there and contemplates my sad face. "Okay, maybe someday I'll let you drive my car. If you treat me nice. Speaking of driving, you ever hear the one about the three blondes that drove to Disneyland?"

Leave it to Josh to turn my lack of driving ability into a dumb blonde joke.

It's lunchtime, and we're hiding out in the prop room in the theater building, sitting on a blue couch probably used for some dumb comedy from years gone by. It's like our private lunch emporium.

During orientation week at good old Stonington Community College, when we should have been going to some kind of meet your classmates kind of thing, Josh and I decided to be anti-social and wander around the school. We ended up backstage of the auditorium where we found this out-of-the-way room where all the props are stored. Nobody ever seems to be around, and it's way better than trying to fight for space in the cafeteria. We spent the whole first semester hiding here without anyone catching us and now we're into the second semester and haven't had problems yet.

P.S. Neither of us are in the theater program. Josh leans toward psychology, and I'm not sure what I want to major in. A Bachelor's degree in Slackerology? Yes, please. When I'm homeless, it will look great taped to my cardboard box.

Anyway, back to the dumb blonde joke. I groan and prepare for the worst. "No, Josh, I don't think you did."

"They were driving in this car for four hours, see, and finally they saw a sign that said, 'Disneyland: Left.' So, they turned around and went home . . . ."

Ouch. I don't know what's worse: Josh's joke or my sorry excuse for a tuna fish sandwich.

Lunch in the prop room may be our daily ritual, but if Josh keeps it up he's not going to make it out alive today. Besides the awful jokes, I'm being forced to listen to him babble on about my taste in women.

Like: "You only picked Barbara because you wanted her for yourself," he says, grinning his silly monkey grin. "I never should have asked you to be my matchmaker. You keep all the good bitches for yourself."

"How can you say that? The only girl I haven't tried to fix you up with is Daphne!"

"Yeah, let's talk about that. She was looking fine last night. Did you see her checking out my moves? Woof." He chomps into an apple as if he's Adam.

"You're desperate." I frown. Without thinking, I pick up a Styrofoam life preserver with the words Anything Goes scribbled on it. I absently trace the letters. "But Alice is seriously messed up . . . I mean, Barbara. Or whatever her name is. I want to help."

"You can. Help yourself and stay away from her."

"I can't!" I squeeze too hard and the life preserver makes a crunching noise. Panicking, I throw it to Josh who raises a skinny arm and bats it aside. The life preserver hits a pile of hats and falls to the floor, not-so-preserved anymore.

And the hats come crashing down.

Too bad, but I'm in no mood for fallen hats. "I may be the only person she talks to. If I don't help her, things could get worse. I think she's on her own, Josh. Probably a runaway. And she's taking something, too. I think. Probably coke."

Josh snorts. "Man, you are such a cop's daughter! How can she be a runaway if she's on that webcam?"

Oh. Hmmm. "I don't know."

"She's on IM with you more than I am!"

"We only talked for a few minutes last night, seriously." Liar. But he doesn't need to know I waited up all night to talk to her. He'd only tease me. And why did I do that, anyway?

Frustrated, I give up on my tuna sandwich and shove it into a crinkly paper bag. "Why? Are you jealous?"

"Yes. Jealous she likes you more than me!"

"Can I help it if she has good taste?" I bat my eyes, flirtatiously.

Josh isn't falling for it. "Why do you think she's a coke fiend, Sherlock?"

"She told me she gets to fly with the angels every once in a while. What else could she mean?"

"She's into nude hang gliding?" Josh finishes off his apple and attempts an overhand toss into the wastebasket located next to a framed portrait of the Mona Lisa. It bounces off the rim and lands on his sneaker. He grins. "Think I should try out for the basketball team? They're having try-outs."

"Great, so you can shower with all the boys?" I smile sweetly and stick out my tongue. Hey, if he can accuse me of having a girl crush on Barbara . . . . "I'm surprised they even have a basketball team at Stonington. I'd think the best they could afford would be a beach ball and some chicken wire."

Josh laughs, but looks at me strangely. "That's why I'm surprised you don't know how to drive. You hate Farnham so much, I'd think you'd want to get your license and get the hell out of here. Maybe even drive yourself to wherever Barbara is and be a part of her world."

"What? Like you don't hate Farnham? Because I know you do."

His voice is soft. "Not as much as you do. Nobody could hate this place that much. Besides, I've lived here all my life. I don't know any better."

I can feel the temperature rising in the room. Why is Josh getting so serious? "Well, I do. And by the way, I do know how to drive. I only need to get my license, that's all. It's one of the things Mom says she'll get around to doing."

"You can do it yourself." I must have given him one of my Mommie Dearest looks for that one. In fact, I'm sure I did, because the next second he's all goofy charm and twinkling blue eyes. "I'm sorry, babyfish. I didn't mean to-"

"It's okay." And I mean it. I'm not going to fight. Thank God Josh is going to this go-nowhere school too, keeping me company during lunch. I don't know what I'd do without him around, and I don't want to find out. And not because I don't have a license. I'd be seriously lost without him, with or without his wheels.

"What about Jeremy?" Josh asks as he bends down to pick up his apple core. "Barbara said she can talk to him. So she's not exactly all alone."

Jeremy. That part of the conversation was interesting. She said Jeremy has what she needs. Who is he? And why does it seem like Barbara doesn't totally trust him? Maybe because when I asked her point-blank, she couldn't say yes.

"How about if she's going to get hurt, Josh? Shouldn't I try to help?" I think about my dad. He spent his career putting his life on the line trying to save people from the darkness. Maybe I should be more like him.

Then again, look where that got him.

It's as if Josh can read my mind. He slides closer on the couch so our knees are touching. "If she's in so much danger, you'd better stay out of it. Call the police. Write to PeoplesCam if you're worried. But keep your nose out of it, babyfish." He leans in and kisses the tip of my nose. "Because it's a nice one. At least, I think so."

He pulls away. His steady blue eyes are staring into mine the whole time. Can he tell I'm shocked? What does that goofy smile on his face mean?

"See ya." And with that, Josh grabs the life preserver and places it around my neck. Then he jumps up and runs to the prop room door. With a slam, he's gone.

I sit on the couch more than a little confused. I look to Mona Lisa for help. Why did Josh McBee kiss me on the nose?

CHAPTER SIX

ATTN: PeopleSpeak Out!

To Whom It May Concern:

I've been on PeoplesCam for about six months now and always see that notice you put on the bottom of your home page that tells you what to do to report abuse.

I'm not certain this is abuse, but I'm worried about this one person. Her screen name is GoAskAlice, and from her profile, it looks like she's involved with a group called the GKS. I don't know what the GKS is, but I'm worried because of the things she's said.

I think Alice might be a runaway and I wonder if what she's doing with the GKS is legal.

Alice asked me to help her, but I don't know where to go. I've thought about telling the police, but I thought I'd check with you first. Have you heard anything about the GKS or received complaints? I'd be interested in anything you know and please let me know if you need any more information.

SEND.

Josh,

Why did you kiss me today? Was it a friendly kiss or was there more?

It was probably nothing, right? Some friends hit each other on the shoulder; others spank each other on the butt. I guess I'd rather have you kiss me than spank me on the butt, and I know you were trying to make things better after going on and on about Barbara and my driving.

You're right. It does bug me I don't drive yet. I keep putting it off and I'm not sure why. I should bug Mom to get it done or maybe do it myself. It would be good to have more freedom. Maybe I'd hate Farnham less if I could . . . I don't know, have an escape hatch?

Anyway, if the kiss meant more, say it.

In a way it'd be weird because we've been best friends for so long. I don't know if I want to mess that up. I like being able to talk to you about anything. I like the dumb jokes you make on the way to school. I like making Pikachu noises by the hanging rock. I like talking about the silly spiders you hit on. And I'm pretty certain we wouldn't be able to do that if we were dating.

But I guess, when you get right down to it, there is someone I haven't tried to set you up with at school. Me, right?

I wonder if that kiss means anything. Or whether my flirting with you means anything. And I wonder if we'd jkjkjkl

I'm not going to send this, am I?

DELETE.

Thank you for using PeopleSpeak Out!

This will serve as confirmation we have received and registered your comments and concerns. At the earliest convenience, we'll be in touch to secure additional information on the nature of your problem.

Here at PeoplesCam, community is at the heart of everything we do. Please let us know whether we can be of any additional service. In the meantime, why not consider an upgrade to your current membership? It's all about options and we want to make sure you've picked the best one to better manage your busy life. That's why we offer you a wide array of features, including . . .

DELETE.

Trash that sucker. Doublespeak, more like it.

CHAPTER SEVEN

More than ever, I can't wait for work to end.

What I'm wanting more than anything is to run to my room, do not pass GO, do not collect 200 dollars, to see if Barbara/Alice is around. She said next time I'd see her would be Friday night. That's tomorrow, but who knows? She might change her mind.

Part of me wonders whether she'll ever be on again.

First though, I have to get through the rest of the day, which means slaving away at Fandango. Josh is there too, but I've hardly seen him. At least, not to talk, you know?

I'm working the register again. Tonight has been especially crazy. Also, I'm stressed out because people keep handing me twenties and looking for change, so I'm forever running out of ones. Robyn keeps having to go into the back room to get me a new stack from the safe. Why can't everyone use plastic? So much easier. One swipe and it's over.

As for Josh, I guess he's busy bussing. There was one point about an hour ago where I looked across the room and caught him staring at me. He knows I caught him, too, because he smiled and pretended to fling a plateful of half-eaten potatoes my way. Is that his idea of flirting?

At long last, 9:30 arrives. As I finish counting the cash drawer Josh sneaks up behind me. "You need a ride home?" he whispers in my ear.

"Oh! 61, 62 . . . ."

"Well? I'm leaving soon."

"Hold on! Sixty—" Oh, forget it.

I close the drawer and turn around. I'm staring right into his bright blue eyes, and he's standing way too close. Why does this seem weird? It wouldn't have 24 hours ago. "Um, Robyn said she'd drive me."

"She did, did she?" He has this look on his face like he read the Facebook message I never sent.

Wait, did I send it by accident?

His face is red, so red it's almost hiding his freckles. "Well, if you're sure you don't need a ride . . ."

I want to. Maybe, in the darkness of the car, I could find a way to talk about yesterday's kiss. And really, would Robyn care if I changed my mind and—

"Okay, see you!" And he's off.

Josh and his mixed signals. If that kiss meant something...anything ...he'd give me time to think.

Thirty minutes later Robyn's pulling into my driveway. The sound of gravel crackles underneath the tires of her car. It's a welcoming crunch. It means I'm home.

The place is completely dark.

"You sure your mom's here?" Robyn looks the dark house over.

"She said she wasn't working tonight." Was she called in at the last minute?

Is her car here? The garage door's closed.

"I'll wait until you make sure everything's okay," Robyn puts her car in park. She's got that firm look on her face, the one she gets when Josh is trying to talk himself out of trouble.

The headlights from Robyn's tiny, noisy Subaru cast a blinding glow against the rain-covered windows. I open the car door, bracing myself for a gust of cold winter air. I shudder and hold my coat closer. It's old and worn and not half as warm as Daphne's fuzzy fake furry coat. "Be right back."

I run to the garage. Look inside. With the help of the headlights from Robyn's car I see Mom's Ford Escort. That's strange. So why is the house so dark? "She's here," I call out, against the wind.

Robyn rolls her window down. "What?"

"She's here," I yell, moving back to her car. "I'll be fine."

"You sure?" Robyn looks as if she doesn't believe me. "I could stick around for a few minutes, honey. Why wouldn't she leave a light on?"

I bite my lip, trying to hold back my irritation. Okay, I know she's worried, but she doesn't understand. Mom sometimes forgets things. Like my birthday last year. She remembered it three days later and felt guilty for weeks. I once heard grief makes you more aware of the people left behind, but in Mom's case it's the exact opposite.

Still, all the lights are out.

Thoughts are forming, nagging in the back of my head. Stupid, unwanted, impossible things. About Dad. About the cases he'd solved as a cop. He had worked in Narcotics and cracked a lot of big cases. Mom doesn't talk a lot about Daddy's work, but I have ears. I know what a big man he was.

Every so often, Daddy's best friend Dom comes to visit. Mom talks plenty when he's around. Uncle Dom was best man at their wedding and Dad's partner on the force. He's a tough guy, very Italian. Sometimes when he's over I hide in my room and listen to them downstairs. To hear her open up.

Would any of the scumbags Daddy put in jail carry a grudge? Would they be angry enough to visit us now that we're so far away? In Farnham? No. NO. I'm letting my imagination get way out of control.

"Seriously, I'm fine." Besides, what good would Robyn be? She's all of five foot two and weighs 110 soaking wet.

"I'm waiting until you get inside." Her arms are folded. That's that.

"Thanks." Truth be told, I kind of like when she plays protective mommy. I close the car door, then run to the house, anxious to escape the cold. With one hand on the front door, I dig my other into my coat for the keys.

No need to bother. The door's unlocked.

Seriously weird. I take a nervous look back at the Subaru.

Okay, deep breath. I enter the kitchen, fumble around for the light switch on the wall. After a few seconds, the room's bathed in light. Huge relief.

Nothing's changed. Same lemony yellow linoleum on the floor. Same photo of me playing Little League in fifth grade stuck to the refrigerator.

Okay, Robyn, you can go now.

I hear a crunch of gravel outside. Robyn's leaving. A trickle of fear drips into the pit of my stomach. Hey, what's the big deal? You've been left alone a million times before.

But not with her car in the garage.

"Mom?" All I'm getting is silence, except for the hum of the heaters.

Which doesn't make sense. Her car's in the garage! Even if she was already asleep, wouldn't I hear some noise? Maybe the soft rock eighties radio station she plays all night long or her ghastly loud snores? Nothing.

Even though it's way warmer inside than out, I hug my coat more tightly. I need protection. Against what, though?

I rap my knuckles against the kitchen table, to generate some noise. I glance over into the living room, covered in darkness. I should go in there. Why can't I move?

I take a few hesitant steps forward. The old floorboards creak under the weight of my footsteps. A chill runs down my spine. I stop, right at the edge of the doorway, scared to take the next step. Staring into the shadows. "Mom?"

If only the light from the kitchen showed more. The inside of the living room is a jumble of shadows. I need to go to the couch, turn on the light.

Something's holding me back.

My hands are trembling. Why am I so nervous? Defiantly, I make a fist and shove them into the pockets of my coat. Be brave. Walk forward. Stop shaking. Mom's in here. Somewhere. "Mom?"

The silence is broken by a loud crash. Glass breaking.

"Shit!" What the fuck was that? I jump back, hands out of my pockets, scrambling to grab onto a kitchen chair for support. "Who's there?"

I try to sound brave, even if my scream a few seconds earlier clearly gave me away. Maybe I should get the hell out of here. Run to the garage. Grab my phone and call Robyn for help. No use risking my life if someone's here and—

But if someone's here, then what about Mom? I can't abandon her. Especially if she's been hurt.

I pace the floorboards, trying to muster up the courage. Wait. My phone has a flashlight. Of course. Christ.

I reach into my coat. Let there be light.

And instantly I can see the couch, the TV, the dresser. Same as it was when I left. Wait, what's that on the floor?

Tentatively, I walk back to the living room and reach my arm out. My hands fumble against the smooth wall, searching for . . . hey, here we go.

"Ohhhh . . ."

What? Mom, I know it. That voice, low, kind of gravelly. Okay, good, she's here, somewhere. Is she okay?

There she is. Behind the coffee table, lying on the floor. On the floor? She's wearing her pink nightgown, the one that makes her look like a fuzzy caterpillar. Spread out. All around the couch are pieces of broken glass.

"Mom?" This time I don't care whether I let the desperation show or not. The fear breaks and I run to her, lift her head, touch her forehead. It feels warm. I brush the hair out of her eyes, pat the back of her head, trying to get her to wake up. Hmm. No bumps or anything...

Her eyelids begin to tremble. That's a good sign. "Mom?"

And then she opens her eyes. Great, she's okay. It must have been an attack, that's all. The thing is, she hasn't had one for a while. She's been doing so well on the new meds. She's okay; it's nothing, so why am I being such a big baby about things?

"Mom." I hold her close. She turns her head, shakes her honey-colored hair, so filled with gray streaks. She reaches a hand up to her face, the hand with Daddy's wedding ring on it. Blinks a few times. She's starting to figure out where she is.

"Kami?" She pulls away, concerned. Good, she's a grown-up again, I can breathe easier. "Is everything okay?"

I tug at her pink nightgown and pat her arm. "I think you had an attack."

"Ann attacked?" She looks at me oddly, then awareness sets in. "Oh, I don't think so, honey." Her eyes grow wider though as she starts looking around the room. I guess reality is setting in. "How did I end up on the floor?"

"Exactly. I'll get you some bread and a glass of water."

"How did you find me?"

"The lights were off when I came home from work. I came in. I heard glass breaking in the living room. It kind of—"

"And there I was." She frowns and places her hands on the coffee table. Pushes herself onto the couch. "I remember sitting here, reading the Carlisle ledger--" She looks around, concerned.

I spot a pile of papers on the floor, near the broken glass. "Right there."

"I don't usually black out like that though." She's agitated. I wish I could take that away from her. "I was tired, that's why I put on my pajamas. Your favorite ones, right?" She tries to smile but then glances over at the scattered broken glass. "Is that the new lamp?"

"Well . . ." I shrug. "It was."

Mom lowers her head and places her hands on her forehead, rocks back and forth slowly.

"I'll get you some food."

"I don't think I had one." Had one? Oh. Ann attacked, right. "I know when they're coming on, Kami. I didn't feel anything this time around."

"Maybe you fell asleep. I would too if I was reading some boring accounting thingy."

"Asleep enough to break a lamp? I think I'd wake up when that fell."

"That happened when I got home."

"Oh." She reaches down to pick up some of the broken glass. "I'd better get a dustpan . . ."

"Mom, take it easy." I grab her shoulders to keep her seated on the couch. "We've got all night to pick things up." I sit down next to her. Maybe that will keep her from cleaning.

She pats my hair gently and kisses me on the cheek. "How are you doing, honey? We hardly see each other."

"I know." I try to play it like it's no big deal. "Maybe tonight?"

"Quality time," she laughs. "Like picking up broken glass, and eating bread and water?"

"Oh, I think we can find more to eat than that." For some reason, my mood's lifting. Jokes, small talk. It's all I want right now. Or ever. "Isn't there some Chocolate Silk in the freezer?"

"Chocolate Silk!" Mom beams and I want to kiss her. "Okay, but only one bowl. I'm still trying to work off your baby fat."

"Hey, live a little. You're in your caterpillar jammers. Caterpillars like baby fat." I show off my crazy mad smile.

She ruffles my hair. "I like it when you make that face. You need to smile more, Kami."

Now that is funny. "You should talk!"

"How about a movie, too?"

"Okay, but no goopy love stories," I warn. "I'm in no mood for a chick flick."

Mom pats the back of my hair, and in an instant I'm five years old. "Maybe you need a good love story. How else are you going to get Josh to ask you out?"

"Mom!" What the hell? "I don't want anyone asking me out. Especially not Josh."

"If you say so," Mom says but it's clear she's not buying it. "No love stories, huh? Okay, where's the remote?"

The movie's over. I've stumbled my way upstairs.

The first thing that catches my eye is the glow from the laptop. That's weird. I never leave it on like that, not ever.

That's when I see it.

There. On the keyboard. Propped up between asdfg and qwert. A business card, completely in black. Like . . .

I pick up the card, my heart pounding. Hold it between my fingers. It's a hologram. I tilt it, a few degrees. In the lower left hand corner, three initials appear.

GKS.

How did that get here?

It's like all the air has been sucked out of the room.

I'm scared for Barbara. And for myself.

CHAPTER EIGHT

Thanks to that little calling card, I've spent the past few hours with the computer on, desperately seeking Barbara. Someone's been in the house. Someone left me a message.

She has to know who.

I'm sitting in bed, the pillows propped up so I can stare with half-opened eyes at the laptop in case Barbara signs on. I don't care about the girls in GroundUnder or the Late Night freaks or any other silly distractions. I'm playing the waiting game. For Barbara. Staring at the ceiling, then the screen, then the clock. Every so often, I close my eyes for a second—but only for a second, before starting everything all over again.

Lather. Rinse. Repeat.

I've got my favorite monkey pillow squeezed around my stomach, my kitty by my side. I hold the black GKS card in my hands. My fingertips trace the edge of the card, over and over, until it wears a line into my skin. My fingers slide across its smooth glossy surface, tracing down until I reach the lower left hand corner. Tilt back, and—

GKS

Were they behind what happened to Mom? She said this attack wasn't like the others. Had someone knocked her out? But no, there would have been a bump on her head, right?

This was a warning. Things could have been worse. If they can find me so fast, so quietly, there's no telling what they could get away with if...

And they could always return again.

No. Chill. You're being ridiculous.

I remember the first time I saw mom have a seizure. I was four, she was driving me to a birthday party. I think I had the birthday present on my lap. It was a sunny, beautiful day, so bright I had plastic white sunglasses to cover my eyes.

And. We were driving through the parking lot. Without warning, the car swerves to the right. Without warning, we're zooming toward a big yellow pole. I let out a scream. We crashed. My glasses flew off. Mom's face was pressed against the steering wheel, her eyes staring sightlessly to the right. I started to cry. Then people started swarming around us, so many people. My door was opened by a nice lady in a blue sweater. Soon an ambulance arrived. Mommy's walking around, looking as if she was going to fall down any minute. I kept crying out for her. I wanted so much to hold her, to be held by her, but she didn't seem to hear me . . .

I remember Daddy in the parking lot. He had his blue uniform on. Someone must have called the accident in. He held me in his arms, held me with my face crushed into his neck. Whispered to me as Mom was loaded into the ambulance. "She's going to be fine," he said. "Everything's fine," he said. Mommy and Daddy weren't going anywhere . . .

Weren't going anywhere. Really, Daddy?

He dropped me off at Nana's house. She took me out for ice cream.

No, the thought of ice cream isn't going to help, not after all the Chocolate Silk I've eaten. I dab at my eyes and reach over to my laptop. Time for my 110th search of all on-line users, in case GoAskAlice is avoiding me.

The clock on my phone tells me it's 2:45. I'll be seeing morning before I know it.

I go to the user ID area and type in "GoAskAlice."

"This Camera is Inactive."

Hmph. Try again later.

###

There's a leopard purr at 2:54.

In three seconds, I'm sitting up in bed.

I throw my pillow to the floor and turn over to check my laptop. The message window glows in the dark.

I refuse to look at it, afraid it might not be her. Well, it's definitely not Josh, not this late. Clicking down to the tool bar, I call up her webcam. Is she on?

It's active! The image comes into view slowly line by line. I watch her face emerge, starting with the top of her head, her golden hair.

Then the screen reaches her eyes.

They look red and puffy, as though she's been crying. Something's wrong. Something's happened. Did they hurt her?

It's clear when the bottom part of the screen comes into view. The left side of her face is all puffy and swollen.

She's been punished.

I can't take it any longer. I glance over at the message box to see what she has to say.

GOASKALICE: Kami are you there please say your there

NIGHTQUEEN22: I'm here.

My hands practically glide across the keyboard.

GOASKALICE: Are U okay?

I stop for a moment. Am I okay? That's a strange question. She's the one looking smashed up.

NIGHTQUEEN22: Of course. Why wouldn't I be?

GOASKALICE: Hey, just checking the temperature of my NYC sistah that's all

NIGHTQUEEN22: Bigger question. How are you?

The next image. Her hand touches the side of her face.

GOASKALICE: been better

NIGHTQUEEN22: I've been waiting to talk to you. I've been worried.

GOASKALICE: Did U say anything to anyone, Kami?

Oh. Should I tell her the truth?

NIGHTQUEEN22: Who did that to you?

GOASKALICE: He did

NIGHTQUEEN22: HE did?

GOASKALICE: Pretty aint it?

NIGHTQUEEN22: But why did he do that?

GOASKALICE: Did you say anything?

I'm almost afraid to tell the truth. No use hiding it, though. I caused this somehow. I owe her.

NIGHTQUEEN22: I did talk to Josh.

GOASKALICE: That's all?

NIGHTQUEEN22: he told me I should report it to PeoplesCam.

GOASKALICE: Oh God U didnt did U

Why? How could reporting that get Barbara into trouble?

The image on the screen changes again. Her eyes are wide. Haunted. Scared.

NIGHTQUEEN22: Is PeoplesCam what this is about, Barbara?

GOASKALICE: I think

She types those two words and hits Enter, then lets them hang there in space for about twenty seconds. I want to reach through the camera and shake her. What's going on? What are you involved in? Tell me before it's too late!

But still, no answer. Simply "I think."

Finally, a response.

GOASKALICE: NO. No theyre not

NIGHTQUEEN22: Then why did Jeremy hit you?

GOASKALICE: He didnt I fell

GOASKALICE: And I didnt say Jeremy hit me

NIGHTQUEEN22: Come on, Barbara, that's BULLSHIT!

NIGHTQUEEN22: I don't believe you.

She keeps her head down away from the camera lens. I have to get it out of her somehow. The truth. So maybe I have to tell the truth.

NIGHTQUEEN22: Barbara, they were here tonight.

GOASKALICE: What?

NIGHTQUEEN22: They were in my house. They left me a calling card. And a broken lamp.

GOASKALICE: No

NIGHTQUEEN22: I found my mom on the floor and the laptop on. And this card by my computer.

I hold up the card for her to see. Next image, her eyes are enormous. She believes me.

GOASKALICE: Get off peoplspeak Kami

NIGHTQUEEN22: Why?

GOASKALICE: Stay off it, K? Hide

NIGHTQUEEN22: Can YOU hide, Barbara?

GOASKALICE: U DONT UNDERSTAND YOURE IN TROUBLE KAMI UVE BEEN INVITED

NIGHTQUEEN22: Invited to what?

Invited? There's no response. I sit there staring at the screen. In the next frame she's out of the picture. All I can see is her black chair and the cherubs peeking out from the red wallpaper. I drum against the desktop anxiously. Where is she?

I wait for a good ten minutes. Each minute kills me a bit more. I fight against sleep, fight against the heaviness in my eyelids. I look at the clock. One more hour left before school. Have I ever been up this late?

I hear a leopard hiss. I look up.

GOASKALICE: Pretend you dont know me

GOASKALICE: It wont matter much longer anyway

NIGHTQUEEN22: Why? Why won't it matter?

GOASKALICE: It wont

NIGHTQUEEN22: Why won't it matter? Now I'm involved in this, too, Barbara. Me and my mom.

GOASKALICE: I

GOASKALICE: I dont want to see them hurt you Kami

NIGHTQUEEN22: I don't want to see them hurt you, Barbara.

GOASKALICE: I

NIGHTQUEEN22: What's the GKS, Barbara?

GOASKALICE: Theyre big really big. They can get into everything

NIGHTQUEEN22: So what are they?

GOASKALICE: I got to go Kami

NIGHTQUEEN22: Wait talk tell me whats going on

GOASKALICE: Its too dangerous.

GOASKALICE: Youre too good.

NIGHTQUEEN22: Is there any way I can get in touch with you?

GOASKALICE: No

NIGHTQUEEN22: Maybe we could Skype? Would that be safe? What's your phone number?

GOASKALICE: I cant

NIGHTQUEEN22: Why not?

GOASKALICE: I cant

NIGHTQUEEN22: How about Facebook?

GOASKALICE: cant cant cant

NIGHTQUEEN22: Tell me where you are? What city you live in?

GOASKALICE: I'm

GOASKALICE: No

NIGHTQUEEN22: What's your phone number? Do you have FaceTime?

NIGHTQUEEN22: Do you have an email address? A private one? Some way you could reach me in secret if you need help?

I look over at the screen. Her face is too close to the camera now. She's practically a shadow.

GOASKALICE: Maybe

NIGHTQUEEN22: Give it to me.

GOASKALICE: rumblebuffinn@dakota.com

NIGHTQUEEN22: I'm going to email you. If you're ever in trouble, if there's anything you need to say, write back, anytime. Any reason.

GOASKALICE: What reason

NIGHTQUEEN22: I don't know. To give me a clue. Whatever you're afraid to say.

GOASKALICE: Okay

GOASKALICE: Thank you

NIGHTQUEEN22: You're welcome

GOASKALICE: I mean it. Thank U

NIGHTQUEEN22: When can I talk to you again?

GOASKALICE: I told you 2night. Its the finals.

NIGHTQUEEN22: The what?

GOASKALICE: Theres your secret I'll send you the password

NIGHTQUEEN22: What?

GOASKALICE: Night

I hear a door close. I look up at the screen. The last image I see she's rising from the desk. I see her upper arm, the one with the strange mark on it. The one I hadn't been able to figure out the night before.

I can see the mark up close now. It's not a bruise or a birthmark after all. It's a tattoo.

A little black circle. Perfectly round. And in the center of the circle—Three little letters.

CHAPTER NINE

My alarm goes off at six every morning, whether I want it to or not. I didn't want it to today.

I'm lying in my bed all wrapped up in my blanket cocoon. With only an hour and a half of sleep, my head feels as though it's stuffed with cotton. I turned off my laptop at around four, but then spent the next half hour tossing and turning. My mind wouldn't turn off.

The soft blanket is so warm against my skin. I wish I could stay like this for ten more hours. If ever a day was meant to bunk school, this is it.

Maybe I could play dead. Fool Mom into letting me skip school. "Dear Stonington Community College: Kami Corley can't go to school today because she's dead. She might be better tomorrow. Love, Kami's Mom"

Wait.

Today's the day.

Crap. I open my eyes with a start and blink as the full force of the morning light streams through my bedroom window. Groaning, I force myself to sit up.

It's Friday. Tonight is Barbara's night. The butterflies in my stomach started fluttering at the thought.

I've got no choice. I have to face the day. I let out a loud angry groan and rip off the blankets like a bandage.

After a quick pit stop, I stumble down the stairs to the kitchen. My bare feet take me from the slightly sticky wooden floorboards to the soft plush carpet in the living room, to—

"Ouch!" I grab at my foot and collapse on the couch.

That hurt! It has to be a piece of glass from the night before. I raise my foot. A thin line of blood is forming at my heel. Yep. I grab it tightly and try to squeeze out the tiny glass shard.

"What's the matter, hon?"

"Looks like we missed a few pieces last night." I call out to Mom in the kitchen. "Do we have Band-Aids?"

"Baby, come in here. Let Mama take care of you."

I rise to my feet and hobble into the kitchen. "Owowowowow . . ."

Mom's moving her breakfast from the counter to the kitchen table. Black coffee and burnt toast with a thick smear of butter on both pieces.

I smelled it before I entered the kitchen, overpowering even the smell of the vanilla air fresheners Mom loves to stink up the house with.

Mom likes her toast on the dark side and likes the butter to soak into the bread so it gets all spongey and chewy. She also likes her coffee black. Ugh, you couldn't get that breakfast through my clenched teeth if you tried.

I throw myself down into one of the chairs. Mom hands me a paper towel to wipe off the blood. Dutifully, I raise my smelly foot in the air and she bends down to examine the cut.

"You'll survive," she teases, and lets go of my damaged stump. "Hold on, let's see what I can find."

She's wearing her blue pant suit today. It's nice, but I've seen it way too many times: blue blazer, white blouse, matching blue pants. Mom takes a bite out of her toast, puts it back on her plate, and turns to rummage through the cupboards in search of a bandage. "You want breakfast?"

"Sure." She knows my poison. A big bowl of chocolate (Chocolate Crunchies, to be specific) and coffee from the Keurig with at least five spoonfuls of sugar. Mom and I are united in our love of coffee at least. Regular Gilmore Girls we are.

She keeps talking, mostly to herself. "Now, I could have sworn I had a bandage over . . . ah!" She locates it in the silverware drawer by the sink. I'll never understand my mom's system for organizing things because it's basically: first place that comes to mind. "How late did you stay up last night, baby? Chocolate Crunchies today?"

"Chocolate Crunchies every day." She nods and grabs her coffee mug from the table first to take a noisy slurp. "Not too late," I lie, glancing down at my cut so she can't see my eyes. "Midnight. Why?"

"Still too late," she clucks. "But it sounded later. It sounded like you were still awake at one."

"I had trouble sleeping. I was worried about you." Ouch. I feel guilty for that lie. Well, half-lie.

Mom seems to find my concern touching. "I'm doing fine, sweetie. Really."

I close my eyes. I want to put my head down on the table and take a nap, but force my eyelids open and fight the feeling. "What were you doing up at one in the morning anyway?"

"I couldn't sleep, either." Mom puts her coffee down and grabs another piece of toast. At this rate, I'm never going to get my Chocolate Crunchies. I sigh in frustration and start opening up the bandage.

"Hey, Mom?"

"Mmmmm hmmm?" Her mouth is full of toast, but at least she's rummaging through the cupboard again.

I want to ask whether she's afraid what happened last night was more than one of her seizures. Oh, and maybe tell her everything—about the card, about the GKS, about my conversations with Barbara. But do I have the nerve?

Maybe it's better to keep things vague. "Ummm, what would you do if you had a friend who was in trouble?"

The merry jingle of Mom pouring Chocolate Crunchies into a bowl stops mid-stream. I look over in her direction.

Shit, I used the "T" word. The one letter no mother ever wants to hear from her daughter. Mom looks like she's swallowed a goldfish. "Why? Is one of your ... friends in trouble?"

Okay. Gulp. Time to do some dancing. Fast.

Nervously, I play with the ends of my hair. "No, not one of my friends. Josh told me something about someone, that's all."

"Do you mean like pregnant?" Mom's eyes are starting to bug out. *I mean seriously, get a grip. You have nothing to worry about on that front.*

"No! I mean ... like, in danger."

Her relief is plain to see. As my reward for not being preggers, the milk starts flowing into my cereal bowl. Oh, okay, danger is A-OK as long as no one is knocked up or anything. "I guess that would depend on the kind of danger she ... or I guess he ... was in. I'd definitely tell this person to get out of danger if they could."

Gee, Mom, how profound. "Like what?" I ask as I dig into my cereal bowl. "What if this person felt she ... or he ... is going to be hurt by someone?"

"Honey, you should be able to answer that." Her fingers push the crumbs from her empty plate into a little pile. I can tell she's wrapping things up. "Your friend should go to the police and file a restraining order. Or go see the campus police."

Mom, this advice isn't helpful at all. I absolutely know my ears are getting red. "The police around here aren't exactly New York's finest, Mom. Most of them aren't smart enough to make bike cop!"

She grins then catches herself. "They're not that bad."

"But how about if you didn't have anything solid?"

"At least you'd have it on record."

"I guess."

She scoops up the last of the burnt crumbs with her finger. "How could Josh's friend be involved in a problem so big the police couldn't handle it? Even the police around here?"

I'm not sure how to answer. I'm way too tired and it's way too early to come up with an intelligent response. "It isn't. You're right." I stir my bowl of delicious chocolate. "How about you, Mom? What would you do if you thought you were . . . um, being threatened?"

She shrugs and brushes some crumbs off her suit. "That's easy. I'd call Uncle Dom. He'd never let anything happen to me. Well, us. We've got our own guardian angel looking after us, even if he's so far away. You know that, right?"

I nod, too busy slurping down my cereal. After I've had a chance to wipe my mouth, I ask, ever so casually, "Have you heard from Uncle Dom lately?"

"Ah, a few months ago. They've been keeping him busy. How's your foot?"

A glance down. "The bleeding stopped."

"Speaking of which, I have to run. You need a ride?"

I consider it. It would be so easy to . . .

"Yeah. Can you wait a minute? I'm not ready yet."

"Need your books?"

"Need my make-up! Do you see these eyes?"

In a second I'm heading upstairs for my miracle bag and to brush my teeth. I'm not going to talk Mom out of driving me to school, although no way am I going to ask her if I can drive. Even if I should. That would be dangerous with only ninety minutes of sleep.

Oh, wait, stop. Josh. He must be on his way. I truly don't want to talk with him about this yet, though. Better send him a text to meet up for fine dining in our luxurious prop room.

The good news: Western Civ II is a great place to get some shuteye.

CHAPTER TEN

He may not have taken me there, but Josh did drive me home from school, and I was totally ready to confront him about the kiss. But then five minutes into the ride a Calypso buzz from my Android tells me I have a message in my inbox and when I see who it's from, nothing else matters.

Kami,

I know I promised you a password for tonight. I spoke to Jeremy and he says the only way to see the show tonight is to go to gks. You know how to do that right? So here it is. Id gnostrime, password orknies. DO NOT GO ON BEFORE 11 THAT WOULD BE BAD

Orknies. There's that Lion, Witch, Wardrobe thing again. It makes me smile even though my stomach's in knots.

But the actual site? She's wants me to go to that place with the black screen and those weird words about the other side of entertainment?

I wonder, how did she get Jeremy to say yes to that? She couldn't have gotten a password for me without him. But if he knows, does anyone else?

I think about that black calling card left in my room and shiver.

Shit got real. And also, what am I going to see?

"Kami?"

Wait, Josh. I look up. Oh. We're parked in my driveway, and I haven't listened to a single word he's said.

He knows I'm distracted. Of course he does. How could he not? "Everything okay, babyfish?" he asks, and the concern in his voice wakes me from my trance.

He's leaning forward in the driver's seat, and his face is inches from mine. His blue eyes look wide and alert. It's the perfect opportunity to kiss him on the nose. Or maybe even the lips. I'm pretty sure he'd like that, too. But I'm too tired and way too distracted to be that clever. Way too focused on the little black box in my bedroom and not the guy in front of me.

So I shrug and pretend. "I'm fine. Have a few things on my mind." I reach for the door.

Before I turn away I see a strange look on his face. "Are you fine?"

Oh, honey, if you only knew. I wave goodbye and run into the house.

The minute I get in, I sprint upstairs, grab a wrinkled piece of paper from my desk, and scribble down the password.

I'm fighting the urge to grab my laptop and log on to gks.com right then. No, no, no. She said not to go on before 11. But why would that be so bad?

Maybe what I should do is call Josh and ask him to come back. Help me figure this out. It's not too late and besides he only lives two minutes away.

I reach for my Droid, but stop before I start texting. I can't bring myself to do it.

Well, if I can't log on and I'm too chicken to let Josh know what's going on, it's time for the next order of business: finding Mom's address book. One thing from her speech this morning actually made sense.

Where would it be? The first place to look is in the everything drawer in the kitchen. That's where she tosses all her odds and ends, the pieces of her life that don't have a place to call their own. That's where I can usually find all the misfit toys.

It isn't cuddling next to the electric can opener or potato peeler, however. But hey, I found my Mayday Parade CD! I haven't seen that in years.

It's also not in her big pile of unpaid bills near the kitchen table either. I go through every single overdue notice. No luck.

Waitaminute. A snapshot image springs into my head, a memory from last night. As I was lifting Mom while she was slumped on the floor, had her little blue address book been on the end table next to the ledgers?

Excited, I sprint into the living room. Yep.

After carefully checking the couch and carpet for stray broken glass, I take a seat. Thumb through the dog-eared pages.

Domenic Torelli. 212/555-4746

Mom's right, he is our guardian angel. I grab my phone out of my pocket and start pounding the keys before I lose my nerve.

One ring . . . two . . ..

I hold my breath. What am I going to say? Where will I start once he gets on the line?

"Hey, this is Dom."

His voice. Warm and deep and definitely New York and Italian with a hint of a gravel. Mom says it's from smoking too many cigarettes.

"I'm not able to get to the phone right now, but if you leave your name and number I'll get back to ya."

Beeeeeep.

My fingers twist at the ends of my hair. This is my cue.

"Um, Uncle Dom? This is Kami. I, uh, know I haven't called in a while, but uh, uh . . . well, I want to talk to you when you get a second. Thanks, bye."

I disconnect. Good for me. I did it.

And maybe it's good he didn't answer. I need time to figure out what the hell I'm gonna say when he calls back.

CHAPTER ELEVEN

I wait until 11:10 to log on. I don't want to seem too anxious.

I'm sitting cross-legged on my bed with a bowl of popcorn between my legs feeling a faint chill from the ceramic bowl against my thighs. Boy, is it cold outside. The news says it's below zero and the coldest day in February so far. And here I am sitting in my room in a sleeveless tee and shorts. I shiver and debate throwing on sweatpants.

For some reason the popcorn makes me feel like I've got this "here we are now, entertain us" attitude about the whole thing. The truth is I'm scared more than anything else. Scared for what I'm going to see. Scared for Barbara.

The entire house is pitch black. My doing. A totally dark house fits my mood. I've been waiting for this moment for hours, counting down the time by napping on my messy bed, wasting time watching some Vines, texting Josh a few hundred times, all the while waiting for the late night show to start. Wondering what the nighttime will bring.

Around six, Mom came home. Totally surprised me; I thought she was working at the donut shop tonight. But no, get this, she tells me she's going to the movies with friends. She has friends? Then she says she's going out dancing afterward! And when she stops in my room to say goodbye, she's wearing a glittery red top and tight jeans. And, she took the time to dye her hair! All those grays ... well, almost all ... were ancient history.

Maybe in a weird way the other night made some kind of difference.

I'm glad she's going out to enjoy herself. I want her to have fun. But if I have to be honest, I'm also happy because I want to be home alone tonight. In the dark. Waiting for Barbara.

The way it all began.

The laptop monitor glows before me like a silicon goddess. Okay, it's time to see what's going on in Barbara's life. I raise my fingers to the keyboard and type in www.gks.com.

The screen turns totally black, the way it did the first time. Three little letters form again in the bottom right hand corner of the screen. G. K. S. I slide the arrow over and click on the hyperlink.

"WELCOME TO GKS, YOUR DOORWAY TO ANOTHER SIDE OF ENTERTAINMENT. ENTER YOUR GKS ID AND PASSWORD."

I search around for my scrap of paper.

ID—gnostrome

Password—orknies

I wait for the laptop to respond, wondering what I'll see.

The screen blinks for a moment.

Access denied

What? I reach for the scrap and stare at my scribbles. Did I type it in wrong? I carefully retype what Barbara sent me, letter by letter. The computer hourglasses for a moment and then

Access denied

I want to scream. What went wrong? I know it's the right password. I double-checked and rechecked it a hundred times. All day long. Now what am I supposed to do?

Well. There's always the old-fashioned way.

I call up PeoplesCam. Type in GoAskAlice hoping she might be on her webcam, too. That screen is black.

Hmm. There's only one other thing I can try, that thing she gave me if I truly needed help. This qualified.

TO: Rumblebuffin@dakota.com

Barbara, are you there? I tried logging on to GKS site and wasn't able to get in, and your webcam is dark. Don't know how to see U. Kami

I hit the send button. She'd better answer right away! I grab some popcorn and shove it into my mouth. Blah, it's burned. All I can taste is charcoal and salt.

Three minutes later, a new message.

FROM: rumblebuffinn@dakota.com

(My breathing returns to normal.)

Kami Jermy gave me his password Try this GKS2.481. Paswrd is highwire

Jeremy gave her his password? How nice of him. I call up the creepy GKS site again and type in the new ID.

It takes a minute, but it works.

Next thing I know I'm in a whole new kind of website. The scary black and white is replaced by a screen that looks a little like PeoplesCam. It's another webcam community.

But different, too.

This one has dozens of rooms to choose from and the site even makes it easy for you because a large bar at the top of the screen reads, "GKS: Drag your selections here." And underneath that, "Let the Games Begin."

The rooms are kind of weird because they all have names like "Desire" and "Innocence" and "Gluttony" on them. "The Black Room" is another option. Don't think this is aimed for the under 18 crowd.

This might be an interesting site to play around in if I had the time. But of course I'm interested in only one thing tonight.

Is GoAskAlice here? I type that name in the browser. Yep, it's on the list. She's a Girl Next Door. And the show is live! I can't help it I'm excited. I call her up on the screen.

Connecting with Alice takes seconds. Yep, there she is hanging around in her room with the angels. And she's in real time, wow. Live action Barbara? She's moving around! This is so 21st century.

I can barely breathe. This is so cool. Never thought I'd be able to see her like this after so long seeing her as a frozen image.

And, wow. That means we can speak.

There she is sitting in her room. Her hair is pulled back and she's wearing a tight black halter top. She doesn't look as natural as she usually does. She's got a lot more make-up on tonight. Thick black lines under her eyes. As much as I worship the goddess of eyeliner, I don't like it. It's like she's trying to impress someone. Or, maybe covering up her bruise?

Can I truly talk to her? I click the cursor on chat and fire off a message.

GKS2.481: Hey there.

No response. I suck in my breath and bite my lip.

GOASKALICE: Kami?

Contact! This is unbelievable. I can't wait to finally talk to her face to face.

GKS2.481: Yep!

GOASKALICE: Heyyyyyyyyyyy

GKS2.481: I'm going to get on my cam now so I can say hi!

GOASKALICE: NO

GOASKALICE: NO DONT DO THAT

Don't?

GOASKALICE: IF THEY SEE ME TALKING TO YOU THEY'LL KNOW

GKS2.481: Who? Know what? So what should I do?

GOASKALICE: Turn your webcam on, but promise me you'll talk to me like this

GKS2.481: Why?

GOASKALICE: Just promise me, okay?

You mean we can't even talk? Shit. But even so . . ..

GKS2.481: Okay.

I glance down for the time. Between my late entrance and the problems connecting to Barbara it's now 11:20. Time flies when you're having fun.

At least I can see her live, and the image is so much clearer. I can see her room, the place she lives in. It's all come alive for me. I can actually see the little white angels on red wallpaper. But without the pixilation, I have to admit, the wallpaper looks a whole lot crummier. And is that a tear in the top right corner of the black leather chair?

Barbara's room seems a lot smaller. Smaller than my bedroom even. It doesn't look that great at all.

GKS2.481: I'm going on cam.

GOASKALICE: Good I want to see you

I click on the cam. And there we are seeing each other for the first time face to face. Or had she been seeing me real time all this time? I never thought to ask. Whatever, it makes me want to cry.

GOASKALICE: There you are! Hello Kami

GOASKALICE: Kamiiiiii

GKS2.481: Did I miss anything?

GOASKALICE: Not yet the fyreworks will start soon

GKS2.481: Fireworks?

I'm squinting in the dark all the time focused on Barbara. She seems different. It's harder for her to hide when the view is so clear.

What is it? She's smiling but it's not the smile that haunts me. Her eyes seem a little glazed, along with something I can't put my finger on.

But the glazed look. I have my suspicions about that.

GKS2.481: Have you been flying with the angels?

And she throws back her head and laughs as if what I said was hysterically funny. Right away I lower the volume. Of course, I can hear her now. Real time, right? Her laughter seems forced, kind of crazy. Her voice is higher than I thought it would be.

GOASKALICE: What makes you think that Kami

GKS2.481: Barbara

GOASKALICE: The only angels around here are on my wallpaper

GOASKALICE: The rest have all fallen, right?

GOASKALICE: Fallllllllllllllllllllllllllllllll.n.

GKS2.481: Barbara, are you stoned?

She shrugs her shoulders, lowers her head. Her eyes look up at the camera and a guilty smile spreads across her face. And then she says clearly, into the camera, "You know I wouldn't do that."

GKS2.481: Seriously?

No response. I wait for an answer, watch the clock tick by. Alice isn't saying anything.

Without warning, she turns her attention back to the screen and says "Well, you'll just have to guess what I was sayin' that about, won't you? What are some of the things I wouldn't do, huh?" Her voice is rough around the edges and she clearly has an accent. From where? It's hard to tell. And then she laughs again as if what she said was hysterically funny.

Oh, I get it. She's not talking to me.

I can't take the silent treatment any more.

GKS2.481: Where's Jeremy? I thought you said you were going to put on a show.

GOASKALICE: Man Leas looking seriously wacked tonight

GKS2.481: Who's Lea?

GOASKALICE: Hey Kami can you do me a favor?

GKS2.481: What?

GOASKALICE: Can you just sit there and smile for a moment? Maybe make it brighter there? Its so dark I want to see your smile

GKS2.481: Hold on.

I jump off my bed and turn on the lamp on my dresser. Then I hop back on and smile pretty for the camera.

Here I am, Barbara. I stare at the screen, stare at her, and try to maintain our connection. She still has that stoned look plastered on her face, but at least I've figured out what else is there besides the dull glaze. I see excitement in her eyes. And maybe a touch of fear.

GOASKALICE: Kami I love your pretty smile. Youre so pretty you know that?

GKS2.481: Gee thanks

GOASKALICE: Pretty blue eyes I always wanted to have blue eyes but my Kami's got them instead

GKS2.481: Since when am I "your" Kami?

GOASKALICE: Youre my Kami. My chica. The best frend I have right now

GKS2.481: Where's Jeremy?

GOASKALICE: I dont know off somewhere I dont think he wants to see me tonight

GKS2.481: Why not?

GOASKALICE: Oh hold on a minute Kami

GKS2.481: What's going on?

Barbara has her head lowered and shoulders bent forward. Her face is a dark shadow looming into the webcam.

GKS2.481: Barbara?

GOASKALICE: Stop it theyre going to make the announsment.

GKS2.481: Who?

No answer. I tap nervously on my keyboard. Who's making a decision?

11:27. Three minutes until the fireworks. But what's gonna explode?

Barbara raises her head and stares up into the camera. Her eyes looked tired. She's smiling, but the smile looks defiant. It's definitely not a happy look.

GKS2.481: Barbara, what's going on?

GOASKALICE: I gotta tell U I always get so nervous Kam I mean I hate them like hell but it is such a relief once you get through the moment

GKS2.481: What moment?

No response.

GKS2.481: What moment, Barbara?

She jerks forward and reaches up her arm and next moment a blurry shadow takes up the left side of the screen. I can still see Barbara beyond the blur though with her confused fake hazy smile.

GOASKALICE: Ive got my hand up to the computer Kami Im touching your hair I wish I could touch your hair I wish I could be normal like U are Kami I wish we could really be friends

GKS2.481: We are friends, Barbara.

"Face to face friends, I mean," she says out loud and on the loud side. She's forgotten herself. She's forgotten the rule she set up at the start of this: no speaking to each other. But I'm glad she did and I hope no one figures out what she means or who she's talking to. And she keeps going.

"I want to talk to you in person. I wish I was far away from . . ."

Then she stops. She remembers.

"Wish I could have some face time with you in Narnia," she corrects herself.

She sounds a lot younger than I thought she would. Is she even 18? From her still life images I thought she was so much older.

And from the sound of her voice, I think she'd like to be anywhere but where she is.

I choose my next words carefully.

GKS2.481: Where are you, Barbara? Maybe I could visit you.

GOASKALICE: Kami I'm

The shadow disappears from the screen. Barbara is staring intently at the camera. It looks like she's reading. Her eyes are wide. And the smile's no longer there. In fact, she looks like she's about to cry.

"Oh shit," she says.

That's it. I stare at the screen waiting for her to fill in the blank. But she doesn't. Instead, she swears again, shakes her head. I see her try to lift herself from the chair as if she has to go.

GKS2.481: Barbara, is everything okay?

I hear a weird noise in the background that I can't identify. She cries out at the sound and her struggling becomes more intense. She can't get up for some reason. The noise grows louder. She falls into the seat, screams out. I see a blur of color, her hand, hitting the camera. She screams again, keeps screaming.

Her screams fill my room. I twist around in my bed. The bowl holding the popcorns slips through my legs. The popcorn spills to the floor. I don't care.

GKS2.481: Barbara?

Silence. Whatever's happened seems to have stopped. She sits back in her seat. Her eyes are closed and she's panting hard and I see blood on her mouth. Blood?

GKS2.481: Barbara?

A sound echoes through my house. Bell chimes. It's 11:30 on the dot. My room seems so dark and cold even with the lights on. The rest of the world seems far away. The only thing that matters is the little window in front of me.

GKS2.481: Barbara, talk to me!

And then I hear the noise again. I can't place my finger on what it is. A weird humming. Next thing I know she's screaming again.

Only this time, her screams are way worse. And then her head is thrown back and I know something bad is happening. She's sitting rigid in her chair screaming. Then she falls back and I see her eyes again. Eyes filled with fright, filled with pain.

Then her mouth is open and blood is trickling down her neck and the next thing I see she's twisting her neck at a hideous angle. Her back is arched against the chair as if she's trying to push away from the desk. I stop typing because I know it's no use, that it's happening and I can't do anything and then her neck is twisted in the opposite direction and her neck looks swollen. Tears sting my eyes. Please make the screaming stop. Please stop hurting her. Barbara is there anything I can do?

The weird noise stops. She goes limp then slumps forward. Her camera seems to freeze. All I can see is the golden crown that's the top of her head, filling the screen.

I know what this means. I don't want to believe it even though it's right there in front of me. This is what she's been talking about all along.

The late night show.

I rub at my eyes and feel the sting of salt from the popcorn. That snaps me out of it. I'm aware again. I can hear myself breathing rapidly while the tears stream down my cheeks.

And then the screen goes black.

I know it's not going to help, but my hands reach toward the keyboard. My trembling fingers type out

GKS2.481: Barbara?

I hit enter. But before I can catch my breath there's a response.

All the breath rushes out of my body. Relief. Maybe she's okay after all. And all this time I've been thinking that-

Then I read the message.

And I realize . . . I realize . . ..

I realize what it says.

GOASKALICE: YOU'RE NEXT

CHAPTER TWELVE

I rise from my bed slowly, never taking my eyes off the screen. I wonder if whoever sent me the message is watching my every move, as if the minute I let down my guard and take my eyes away from the blinking cursor, I'll give them the chance they need. To attack.

And the whole time the image of what I've seen replays in my mind. Her head thrown back, the look of fear in her eyes, the thin line of blood making its way down her neck. Her final scream, the way she pushed back right before her—

Death. Barbara's dead.

So this is what she meant when she asked for help that first night. She was looking for a way out but was too scared to spell everything out. I was too stupid to pick up her clues.

A crunch of popcorn. The kernels are like tiny pebbles digging into my socks. I want to fall onto the bed and break down, crying for Barbara.

I can't. The power of the words on the screen keeps me numb. They know who I am now. Her trap is mine.

You're next.

I have to do something. Of course, I need to call Mom. Screw girl's night out. She needs to know about this.

Okay, so where's my Android?

I search around, lift the blankets, sort through a ton of needless crap. Maybe under the bed? Shit! Why am I such a slob?

Frantic, I crouch down to look underneath. YES.

Her number's on speed dial. The phone starts ringing. Come on, come on . . .

Dammit! It goes right to voicemail. She must have silenced her phone. Maybe they skipped the movies and went dancing. She never checks her messages. It'll be weeks before she gets it.

What else can I do? Run downstairs and hide underneath the couch? Hide in the cellar? Could I get that far? No, I'd be a sitting duck.

I could leave the house. Josh isn't that far away.

Josh! I should call him. Or send a text. Either way he'd—

Or maybe call the police. Why am I being so thick? What can Josh do they can't? Easy . . . easy . . .

I can see my phone wobbling in my hands as I try to hit the right numbers with my thumb. Stop shaking, dammit. Get to work. It's three keystrokes, after all.

A southern-sounding lady answers the phone on the first ring. "9-1-1, please state your name."

"Kami Corley." My voice echoes back in the phone. I wince. I sound way too high-pitched, way too frantic. Like I'm 12 years old. "I need the police. I . . ." How do I say this? "I saw somebody die."

I hear a rapid inhale of breath. "Hold, please." Then a click, a dial tone, and a deep voice on the other end of the line.

"Farnham Police."

"Hello? I, um . . ." I wipe a tear from my cheek. "I think I saw someone get killed."

There's a long pause. Too long. Didn't the guy hear me? "What do you mean 'think,' ma'am?" His tone doesn't change at all.

"Well, I mean, I saw it. On line."

"On a line?"

"No! On a webcam. On-line. Her name is Barbara."

"On a webcam, ma'am? And you're sure she was killed?"

Am I? What kind of stupid question is that? "Yes, I'm sure. I mean, it's hard not to . . ." I stop, bite my tongue. "Yes, sir."

"How was she killed, ma'am?" The officer's tone is brusque, impersonal. The way he keeps saying killed is annoying.

"Well, um, I don't know, but she . . ." How had she been killed? "Listen, you have to get over here, because--"

"Did you know this person, ma'am?"

"Yes, of course, but listen--"

"What's her full name, ma'am, and her address?"

Wait. What is her full name? Funny how during all the late night conversations we had, that never came up. "Um, like I said, Barbara."

"Do you know her last name, ma'am?" He says it slowly, as if he's talking to a child. I'm not, dammit. He also sounds kind of annoyed, as if I'm wasting his time.

Every word he slowly speaks makes me feel more unsure about everything. "I don't know what her last name is. We talk online a lot. She lives in another city."

"What city, ma'am?"

What city does she live in? She never would say. She never even gave me a hint. She didn't trust me enough to tell me. Frustrated tears flood my eyes. I blink them away. I realize how little I know. "I'm not sure."

"What did you see, ma'am?"

What did I see? What did I see, exactly? I saw her gasping, that awful look on her face. I saw blood, lots of it. "I told you. I saw someone get killed. Right before my eyes. I saw..." Oh, why can't I find the right words?

"Does she live in this town, ma'am?"

"No. No." Stop calling me ma'am. Stop using that tone. "No, she doesn't."

"Then I'm not sure I can help you." Why does he sound so pleased? It's as if he knows he's five seconds away from a donut break. Why would this make him happy? Maybe he's right. Maybe I don't know what I'm talking about. Even so, shouldn't he at least pretend to be helpful?

Screw being nice. I am so done with this! "Help me? I want you to help her!" Dumbass!

"Ma'am, how old are you?"

"What difference does that make?"

The laugh on the other end of the line tells me it makes a huge difference. It means I'm a child, not worth his time. For all he knows, this could be a prank call. Who would pull a prank like this, though? Why can't he take me seriously?

"Is your mom or dad home?"

"Mom's out. Dad's . . . what difference does that—"

He cuts me off again. "Let your mom know you're talking to a girl on some webcam and then, if you still think you've seen someone killed, come into the station and fill out some paperwork."

"You don't understand!" I reply, letting the desperation show in my voice. "You've got to come here. I think they're after me, too."

"They are? Who are they, ma'am?" The way he says it makes it clear he doesn't believe me. I might as well say my house is being invaded by aliens.

I don't know what to say anymore. Nothing I could ever say will get him to believe me.

"Why do you think they're after you, ma'am?"

"Because . . . well, they wrote on her IM . . ."

"Is this some kind of a joke?"

"NO! Why won't you listen to me?"

"Maybe someone's playing a joke on you. There are lots of weird people out there, honey. Get in touch with your mom, let her know what's going on, and then come on down and tell us all about it. Okay?"

His voice is firm and tells me all I need to know. He thinks I'm overreacting. Even worse, playing a joke on him. Why couldn't he send a police car over to check out my story? Would that have been too hard?

This call is over. This call is a waste of time. I can't allow myself the smug satisfaction of knowing I was right all along about Farnham's finest being totally useless. I sit back down on the bed, out of breath and unsure about what to do next.

What if he's right? What if this is all a joke?

I throw the phone down and glance over at the blinking cursor on the screen.

GOASKALICE: You're next.

I minimize the message box and call up my browser. One thing I haven't tried. Barbara's email address. Her secret weapon.

rumblebuffinn@dakota.com.

Maybe there's a . . .

The sound of my Android snaps me out of my trance. The funky calypso beat, like a song they'd play at the Fandango Café, seems so out of place now. The ring tone echoes through the empty house.

Did the cop grow a brain cell and decide to call back? Yeah, right. Mom? Josh? Josh, yes. Who else would be calling this late at night?

I hold my breath and reach for the phone, tucked between the folds of my bedsheets. Josh, help me. Please be you. Please help me.

But the caller ID says "Unknown."

Who cares? I hit the bright green answer icon. "Hello?"

Only silence on the other end. Nobody says a word.

"Hello?"

Dead air. Not Josh. Who is? This is crazy. What has Barbara gotten me into? What was the game she was playing and why hadn't she given me more of a warning, why didn't she give me more than her first name and a pretty face and not much else?

My hands are trembling so badly. Stop it, stop it! It's all I can do to turn off my phone.

Maybe the dumbass cop was right about one thing. Maybe I need to get out of the house or find someone that can really help. Someone like Josh, or . . .

Or Uncle Dom. Uncle Dom!

No time to waste. I flip through my call history. Josh, Josh, Mom, work . . . New York area code, New York area . . . yes, there it is. Domenic Torelli. 212/555-4746

I hit send, wait for the phone to ring. Please be there . . . please be there . . . please be . . ..

After the fourth ring. "Hello?"

His voice. His voice!

"Uncle Dom!"

I hear a crash downstairs. The sound echoes. Bounces off the walls. A thin trickle of cold sweat slips down my back.

"Hello?"

CHAPTER THIRTEEN

"**K**ami, is that you?"

Maybe I'm having an out-of-body experience. I can hear Uncle Dom's voice on my Android, but at the same time I'm having trouble focusing with all the noise I'm hearing downstairs. I hear voices. Voices! And footsteps, moving around, bumping into things. From where? There's the sound of glasses slamming together and the kitchen table being pushed aside. Someone swearing. Oh God, they're in the kitchen.

That crash of glass. A window, maybe? Someone breaking in? If it's in the kitchen, that must be the door, of course. Now they're in, and—

"Kami?"

Uncle Dom. Snap out of it! He's my link to safety. But how can he help me, so many miles away?

"Uncle Dom," I whisper. Quietly as I can, I rise from the bed and tiptoe to the door of my room. I hear two guys talking to each other. Their voices are terrifying.

"Kami?" Uncle Dom's voice rises.

Oh, right. "Yeah, it's me."

"What's going on, honey? Why are you calling this late at night?" Even from a distance, his blunt, take-charge voice makes me feel safer.

"I'm in trouble."

"What? Why would—"

"I saw somebody get killed."

His voice rises. "Is your mom okay?"

"Mom's fine. I'm at home and I've got to get out of here."

"I can get the police over there in—"

"No time!"

"But Kami, I—"

"I've got to get out now. I don't know who's listening or anything. Uncle Dom . . . look . . . I have to hang up . . . but I saw someone get killed tonight. On a webcam. You've got to believe me. I saw her die. People . . look . . . Uncle Dom . . find out about GKS and . . ."

"The what?"

"GKS. GKS! They're . . ."

The sounds are getting closer. My hands are shaking. I know I need to hang up. I also need to tell him as much as I can while I still have time. "The girl. Her name's Barbara. Her email address is rumblebuffinn—

two n's, Uncle Dom—at Dakota.com. Don't know if that helps, but it might. And there's this card . . . I'm going to hide it under my pillow . . ." More rustling. "Gotta go."

"Kami! Listen, where are you going?"

"I don't know. I've got to try to get out of—"

A dull thud. I can picture someone walking across our linoleum floor.

"Gotta go love you bye." I shove my Android into my pocket and look around.

Not much time. But if anything happens, I have to be able to leave some clue about what happened. A note? No time and they'd probably see it. The card, yes! I promised Uncle Dom. I search around for my jeans in the pile of dirty clothes by my bed. Reach into my pocket and slip the GKS card under my monkey pillow. Should I throw on my jeans? No, no time! I close up the laptop so the glow of the screen isn't bathing me in its blue-white light. I rise from the bed and take a quiet step forward.

I tiptoe to turn off the light Barbara made me turn on. Lights out.

Even though I'm completely in the dark, the house is alive around me, full of sounds and electric energy. I can definitely hear footsteps downstairs. How many people are down there?

I creep over to my bedroom window. It's the safest way out. I slide it up as quietly as possible.

Another crash echoes through the silence. It sounds like someone fell. Good, I hope they broke a leg.

Still, they're closer now. Probably in the living room. They'll be upstairs soon enough. I hear a mumble of voices and the hall brightens. Someone's turned on a light downstairs.

I have to go. Using all I've got, I raise the stubborn window screen. This is easy, Kami, you can do it. You've done it before, many times. This past summer, sneaking out to go walking in the town park after midnight. With Josh, singing off-key crap, laughing like idiots.

There's a drain pipe right next to the window. Close enough for me to grab and sturdy enough for me to slide down. At least, I hope it is.

I have to hurry. Swallowing hard, I raise my leg over the window sill, place my left hand on the drain pipe. It's freezing outside. I try not to look down because I know the ground so far away will only make me dizzy.

The cool night air bites into my skin. The drain pipe is freezing cold. Dammit, maybe I should have put my jeans on. This is nothing like sneaking out last summer. This is not going to be fun.

Here goes nothing.

I push myself out, grip the drain pipe with both hands, my feet still touching the edge of the window. The cold nibbles on my hands, my legs. The pipe seems wobbly and groans from my weight, but holds.

I close my eyes for a second, trying not to think about being seen, being caught, being dead. I push off.

Footsteps on the stairs. Low angry voices grow louder by the second. The lights in my room flash on.

I don't want to know what happens next. I kick away from the window, holding tightly to the drain pipe. I hear a shout. Someone's yelling, someone with a deep voice. It doesn't matter, because something else, something far worse is ringing in my ears. With a loud screech the drain pipe snaps apart from the roof.

Shit! I try to hang and ride it down. Maybe it will hold for a few seconds longer. Please please please let it hold. Think Mary Poppins gliding to the ground with her umbrella. Please please don't let me fall, don't let me—

The surface is too rough. My hands aren't strong enough. It's too cold. I lose my grip. I'm falling through space, screaming at the top of my lungs, bracing for the fall.

I hit the ground. It feels hard like stone. All the breath leaves my body. My eyes snap open, and I look around wildly at the cold night sky, my bedroom window lit up against the darkness.

The stars are so bright tonight, the sky's so clear. The moon is almost completely full; it looms over me. I wish I could reach up and touch it. My head is so dizzy. I feel as if it's stuffed with stardust.

A loud slam, from up above. Voices, in my room. That pulls me out. It's getting colder outside by the second. My teeth chatter as I lie there, stretched out on the cold ground in my T-shirt and shorts. Why didn't I put on my sneakers? Not even my fucking yoga pants? So stupid. Too much of a rush. Too stupid to think it through . . . No time. Gotta go. I try to take in a breath and lift myself up. The second I do, I feel a sharp pain in my chest. I can't breathe. Can't breathe? Panic starts to set in. Can't breathe?

I know those deep voices must be running out of the house after me. I try to lift myself from the ground. Gotta get up. Gotta get away. I hate this feeling of helplessness. I can't lie here on the ground like a fallen statue, like a stuffed animal, like Mrs. Tibbs falling from my bed. I'm stronger than that. I've got to lift myself up and—

"Ahhhhh!"

Another sharp jab of pain shoots through my chest. I claw at the air, try to push through it.

The kitchen door bangs open on the other side of the house. They must be coming.

I have to get away. The woods are close. If I can reach the woods, I can go to the Bigelow's house next door. Or run to Josh's house, wake him up.

I picture him standing there with his hair sticking up like a pine tree. He'd run with me to Daphne's house. We'd steal her little yellow car. We'd get the hell out of Ohio. Maybe there'd be a car chase? Man! I hope Josh knows how to use a stick shift.

Gotta go. Gasping for breath, I try to sit up to stumble forward. The ground is like ice. I'm in agony. It's too much. I can't breathe. Can't catch a single solitary breath. The pain. I cry out, grab my side, fall back to the ground.

I hear voices. They're close now.

I clutch at the cold, thin, unforgiving grass. Try to crawl forward. The voices grow louder.

"There she is."

I feel a sharp pain to the side of my head. I let out a gasp and look up. The pain's too great.

Rough hands grab my shoulders, yank me off the ground. I scream out from the pain. I try to kick away. I squint and strain to see who's doing the grabbing, but all I can see are shadows and glimpses of a dark hooded sweatshirt. I claw at the big shadow towering over me, try to scratch at what has to be his face.

I'm pushed away before I can make contact. I hear a harsh laugh, then the hands squeezing my shoulders release and I'm pushed forward. I stumble and fall to the ground. A stab of pain slices through my side when I hit the frozen earth.

No, I have to keep fighting. Blindly, I use my legs to kick at whatever's around me, to keep them away. I scream out, loudly, so that anyone who is nearby can hear me, might come running, might try to save me . . .

"Stop that!" The voice is angry, clearly pissed off. Then he kicks me, right to my head. The pain is unbelievable. A ringing fills my ears.

The world goes hazy, soft around the edges. The voices are softer, far away. The world blurs. The voices fade.

CHAPTER FOURTEEN

"**D**at turn. DAT ONE, asshole. There. Fuck!"

"For Chrissake, shut da hell up and let me do the—"

"Not if you're goin' da wrong way, dude!"

"Damn."

Cold vinyl against my cheek. My heartbeat pounds in my ears at odds with the thudding techno on the radio. My head hurts. My left side aches like hell. Whatever my right hand's touching, it's squishy. Where am I?

I open my eyes. Look down. My hand's dangling inside an old McDonald's bag. Gross. I yank that hand out and wipe ketchup ooze on the carpet.

Try to get my bearings. Where am I?

Besides the steady beat of the techno from the speakers somewhere above me, I hear a thumping underneath. Tires against pavement.

I must be in a car. I raise my head an inch to see if I can get a better view. From the looks of it, I'm in an SUV. The back seat, apparently. At least, from what I can tell. The only other thing I can see is a ton of trash around me. Lots of fast food. Taco Bell, Wendy's, Drunkin' Donuts, you name it.

The car has a new car smell, but mixed in with the completely gaggable smell of rancid sour cream and decaying burritos. Way to ruin a new car fast.

"I did da right thing, asshole. I fucking got onto 95, took a left at the third exit, now I'm—"

"You got on 95, yes. The opposite way. You went da opposite way!"

The one who's speaking laughs. Way too loudly, like he's trying to piss off the guy driving. Sure enough, the sound of a fist pounding an arm punctuates the air, and he's no longer laughing.

"Fuck!"

"Go fuck yourself. You pull shit like that again and I'll—"

"Okay, okay. Calm down, Rick."

Rick. An actual name. These are the guys who broke into the house. Must be. Their voices are deep, rough, hyper-masculine. Angry.

I strain my neck to look into the front seat. All I can see are two dark shapes. Thing 1 and Thing 2. That's what they are to me.

They sound like punks, not trained killers at all. Older than me, but not by much. With a strong accent. From where? Can't place it. Not Brooklyn.

I can't see them from where I am. Should I raise my head and get a better look? That would be stupid. I need to keep playing dead and listen to them speaking their thing-speak.

But I don't. Instead I lift my head slowly.

That's not much of a help. As careful as I can, I lift myself higher by pushing against my left arm. Right away, I feel a rush of pain down my left side. I cry out from the sudden shock and collapse. My hand ends up back in the McDonald's bag in the cold, squishy ketchup. My left side's on fire.

"The princess woke up!"

We drive under a street lamp. In the shock of the light a face looms over me. He has dark hair, a unibrow, brooding eyes set close together. Shark eyes. Dead eyes. Not someone to mess with.

"She's pretty," he says. His breath smells like old socks and cigarettes. "Think maybe we could pull over and have a little fun with her before we—"

"Not unless you want your balls cut off, asshole."

Shark Eyes keeps looking at me. I try to ignore him, nursing the pain in my side and scared of what he might do next.

He leans down closer. I let out a whimper. Oh please don't please don't please don't . . .

Then there's a pinch in my side and the shadows run together. The hard beat of the music loses its edge. Then pretty much everything . . . starts to . . .

Fade away.

I wake and I'm in . . . bed? My bed?

The mattress is cushiony underneath me. Mom tucked me in. The blanket is soft and warm. A soft buzzing like mellow bees drifts closer.

I open my eyes. Wow, so bright! My arm immediately goes up to shield myself from the glare. I toss around in the bed, squint my eyes closed. Where is that damn buzzing coming from?

I can still see the glare of the light from behind my eyelids. Where am I now? I try to adjust to the light. Slowly, slowly. Okay, try opening your eyes a tiny bit. I can see . . . shapes. A person? I can't see the face clearly.

The figure comes closer. I see a flash of blonde hair. The face swims into view. Warm inviting eyes and a Cheshire cat smile.

Barbara.

How could it be Barbara? Barbara's dead. She's dead!

Am I dead too? It can't be her.

How nice it is to see her face, her soft eyes . . .

I reach out to touch her. Even if she is a ghost. I mean, she has to be, right? But what if--? No, I saw her die. She's dead.

Fingers wrap around my wrist. My arm is forced down to my side. I'm weak. No strength to struggle. I look up at Barbara. Her face is fuzzy, indistinct. She's fading.

I feel hands on my shoulders. Someone pushes me into a sitting position. The pain in my left side is unbearable. I can't breathe. I want to scream. I can't. No air. "Barbara!" I whisper. "Barb . . ." I can't get the words out.

Next moment, I feel a sharp sting in my right shoulder. What the hell?

The bees woke up. The sting pushes me out of my drugged state. Because I must have been drugged. That must have been the pinch I felt in the car, before I passed out. A needle. Shark Eyes must have shoved it into me. And now? Now I'm awake, and I need to get the hell out of wherever I am. I struggle, scream out. "Stop that!"

Someone clamps a hand over my mouth. I feel another pinprick in my side. A hand covers my eyes, presses me back. Before I can think or act, before I can breathe, I'm jabbed again and again and again. Beneath the silencing hand I grit my teeth and jerk my head to the side.

I need to breathe. I need to scream. The clammy hand presses harder. I jerk back, bare my teeth, bite down.

A firecracker of pain bursts in my chest. I stop struggling, shoulder throbbing, the pain in my chest unbearable. Another jab and another jab and another like a hive of angry bees stinging me. Black spots swim in my eyes. I'm being dragged back into the darkness.

Then the jabbing pain stops without warning. The pain recedes. I've been drugged again, but I don't care. It feels good to feel nothing. I drift down onto the cool comfort of the pillow under my head, warm blanket folding around me. Receding footsteps echo into silence, but I hear a soft whisper of voices next to me. Barbara?

"She's in brand."

In brand? What the hell does that mean? Why does my left side hurt so much? What were the stinging bees all about?

It's too much. Can't hold onto my thoughts. Everything slips sideways, melts, blends into the shadows.

Barbara, where are you? I want you back smiling at me. What does your face look like? I need to remember. Barbara are you there? I need to open my eyes, to see if you're there.

Barbara?

I can't hold onto the thoughts. They're all slipping away into a beautiful glimmering darkness.

The darkness is complete. I give in. I drift.

And.

Then.

My eyes flutter. It's hard to see at first.

Where am I? I know I'm not dreaming, but where am I?

Soft cotton and a pillow under my head. It triggers a surface sensation memory and a jolt of the dream. Barbara stood over me.

There's a dull steady throbbing on my shoulder.

I'm in a bed.

Other surface sensations take hold. The space I'm in doesn't have the same feel as my bedroom. It's definitely not home. Not cozy. No smell of vanilla or the sound of eighties music from my mom's radio in the bedroom. It's way colder, too.

I wiggle my arms about. Can't feel any books or pens or even Mrs. Tibbs by my side. I open my eyes wider. There's no laptop resting on a TV tray by my bed.

This space seems smaller, cramped.

I clutch at the blanket beneath my arms and raise it up. It's thin and dull orange and nothing like the blue and white checkered spread I brought from New York City. The one I've had on my bed since I was ten, since before dad died. The one that's worn and comfortable. The one I love so much. The one that reminds me of home.

I can see light coming from my right. I try to sit up and turn around to figure out where I am. As I shift my place I feel a burning pain in my left side. I fall back down again totally winded.

Out of the corner of my eye, I glimpse a headboard. White, the same as the one in my bedroom. Wait, maybe I am home again? Was this all a bad dream?

I twist my neck upward for a better look. The headboard at home is metal and painted white to make it stand out. To make the room look cozy.

No. This one is made out of wood. Looks like a bed you'd find in a kid's room. Like, maybe a girl around the age of 10 or 11. From all the dents and nicks on it, though, it's seen better days. It's not cozy at all.

This isn't my bed.

Where did they take me? Where am I?

The men. The car. The pinch in my side. It all comes flooding back. Two men in my house, in my bedroom, in the car.

I shift to the right, trying to breathe in a way that won't hurt, and trying not to think about what happened.

What did happen? Where am I? I stare at the dingy red wallpaper in front of me. Fear eats away at me, erodes me, and pulls me out to sea.

Where am I?

The wallpaper is red.

Where am I?

With white dots.

No, not dots.

Cherubs.

Slowly I reach out a hand and touch the surface.

Now I know why Barbara had been hovering nearby. Why I felt her presence. Why she seems closer now.

Cherubs.

I went through the rabbit hole. I'm in Alice's world.

I'm flying with her angels. I'm in a dead girl's bedroom.

I'm stuck inside her late night show.

CHAPTER FIFTEEN

I'm lying in that strange bed, focusing on simply breathing. The dull pain in my chest turns to fire every time I turn the wrong way.

I'm also trying to figure out what happened, without freaking out. I want to. I can't afford to. Even if I had the strength for a meltdown, I can only imagine the shape I'd be in after tearing up the place. My place. Barbara's place.

I've been sitting in the same position for what seems like three hours. At least. Breathing. Trying to stay in control. Thinking through all the possibilities and asking myself a million questions I don't have answers to. Like, how long have I been out of it? Where am I? Hell, what day is it?

What is Mom doing? I can see her coming home from her night out tired and excited, maybe a little drunk. The first thing she'd see would be the broken window in the kitchen. She'd call out for me and look around the house with a sick scared feeling in her stomach. The same way I had the other night.

She won't find me.

Wait. What if she came home and someone was waiting?

No, no. Stop it!

I blink away the tears, focus on my breathing again. Mom's fine; she has to be fine. If they did anything to her, it would only make things worse for them, especially with my call to the police and to Uncle Dom. Even if the locals don't care, Uncle Dom won't let things go. He'll be like a pit bull.

Did he call Mom yet? He must have.

Wait. Do I still have my Android? I shoved it into my shorts before taking the jump. Maybe they forgot to search my pockets? All I need is one call.

I pat myself down. Nothing. No calls today.

I'm alone. No one can help me here. Wherever here is. Whatever's going to happen, I'm facing it alone. No Uncle Dom. No Josh.

No Mom.

It's hard to stay calm thinking like this. I give up trying. The tears come and I let them, grabbing my blankets in handfuls, in bunches. I cry and I cry and I cry until my sides can't stand the pain any longer.

Then the crying is over, and I'm lying there staring at the ceiling in a room I don't know, in a bed that I've trashed and sheets that aren't mine. Nothing here is mine. It's all strange. And even though I know the tears will dry on my face and my breathing will go back to normal and my heart will stop pumping a million miles a minute from all the crying, even though everything will seem outwardly normal again, all I can think is:

What now? What the hell am I going to do now?

Okay. Time to pull myself together. Figure out where I am. See how much trouble I'm in.

With an effort, I grit my teeth. Suck in my breath. Push myself up.

It's agony. I want to scream, but only a little cry squeaks out, like that little panic noise you make before you reach the highest point on a roller coaster.

I form a dead spot inside my head, shake off the pain. Pull myself up into a sitting position.

I'm up. I gasp for breath, my hand to my side. Breathe. Breathe. Slowly. The pain starts to fade. Breathe through it. Breathe.

I push the blankets aside. Hmmm, someone's taken off my T-shirt. I'm wearing my pink and black bra, which is not one of my favorites, because it always squishes my boobs. At least they left my shorts on. My feet are bare. So long, monkey socks. Well, no time to stare at my Pretty in Pink toenail polish. No more stalling.

Time to stand. I take my hand and touch it to my kneecap. Carefully I push against it until my leg is touching the ground. Now comes the hard part.

Pain jabs my side as I twist my hips around. I bite my lip and enter that dead spot again.

Ooh, head rush. I grab the side of the bed to steady myself.

The room is small and narrow and bare. The worn carpet is hard and cool beneath my feet, not like the soft shaggy feeling of Mom's living room carpet. I used to love to squish my toes into the throw rug by the couch. This carpet is rough and is about as warm as an ice cube.

Even though it's only a twin, the bed with the white headboard takes up most of the space, except for a small brown nightstand with an eighties-style red lamp to my right. It looks like a red ball with a white lampshade plopped on top of it. The lamp has chips all along the base and the lampshade is bent on one side. Must have fallen once or twice. Or been thrown.

In front of me, almost touching the foot of the bed, is a dresser with a small television on top of it. The dresser is white with dust. Then again, the whole room is covered in dust. Guess the housekeeper hasn't been to visit in a while. An interior decorator, either: all of the furniture looks as if it was randomly thrown together, like overstock from a cheap warehouse that went out of business a long time ago.

There's a door to my left. It's open. Could it be freedom? Could it be that easy?

Where are the windows? What kind of bedroom doesn't have windows? It'd be nice to look outside and get an idea where I am. Barbara lived in the city. Which one? Did she even know?

Hmm, interesting. If I stand still, the throbbing in my side goes away a little. So standing isn't a problem. Is walking?

I take my first step. No, walking doesn't hurt that much. One step at a time, I shuffle to the dresser. I raise my arm and draw a line in the dust around the TV. I was here.

What's in the next room? I twist my body too quickly and ooh, sharp pain. Shit, this hurts!

I peer into the room before me, not sure what I am going to see. Will it be a big open room surrounded by little rooms like the one I'm in? Is anyone waiting outside? Are there guards?

Wrong on both counts. No one's home, and while it's not a big open space, it's not exactly a luxury spa, either. The room is larger than the bedroom, shaped like a rectangle. Is it a waiting room? No, not exactly.

No angel wallpaper here, but a dingy off-color white paint with random crayon scribbles all along one wall. The lights are on, but it's not exactly blinding. A spindly black lamp stands to my left around the center of the room, shining three thin beams of light in arbitrary directions. It's placed next to a gross lime green couch covered in stains. Don't think I'll be sitting there any time soon. The rest of the room is pretty much empty. Not even a wastebasket.

It's an apartment. Like a tenement in New York City. I think I'm in the living room. At least, it's probably the largest room, from the looks of it.

Am I in New York City again? I always wanted to go back, but not like this. That wouldn't make sense, though, would it? It took us three days to get to Ohio when we moved out of Brooklyn after dad died. Sure, we made some side trips along the way, but even so, I couldn't have been out that long. Besides, Barbara had been clear about not living in New York City. So where?

A kitchen area takes up the far end of the room, although it doesn't look as if a meal's been cooked there since the Stone Age. A grimy bar area separates the crumbling kitchen from the living room. The Formica countertop is dingy yellow and covered in what looks like rust and layers of dust. The fridge and stove have been removed, so all that's left is a rusty old sink and saggy kitchen cupboards. Hmm, interesting. Wonder what's in the cupboards?

At the far left, an open door. Maybe the bathroom? And another door next to that, on the far wall across from my bedroom. It's mahogany, I think. I mean, I guess. Looks thick. Seems out of place. It's closed. Maybe it leads to the outside world. Freedom?

Better figure that out soon. But first, I turn to get the full tour. Next to my bedroom, another closed door. This one looks interesting. It's painted jet black and even has a black doorknob. A Black Room. Wonderful, I have a Black Room.

Unlike the dirty crayon colored walls in the living room, this door looks as if it's had a fresh coat of paint recently. It looks shiny. Why is it so different? Cautiously, I walk forward to see what's inside.

It's not locked. I open the door and look inside.

The room's small, about the same size as the bedroom. Cherub wallpaper covers these walls, too. Guess someone didn't want to bother changing that. No windows.

A large black desk has been pushed against the wall to my left. It's modern and shiny. Seems completely different from everything else. On top of the desk, a computer. Very high tech looking. Other than that, the desk is empty, except for a small desk lamp.

The only other thing in the room: a black leather chair. It looks comfortable at least. There's a tear in the top right corner and stuffing coming out of it.

Oh. Wait.

Realization sets in.

This chair . . . this room . . . this must be where Barbara spoke to me every night. This was where she—

No, I don't want to think about that. Not now.

All I know is, it's clear she's not here anymore, and I'm pretty certain she didn't end up somewhere else. So what was I seeing in my dream? Was it a hallucination? Her ghost?

I can't deal with ghosts or hallucinations right now. I turn around, close the door. There are other things to see.

As fast as a zombie, I walk away. Need to check out the rest of the apartment I seem to be living in rent free. Past the couch, past the kitchenette. Where does the other closed door lead to?

Although I want to smash it down, I stop when I get there. Who knows what's on the other side? Better be smart about this. I stop and lean my ear against the door, careful not to irritate my side, to see if I can hear anything.

Nothing. It sounds as empty as the room I'm in. I turn the knob. That's easy. I pull.

Nope. Locked.

I jiggle the doorknob back and forth, push against it as hard as I can. No luck.

So, that's as far as I can go. My space. Hers, too. Here I am without a clue why I'm here. Until someone decides to pay me a visit.

Will it be one of the guys who brought me here? I remember their voices, deep and thick, and that face, looming over me. Rick, that's his name. And Shark Eyes. I bet both of them are dark and hairy with broken noses and ape-like faces. The ape twins.

Are the ape twins in charge? Probably not. They didn't seem like the brightest lights on the Christmas tree. So who is in charge?

I hear noises outside the door. Footsteps. Panicked, I turn. Pain jabs my side. Can't breathe.

Have to hide. The open door. The bathroom. I shuffle as fast as I can toward it, slip inside, scrabble for the light switch.

Lights on. I jump. Breathe.

It's only my reflection. A mirror in a dirty gold frame hangs over the sink. No medicine cabinet? Weird. God, I look awful.

I hear a door creak open. I peer around the door frame. Not my door. Muffled voices. As hard as I try I can't hear what they're saying.

My reflection stares back at me.

I look pathetic. I hardly recognize myself.

My hair's a total mess. Eyeliner's smudged all over my face. A splotch on my cheek. I look closer. No, it's purple. A bruise. Lovely.

I look over my half-naked body. Standing there, wearing nothing but a too-tight bra and a pair of loose-fitting shorts. Strange. My left side, the one that hurts so much, doesn't look bad. I touch it. No bruises. A few scrapes here and there, but that wouldn't account for the pain. Shouldn't there be a bruise?

Hold it. There is something. On my right shoulder.

Some kind of bandage. I reach up to touch it.

Ooh, head rush. I close my eyes for a moment.

Looking in the mirror, I see a bandage. I watch my mirror image grab hold of the bandage, rip the bandage off. I bite my lip. OUCH! Yeah, fast is better.

I drop it into the sink.

I stare at my shoulder. It looks darker than the rest of my skin. Why is it darker? I don't tan easy and it's the middle of winter. Is it a bruise, or...?

A bruise. Like the bruise Barbara had.

I look closer. Tilt my body forward. No, not a bruise. It's....

A snapshot memory of sharp stabbing pain and voices swarming all around me.

"She's in brand."

Bright lights. My visit with Barbara. Bees stinging me.

Not a bruise. It's red and raw and puckered at the edges. Three letters enclosed in a circle. I touch it and wince. Three letters burned into my shoulder.

"She's in brand."

The same letters I saw on Barbara's upper arm another lifetime ago when I was safe inside my own house. When I'd been able to hide behind my computer screen.

No wonder her ghost came to visit while the bees swarmed around me. After all, Barbara and I are practically sisters, now.

G.K.S.

I'm in brand now. The way she was.

I'm branded.

CHAPTER SIXTEEN

GKS.

I'm sick inside.

Noooooooooooooo!

Fuck control. Fuck the pain in my side. Fuck it if someone hears me scream. Fuck it. Fuck. It.

None of it matters. I run to the locked door, screaming as loud as I can. Hitting, kicking. Twisting at the doorknob until the pain gnaws into me. I stop. I breathe. I slip to the floor. I cry.

Tears blinding me, I crawl back to the bedroom, gasping for breath and clutching my side.

What can I do? What the hell am I going to do now?

I lean my head against the dresser for support. My head spins. Black spots swirl in front of my eyes. My head is swimming.

This isn't real. None of this is happening. How could I have fucked up so bad? I'm so angry I could—

In desperation, I reach for the TV. I pull it forward and stagger back. It crashes to the floor, the screen cracking into a thousand pieces.

Crying with pain, I collapse onto the bed and curl up into a ball, letting the tears come in waves. I'm drowning. I've drowned.

I only hope sleep comes soon.

###

I don't want to wake up from the dream I'm having.

I'm at the Fandango Café and getting someone's ice cream order messed up.

"Why did you put pickles in my hot fudge sundae?" A middle-aged woman with beet red hair shoves the bowl at me, hot fudge dribbling on the table. I wipe it up. I notice two little dark-haired girls, standing on either side of her, wearing blue baby doll dresses. They scowl at me, silently.

Robyn comes over. "I'm sorry, ma'am." She takes the dish away from me. "I'll make it right."

"I should hope so," the woman says. Her minions shake their curly heads in disapproval.

"No pickles next time," Robyn says to me, speaking in the tone she usually saves for Josh. "This sundae is free, ma'am." She shoves me out of the way and comments on how cute her little monsters are.

It's a totally boring dream, but maybe that's why I like it. Maybe the fact I know it's a dream means I'm waking up. Yep, I can feel the pillow under my head and my toes wiggling under the blanket, so clearly . . ..

Wait. This isn't how I fell asleep. Is it possible—?

Wait. Do I smell bacon?

Bacon? Like Mom's bacon? Am I home?

"Mom?" I rub the sleep out of my eyes and open them.

Crummy angels. Red wallpaper. The red ball lamp. I'm still in the same crummy room. My mood nosedives from excited to suck. Deflate, little balloon, deflate.

I've been moved. I had fallen asleep on the end of my bed and now my head's by the white headboard resting on a pillow and a blanket covers me. Someone took care of me after my rampage. Again. Weird I didn't feel anything or even wake up. Was I drugged? They like to do that around here.

My body's aching worse than ever, too. Tossing the TV to the ground hadn't been a smart idea. And was I . . . ? I push aside the thin scratchy blanket I'm covered in to check. Nope, still in my bra and shorts. Wonderful.

But I smell bacon.

My eyes follow my nose on a wild bacon hunt. Yes, a tray rests on the battered nightstand next to me. Bacon, eggs, and toast. Orange juice too.

My stomach starts doing flip flops. I don't care if it ends up being chewy and cold, the sight of cooked bacon looks so good I want to shove it all into my mouth right away. It seems like forever since I had food to eat.

"Go ahead. It's for you."

Wait. I have company?

The voice is masculine, but soft and friendly. Nothing like the deep animal growl I expected.

Company? I grab the blanket and pull it around me to hide the sight of that ugly pink and black bra.

What does he look like? Head lowered, I glance over.

He's at the end of the bed standing in front of the dresser. Wait, where's the . . . ? Nope, no television.

He follows my gaze and smiles at me as if the two of us are sharing an inside joke. "That was quite a mess. Even with two fractured ribs, you're pretty strong."

Oh. I have two fractured ribs. Ow.

Knowing what's wrong with me makes me feel bolder. I look right into his eyes to see who I'm up against.

Interesting. This guy doesn't look like an ape at all. He's tall and thin, maybe twenty-ish. Reddish blond hair and a scruffy thin goatee. His eyes are golden brown. When he smiles white, slightly uneven teeth show against the red of his lips. His skin is pale with a sprinkle of faded freckles across both cheeks. For some sick reason he reminds me of Josh, maybe ten years older.

"Go ahead and eat. It's okay." He shrugs and grins, hands in pockets. He's shy?

Even though I don't want to listen to a single thing anyone in this place says, my stomach doesn't care. It growls. Loudly. Okay, okay. I'll move. Still holding the blanket against my chest, I try to sit up.

I gasp as the pain stabs me with a hot knife.

"Oh, right," he says, "Your ribs. Let me help."

He walks over and lifts the tray. I gingerly shift into a more comfortable position. He places the tray on my lap while I sit there, panting, helpless.

He smells good as he bends over me. Slightly sweet, but not syrupy. Subtle. Rain washed earth and corduroy. It's nice. He steps back a couple paces.

And bacon.

I dig into the feast. I can't help it; I stuff forkfuls into my mouth, juices dripping down my chin. It's greasy and cold and heaven. As good as Mom's Thanksgiving dinner.

My mystery man leans against the dresser, watching me eat, his hands shoved into the pockets of his jeans. I should probably be creeped out, but I'm so hungry I don't care.

In between slurps I size him up.

He's a good dresser. I'll give him that. Definitely metrosexual. His blue sweater looks casually expensive, and the sleeves are pushed up the exact right way. His work boots look as though he stepped out of a catalog. All show, no work.

After a few moments, he takes out his phone. His phone case is cool. Looks to be made out of wood. Probably cost him a bit, not like the cheap one with pandas I bought at the Dollar Store.

Gee, I miss my Android. But his will do if I can get my hands on it to send a message.

He scowls at what he's reading, then bangs out a response with his thumbs. By the look on his face and the way he's tapping his keys, it's clear he doesn't like the news. "I have to go for a smoke," he says. There's the growl I expected. "I'll be back."

Don't hurry back.

I grunt and keep on eating. He walks into the other room. A click and the door to my room opens. Closes.

He's gone. The room is as quiet and still as the inside of a library at midnight. Even worse, a tomb.

A wave of panic stirs up the bacon and eggs in my stomach. I cover my mouth as it fills with saliva. The greasy food settles in a cold, heavy lump.

Breathe. I shove the tray aside. Breathe. My stomach churns. Breathe.

I have to get out of here. I shiver, clutch the blanket closer, double over, and . . . the churning stops.

I close my eyes and breathe slowly, licking my lips, swallowing.

I'm alone. All alone. I push the tray to the foot of the bed and sink back onto the pillows.

Will he come back? Will someone come to take the tray away?

Why? What do I care if he goes away forever?

I don't. He's the enemy. He may not look like an ape, but he's still a monster.

Don't trust him. Don't trust anyone here.

Look what happened to Barbara.

Fifteen minutes or so go by. Angels and demons in my head wrestle. Is he coming back? I don't care if he comes back. I don't trust him. I want to smash his smiling face with the tray. Break the plate over his head. Throw the orange juice in his face.

Orange juice. My throat's raw and it did taste good.

I reach for the tray and pull it closer. Take a deep, soothing drink.

Metal scrapes in the door lock. He's coming back again. Footsteps. He comes in, holding a pillow in his hands.

"I thought you might need another one," he says, squeezing the pillow. "Can you sit up?"

Sure. By now I have the drill down. I grit my teeth, enter the dead zone, and push myself forward. He tucks the soft pillow behind me and eases me back into it. Fresh washed earth. No, fresh turned earth warmed by the sun and corduroy. I breathe deeply. He smells so good, comforting. He smells like the country, like a walk in the meadow on a warm summer day.

He glances over at the empty tray still in my lap. It looks like I licked the plate, but I didn't. He came back before I could. "Want more?"

I shake my head. I refuse to look into his eyes. The devils are not going to win this one.

"Okay then." The smile on his face is still there, though. Wrinkles have formed in the corners of his eyes, too. I don't think he believes me.

That's irritating as hell.

"I know, it's not five star dining. I did the best I could. Sure you don't want anything else? I can get you other things. You still thirsty?"

"Maybe," I concede, staring at the dresser. My voice sounds so freaking scratchy. It's the first time I've used it in a while, besides screaming. "Some more juice?"

He nods.

I look down at the thin blanket covering my chest. "Um, and a shirt."

He seems pleased. "Coming up." he says. "I know another thing that'll help, too." He takes the tray and walks away.

Another click. Is he locking the door each time he leaves? If he leaves it unlocked even once, I'm out of here.

Maybe someday. Soon.

After a few minutes, the jingle of keys. He's returned and is holding a big glass. "Here you go."

I take it and smile. Then he opens up his other hand and holds out two small white tablets. "Take these, too."

I stare vacantly at his pills.

"It's Roxicet," he explains. "It'll kill the pain. They're strong but make you feel a lot better. Go on."

Says the pusher.

Don't trust him. What if the pills aren't what he says? I stare at the dresser.

It's like he can read my mind. Or maybe it's pretty obvious. "They're not poison," he says, sounding like I'm acting childish. "Why would I feed you eggs if I wanted to poison you?"

Hmm. Good point.

"They take the edge off. Seriously."

I think about the excruciating pain I feel every time I try and stand up. Or breathe, even. A softer edge might not be a bad thing. Still . . . I have one hand holding a blanket and the other holding a glass of orange juice. "Um, I kind of can't."

"Oh. Here, let me help. Open up, okay?"

Like a trained seal, I open my mouth wide. He leans in and pops the pills on my tongue. The whole thing is weird and way too intimate. I raise my arm to take another drink and push him away.

He backs off.

I swallow the pills.

"That's good," he says. "You'll feel better. Promise."

Cross your heart and hope to die? I sip the juice.

I can't help it. His voice is too nice and gentle. Even though I know I shouldn't, I peer up through my bangs and stare directly into his eyes. "Thank you."

I think he notices the change. "Are you scared?" He actually sounds like he cares.

Of course I'm scared. I've been kidnapped, drugged, and locked in a room somewhere. Why wouldn't I be scared?

"I think you're scared," he says softly. His brown eyes bore into mine. He waits.

For what? For me to say it's all right that you kidnapped me because you smell nice and you dress well?

Screw that. "Where am I?"

He keeps his calm gaze fixed on me. "You're here."

"Why am I here?"

He ignores my question. "DM told me you jumped out of your bedroom window. No wonder you hurt your ribs. Musta hurt like hell."

DM and Rick. Okay, so I know the names of the Ape Twins. Now all I need is the name of the guy standing in front of me.

"Are those pills really going to help me get better?"

"Those pills help kill the pain. Nothing you can do for a fracture, except wait it out. I fractured my ribs when I was about 12. Got between Mom and Dad during a friendly family conversation. Fractured my wrist too. I did get a cast for that." He holds out his left arm all nice and friendly. See? He's just a guy talking to a girl. Nothing scary about that.

He flexes his long, white fingers and bony wrist. "See how my wrist bends back? Thanks, Dad."

I cut him off. I don't care about his ancient family drama. "Why do I have a brand on my shoulder?"

He looks at me and flexes his wrist. Doesn't say a word.

"What's the GKS stand for?"

No answer.

"What's your name?"

He stops flexing. He smiles sweetly, showing his uneven teeth. It's like he's been waiting for that one. He plays a little with the sleeves of his blue sweater before answering, adjusting them back into place.

"I'm Jeremy."

Jeremy. Barbara's Jeremy.

Maybe I react, I don't know. It would be hard not to. His eyes light up, and he looks pleased. "She mentioned me, huh?"

Interesting. He didn't call her by her first name. His voice sounds softer when he talks about her. What went on between the two of them? Who is he?

Maybe I can get him to tell me. "She mentioned you."

His look turns serious. "I didn't do anything to her. You need to know that." He says it in a whisper, as if he's afraid someone is listening.

I want to believe him. I also want to know who's doing the listening.

And ask a lot more questions. Before I can say anything else, his phone buzzes. He glances down, bites his lip, and heads to the door.

"Business. I'll come back to check on you. Let me know if you need anything."

What? Why are you going? Tell me more about Barbara! "But—"

He stops, turns around. He wants to say more. His mouth opens and then he takes another look at his phone. "Oh wait. I forgot about that shirt you asked for. I'm sure you're having fun covering yourself with that blanket, but don't worry, it's on its way."

Well, that's a start. "Thanks."

"The Roxicet's gonna make you sleepy. I'd turn on the TV, but . . ."

Oh. Ha ha. You would but I smashed it to the ground. Go ahead and make a lame joke all you want, but by the way you're playing with your phone, it's pretty clear something's keeping you here. What?

"You sleep. I'll be back," he says.

Sleep? I do feel a little weird. Kind of tingly. I yawn. Just the mention of sleep and my head drifts down into the pillows. The one he brought in is way more comfortable than the other one.

But, Jeremy! This is Barbara's Jeremy. I mean, I guess I should have figured he'd still be around. Could I ever trust him the way she did? Stupid question. Don't trust him. Maybe I can get some answers out of him if I try hard enough.

I have a million questions. Maybe after I take a nap.

Questions. I have to remember the questions I want to ask.

Sleepy. It's hard to concentrate.

Maybe I will close my eyes for a minute or two.

I don't even hear the door close. I'm too busy asking questions and dreaming dreams.

CHAPTER SEVENTEEN

I'm not sure how long I slept, but it feels like nighttime. Without a clock to check. Without windows to see outside—or escape from—I can't be sure.

I rub my eyes. Sandy from sleep, and probably the Roxicet.

The tray is gone and there's a blue T-shirt. Wow, Jeremy's made it so I can wear more than a blanket. What a guy.

He's right, Roxicet is amazing. For a while all the pain disappeared. However, the sweet medicated velvet fog's lifting, and the dull pain in my side is back. The last time I tried to turn around I felt an enormous jab of pain.

I grimace. Yuck. My mouth tastes nasty. How long has it has been since I brushed my teeth? Maybe I'll find some toothpaste in the bathroom. Hmmm, what else is in Barbara's medicine cabinet? Razor blades to cut my way out?

To find out, I have one hurdle to cross.

Getting out of bed.

I grimace and push myself . . . forward—

Damn! Is this ever going to get easier? That push forward is like running into a brick wall. I have to keep going. Grabbing the side of the bed for support, I force myself to rise, then stumble to the table for the T-shirt. The red ball lamp makes for a good crutch.

The soft cotton between my fingers feels good. Comforting even. Oh, look. John Lennon's on it. That's cool. At least it doesn't say "Property of GKS."

Now I have to put it on.

What a horrible thought.

It's amazing how such a simple act can be transformed into a bigger drama than Romeo and Juliet. I inch my arms up and raise the shirt over my head, slowly wriggle it down. Every inch makes me want to scream.

Success! The shirt falls around my shoulders. Go me, but now I have to get my arms through the sleeves.

This is where it's going to get tough. The problem is, I have to lift my arm at a weird angle to get it through the sleeve.

Small steps. I lift my right arm and slowly and carefully hunt around for the sleeve. I twist the wrong way. Stabbing pain. Wrong move. I gasp but keep moving my elbow around to find the hole. I cry out. My side feels like it's being scraped with a sharp, rusty can lid. Each twist drives the jagged edge into my side.

I catch the sleeve! Yes! Now it's a matter of shoving my arm through. Oh, come on, you can do this.

I grit my teeth. One more inch. Another inch and . . . it's over. Mission accomplished.

Except for the left side.

Deep breath. Clench my teeth and . . . go.

The shirt is on, and I'm panting like I ran a marathon in August in 150-degree heat. I exhale. That smells nasty.

Toothpaste. Toothbrush.

I raise my arm to grab the nightstand. Oof! I smell like a dead sewer rat. The distance from the bed to the bathroom seems way too far. Deep breath, stand up, shuffle.

At this rate, I'll get there in a week. Come on, granny, you can do it. Toothpaste. Must have toothpaste.

The living room is completely dark. The only light on is in the bathroom. Wasn't it off before I fell into the arms of Roxicet?

Maybe Jeremy turned it on when he left the T-shirt. No matter. A little farther to go. I follow the light.

I barely glance at my reflection in the mirror. I'd rather not see. Oh wait, this bathroom doesn't have a medicine cabinet. So where's the toothpaste? Well, there seem to be drawers under the filthy sink. Which means I need to squat down. Wonderful.

Carefully, I lower myself and open the dingy white doors, afraid of what might be inside.

It's messy but not completely disgusting. And wow, toothpaste and deodorant, what a treat. A few other things, things that make a girl feel human. No razors, so no cutting my way to freedom.

The tube of toothpaste is half empty. Whoever did the squeezing was sloppy about it. They didn't roll up from the bottom the way I do. I scrape the dried goop around the opening away from the hole with a fingernail. Messy.

Come to think of it, I know exactly who the slob is. Was. This is Barbara's stuff. All she left behind. No one bothered to take it away. They left it all for the next person.

Wait. If they left all this, what other stuff was left behind?

Now that's interesting. I stand up and run a finger full of toothpaste through my mouth as fast as I can. As primitive as it is, it's good to have minty breath again.

As soon as I'm done, I re-enter the darkness to begin my hunt. The first place I want to see is the Black Room. This time I'm not going to waste time listening outside the door or smashing TV sets. It's time to figure out what I've gotten myself into.

I stumble through the darkness, still trapped in the lingering embrace of the Roxicet. I'm going to fight the groggy feeling, though.

The door to the Black Room's closed again. I push it open, turn on the light.

The lamp casts odd gleams over the black smooth surface. I brush my fingers against the leather chair. It's soft and cool to the touch. I try to imagine her sitting here, typing to me.

This is where Barbara spent her days. Where her eyes met mine. Now she's a lingering memory, like a half-squeezed tube of toothpaste.

I clutch the back of her chair. This is solid. This is her desk and her chair. Her computer where she trapped my image and then trapped me. Alice through the looking glass—computer screen. I was on the outside looking in, and now I'm right where she was. So what was her life like?

Her. I'm as bad as Jeremy? She had a name. Barbara.

I push the chair back. Sit in front of the monitor. Reach down. One click and a soft smooth buzz starts up. The computer screen flickers to life. I'm not used to having a computer built for speed.

First thing, the time in the lower right hand corner. 11:14. I was right. Night time.

I half expect the screen to be black, like the GKS "portal" I entered. But it's purple and blue. PeoplesCam colors.

Interesting. Is there a connection? Barbara wasn't exactly happy about me emailing them. Why would PeoplesCam be connected with GKS?

I hear keys jiggling. Shit, Jeremy's back. Quick as I can, I push away the mouse.

Footsteps to my left. A hand grabs the back of the chair. The sweet musky smell of his cologne fills the room.

"Exploring?"

I want to turn around, but it hurts too much. So I sit there and nod, stone cold quiet.

He leans in. The chair squeaks. "That's cool. They want you to. I'll get you an ID and password. Shouldn't take long."

I try to appear confident. "So, I can't do anything without a password?"

"Nope." He leans over farther still, his lips against my ear. His voice doesn't sound half as friendly as it did this morning. "Don't try anything cute. Big brother watches everything."

A shiver of fear runs through me. My spine prickles with cold sweat. His voice is soft; his words aren't.

He sounds as playful as a butcher knife. I don't like his night time voice.

I try to laugh it off. It sticks in my throat, so I smile. My heart's pounding, and my fingernails are digging into the soft squishy sides of the chair. "What? No email to tell Mom I'm all right?" My pout is more successful.

"Nope." He steps away. The chair falls back with a thud, causing a shock wave of pain throughout my entire body. I bite down on my lip to keep from screaming. "No postcards to Mommy. Or any of your other friends either. GKS only."

I force my hands away from the arms of the chair, fold them in my lap so he can't see them shaking. I want to pretend he's still the nice Jeremy from this morning, but I'm doing a shitty job convincing myself he's the same person. What is this, Mr. Hyde? I want Jeremy Jekyll back. I can deal with him.

Steady. Keep your head down. Focus on the smooth black surface of the desk. "Gee, what did I do to deserve this?" That's it, keep your tone light. Hide the fear.

"Oh, I think you know what you did. Jeannette."

Jeannette. The fake name I gave Barbara that first night.

He's pleased with himself. He grabs the back of my chair again and slides it away from the desk slowly. He rocks the chair back and forth. Each movement brings with it another stab of pain to the ribs.."Like I said, big brother watches everything."

With a jerk, the chair spins around. I can't help it, I let out a cry of pain, and next thing I know, I'm staring at Jeremy's sweet little boy face. He doesn't look so sweet any more. He's smiling, but without a trace of friendliness in his smile. What big teeth you have, Jeremy. I see anger there, instead. Is this the real Jeremy?

I try to shrug. It hurts my ribs to shrug. "Great. At least I'm not alone."

"Oh no, you're not alone." He smirks. "You weren't alone then and you aren't now. Never forget that."

Tears burn behind my eyelids. It's so hard to keep it together, almost too much. He's pushing me too far. In desperation, I use the only weapon I have. "Barbara's dead, right? Of course I'm alone."

Barbara. I said the name.

The look of sneering confidence leaves his face. He lets go of the chair, takes a few steps back.

"Why did you kill her?" I ask, trying to push my advantage and also trying not to sound like the little girl I know I am. "To make room for me?" Trying to sound as if I have power when deep down inside I know I have nothing at all.

He holds his hands up. We stare at each other. The silence stretches between us. I peer up at him through my eyelashes. I find it hard to catch my breath, and it's not my ribs.

"Isn't that why I'm here? To take her place? You wanted me instead of her?" I push myself to my feet, stifling the pain. "I'm what you wanted." The pain bites deeper. I'm too weak to fight through the brick wall this time. I gasp and collapse into the chair, gasping.

He lowers his hands.

"You're not alone." His voice sounds like steel.

"Big brother's watching, right?"

He grins. Not an evil night time smirk, but the smile I glimpsed when he told me his name. This is the Jeremy that likes surprises. Guess he has another up his sleeve. "Not what I meant. There are others. Other girls. You'll meet them soon."

What?

He shoves his hand into the pocket of his jeans, pulls out two Roxicet, and drops them on the desk. "You look like you need these," he says and twirls me around so I'm facing the computer again. "Coke's by your bed. Still cold if you're lucky."

He presses against me, hands on either side of the desk. Then he's gone, and the key rattles in the lock. I stare at the flickering cursor on the computer screen.

I'm not alone. Other girls.

That went well.

I'm not the only one. The world slips sideways. Once again, Jeremy's managed to turn my world upside down.

CHAPTER EIGHTEEN

After the shock starts to wear off, I blink my eyes, wipe my nose with the back of my hand, and take a good hard look at the screen in front of me.

"I'll need to get you an ID and a password," he said. "That won't take long."

I wonder. What about the old ID that's in the system?

Of course, an ID isn't exactly like a half-used tube of toothpaste. Even so, they probably wouldn't think I have a clue what Barbara's ID is, so why bother removing it?

What if it's the one she gave me for finals? That might explain why I wasn't able to log on, since she was already using it.

If it doesn't work, I can always try remembering the password she said was Jeremy's. That doesn't seem like the best option though under the circumstances. Might push Jeremy's buttons if he found out.

It's worth a try. All I have to do now is remember what she sent. Easier said than done, right?

Think! That night seems so long ago. I try to picture myself sitting in the dark in my bedroom. Warm and safe. A bowl of popcorn between my legs. Here we are now, entertain us.

Wait. It was a Lion, Witch, and Wardrobe thing. Orknies. Of course. It made me smile to think about it the first time, and I smile even more now.

This might work. Excited, I go to type the password into the PeoplesCam-like screen. But wait . . . one problem. I need a screen name. What's her screen name?

Damn memory. Of course, I kind of was abducted since I last used it. The Roxi isn't exactly helpful in focusing either. It's a weird word, reminded me of another language, something crusty old, like Latin or Greek. One of those dead languages, back when all the men walked around in bathrobes and spent their days in coliseums watching people get eaten by lions.

No, not a language. It looked like Latin, but was more of a religious thing. I've definitely heard the word before, when I wasn't dozing off in history class. Stoic? No.

Agnostic? Hmmm. Something like that. It's worth a try.

USER ID: Agnostic

PASSWORD: Orknies

The screen blinks for a minute. "User ID not recognized."

Okay. I kind of figured that wouldn't be it. It's a shorter word. More guttural. More like . . . .

USER ID: Gnostic

PASSWORD: Orknies

I click. No go. But I think I'm getting close. Gnosto, Gnostastic, Gnostro . . . I let my fingers play across the keys, trying to remember the right combination.

Why do I think it has to do with dirt? Grime? Yes, grime! It's a grimy word. Maybe a combination of the two? Gnosticgrime. Gnostgrime. No.

USER ID: Gnostrime

Gnostrime. Yes, that sounds right. After all, I spent a whole day memorizing that word, staring at that paper.

PASSWORD: Orknies

I hit enter. The screen twitches.

Access granted. Wow. Now I'm truly in Barbara's world.

A web page pops up. It's the site I used the night I saw the late night show, even down to the rooms with all the weird names. Most of the webcams are active. They all feature girls around my age, different shapes and sizes. Underneath each screen name is the name of the room they've been assigned to. They have strange names like "Desire" or "Gluttony." From a quick glance, the labels kind of fit the screen names. Along the right side of the screen is a chat room with twenty or so names logged on.

I scan the cameras to make certain Barbara's webcam isn't active. Good, GOASKALICE is asleep. Oh, she's listed as a "Girl Next Door."

Am I a Girl Next Door?

Really? Is it that obvious?

My heart's pounding. I keep expecting Jeremy to burst in at any second. I'd better make my move while I still can.

Do I have internet access? Should I try Facebook? But Barbara didn't sound like she had Facebook. She made me send her an email instead, so it probably wasn't an option.

Okay, then. I type in my email address. Well, one of them. And not the PeoplesCam one either. Plain old Yahoo.

It opens up. My heart is pumping like crazy. I can't believe I've gotten this far. Who should I write to? Uncle Dom? No, I don't have a clue how to send him an email.

Josh. Has to be. With my fingers trembling and my stomach doing flip flops, I type.

TO: wirehanger@ittp.com

Josh listen to me I don't know what's goin on out there, but if you get this please pass it on to my mom. Tell her I love her and ask her to talk to Uncle Dom. Im in big trouble. I don't know where I am exactly except I'm in a big building in a locked room and I have broken ribs and the room used to be the room of someone I saw die and

I blink away the tears that are stinging my eyes. Even after what Jeremy said, I don't want to think of her like that. I can't. Not dead.

It was that girl you were flirting with that night, the one I told you about. GoAskAlice. She said she livd in a city. Anyway they have me now and this is all about this thing called the GKS, so could you have mom ask Uncle Dom if he looked into that. I told him that the night I saw her die. My ribs are hurt and its hard to type but

I know I'm babbling. I don't care. I need to get it down and fast.

The sound of footsteps outside the door. I stop typing. The footsteps move away.

Gotta go better send this Love Kami

I finally let myself breathe after I hit send. I watch the hourglass clock and feel a dull pain in my ribs from all the typing. My head is throbbing.

The screen blinks. Message sent.

Did it go? No way to tell. For all I know, I'm in more trouble than five minutes ago.

I can't wait around to see if Josh writes back. It's too risky to spend any more time on the computer. Time to log off, grab my Roxicet, and prepare myself for my next big challenge.

Getting out of the chair. Time to swim through that brick wall once again.

CHAPTER NINETEEN

Sometimes, without anything else really to do in my room, I sit still on the bed and try to pick up clues about where I'm being kept. You never know, I might get a chance to tell someone where I am. Someday.

If I ever talk to someone.

I'm still not sure my email to Josh went through. That's the other thing I do a lot: check my email using Barbara's ID. I try not to do it too often in case I get caught, which is why I spend so much time sitting on the bed listening. Besides, it hurts to get up.

Picking up clues isn't easy. Without a window (and what's bugging me is, why isn't there one?) it's hard to tell whether it's day or night. It's funny though how accurate my internal clock is. The afternoon feels like the afternoon. Night time sounds a whole lot lonelier. The times I've checked the computer to see what time it is, I've usually been pretty close.

One thing that always breaks up the boredom: Jeremy's visits. I hate to say it, but I'm starting to look forward to them. Except for the incident in the Black Room, he's been the Jeremy I met at breakfast that first day. I haven't seen a glimpse of the other Jeremy at all.

It's nice to be able to talk with someone. It breaks up the sameness, the quiet within my angel-covered walls.

A big part of me hates that I look forward to seeing him.

When I lie in bed perfectly still, I can pick out certain sounds. I hear footsteps down the hall and pieces of conversations. One time I heard two girls talking and the sound of laughter. Who are those girls? Will I get to meet them? How can they laugh in this place?

I get this sense the wall by my bed's white kiddie headboard is closest to the outside. Not sure why, but I do.

So I spend a lot of time lying there. Listening.

I'm pretty sure it's a fake wall. Remember what I said about how strange it is there are no windows here? I think that's where a window used to be. Still is? I've spent time staring at it, you know, whenever I'm getting up to go to the bathroom. Even tried touching the wallpaper a few times, too. Although it's covered in cherubs, I swear it hollows out in the middle. Right where a window should be.

That's the area where I do most of my listening.

It's about a foot away from where my pillow is, so all it takes is a slight adjustment. I lie there kind of off center and my ears strain to hear ... anything really. A plane flying overhead. A truck passing by or a car sounding its horn. I can hear dogs barking in the distance. And music, of course. Mostly rap.

Maybe Barbara spent hours lying in bed trying to figure things out. I can see her living the exact life I'm living. Staring at the angels and a little strung out. Hoping for escape.

This morning during breakfast, I heard the loud wail of a police siren right outside the building.

I stopped eating and put down my fork. I locked eyes with Jeremy standing by the dresser. He was looking extremely urban with a shiny red sweatshirt and designer jeans. His Sketchers matched his sweatshirt. Of course.

Without the TV on top of it, the dresser's kind of wobbly. Every so often Jeremy leaned up against it causing it to bump up against the wall. It's kind of a thing he does every morning.

Bump, bump, bump. The siren's wail stopped abruptly. A dispatcher loudly squawked out orders that sounded like gibberish.

Jeremy and I kept staring each other down. Even though I wore a poker face, inside I was doing backflips. Is it possible ... could it be ... Uncle Dom received my message and tracked down where I am? Oh, please, let it be him. Let this be over. Let them burst in and bump Jeremy against the wall ....

Jeremy's poker face was way better than mine. He didn't look worried at all. Bump bump bump. Every time he leaned back the dresser hit the wall. It was almost like he was doing it on purpose.

Then the tires shrieked and the siren blared again. Soon enough, though, it faded into the distance.

Jeremy smirked. "See? You wouldn't believe how close they are either. But you're under special protection here, Kami. The cops won't think of visiting. They get paid a little extra to keep their mouths shut."

Bump.

I gritted my teeth and tried hard to hide my disappointment, even though I was dying inside.

Bump.

Bump.

I swear, if he pushed up against that dresser one more time I might throw my tray of food at him.

Maybe he sensed my irritation because he stopped what he was doing and walked to the bed. He smiled his crooked smile and said ever-so-pleasantly, "Hey, think you can be trusted with a TV? You've been a good girl. I can talk the bosses into bringing a new one in if you want."

"Sure. Sure, that'd be nice," I managed to say.

He nodded. "It's a deal then."

I pushed my food aside. I wasn't hungry any more. Jeremy took that as his cue, grabbed my tray, and left me to my thoughts.

I pushed my back up against the head of the bed, ignoring the pain. Well, at least I knew we're close to a police station. That was a clue.

I spent the rest of the morning listening for more sounds. That's what I'm still doing now.

Come to think of it, though, maybe I should be doing something else.

Something that will make me stronger.

"Knock. Knock."

Hours later and it's after dinner. Jeremy's standing at the outside of my bedroom holding a small television in his arms. I'm lying in bed, learning to live with a secret. Well, a new secret.

I grimace and struggle to sit up straighter in bed with my back against the pillow. My ribs feel like they're on fire.

Jeremy places the television on the dresser. His pale face is red, probably because he had to carry the TV up a few flights of stairs. "You do know how to work this thing, right? You turn it on by flicking the switch. It doesn't work if you smash it to the ground."

"So that's what I did wrong," I reply, going along with the joke. "Don't worry. After all this time in solitary, it's in good hands."

"It's not the hands I'm worried about, kid. It's the brain controlling them. Oh!" He reaches into his front pocket and slaps two tablets on the night stand. "Here's your Roxi. And I've got another treat for you. Took longer than it should have, but it's ready." He slaps down a scrap of paper next to the pills. "Your ID and password."

I act surprised. "Oh. Great!"

"It'll give you more to do than signing on and signing off." He grins, shows me a glimpse of the charming little boy.

Ah, so they have been watching me. But not close enough. I don't know what to say so I look away, afraid to let down my guard even an inch.

He doesn't pursue it. "Like I said, go and play around. Check out the site. Talk to the other girls. Do you want me to walk you through?"

No I don't, not at all, but I don't want to get him angry. Jeremy isn't fun when he's angry. "Is it hard to figure out?"

He shrugs. "Why don't you try it first? Get to know your way around?"

"Sure."

Then his tone turns serious. No jokes now. He leans in to make his point, placing a well-manicured finger close to my lips. "Listen. If someone says hi, say hi back. Play nice, you hear?"

Play nice, it is to laugh. Clearly he hasn't met the Queen of the Night yet. I smile, resisting the temptation to bite his finger off. "Of course I'll play nice, Jeremy."

"You can even turn on the webcam if you want."

Oh. So not sure I'm ready for that one. "Maybe."

"Try it!" He seems excited about this. Why is he trying so hard to sell me? "Seriously. The girls are nice. Well, most of them. And you like being seen on camera, right?"

Well, I did. Past tense. Back when I had nice people to talk to, like JadeMermaid and Nautical Ninja. And Josh. But now? Here? Like this?

I shrug and I wince. It hurts. "Can you help me up?"

Jeremy holds out his arm and I grab on.

It's the first time I've touched him. His skin is warm. Softer than I expected. His sweatshirt is soft and smells of a mixture of fresh linen and his sweet cologne. I hate to say it, but there's an electric thrill.

Enough. Stop thinking like that! Before I can have any more electric thoughts, I bite my lip and with a sharp inhale, push myself out of bed.

Jeremy whistles. "Still hurts, huh?"

I nod and let go of his hands to grab at my side. I place my feet on the ground and reach over for the Roxicet. "Thanks for the TV. It gets way too quiet in here."

He backs over to the TV and pats it, giving me space. "Certain channels are blocked, in case you're wondering. Oh, and you'll be getting out of your cage soon."

Ah, there we go. One of those little bombshells Jeremy likes dropping when I least expect it. I think I'm almost getting used to them. "What do you mean?" I try to make it sound like it's nothing, like I get sprung all the time.

Cheshire smile. "You'll see."

Oh, he is so full of mischief today.

Well, he seems to be in a good mood. Might be time to press my luck. "Jeremy, can I ask you a question?"

He winks. "You just did."

I'm nervous asking. I don't want to get him angry, but it's been on my mind for a while. "Can I have a pair of yoga pants? I'm sick of wearing jeans."

I know, yoga pants. Stupid, right? Every morning I get clean clothes laid out in the bathroom, so it's not as though I'm wearing the same pants every day. Still, it'd be nice to be able to wear something different, especially since the jeans they give me are usually too big.

He seems surprised, like he expected worse. "Since you're going to be on camera, I can get you anything you want. You need anything else, princess?"

Hmm. On camera? Better not to ask. "I wouldn't say no to eyeliner."

This clearly pleases him. "Consider it done. It's good to see you going along with this. For a change."

Shit, I didn't mean to 'go along' with anything. Not here. I grab at the piece of paper on the table so I'm spared from seeing the look of pleasure on his face.

He's oblivious. "Enjoy yourself. I'll be back in an hour."

I wait until I hear the click of the door closing. Then I shuffle my way through the dark living room into the bathroom. I lift the toilet seat, open my hands. Let the Roxicet fall, then flush.

There. That's my new secret. I'm not using the Roxi anymore. They may like me drugged up and spacey, but I'm not going to end up like Barbara. My story's going to have a different ending.

Somehow.

Feeling braver, I walk back through the dark living room and to the Black Room. The door's open, the light's on. Before I make Jeremy happy and go exploring, I think I'll log on as Barbara again. Who knows? Maybe something good happened while I was dining.

I sink down into the plush leather seat and for show pretend to log on under my new password, glancing every now and then at the paper in my hands.

Her ID still works. I'm ready to check my email.

I sit back in the chair, say a little prayer, type in my password. My inbox is empty. Not even a stupid chain letter.

Dammit! I stare at the screen, alternating between despair and anger. Why isn't Josh saying anything? In desperation, I click the mouse and move it around the desk a few hundred times, hoping to call up even junk mail. Anything.

Maybe I should send another email. Maybe another message in a bottle is needed. Maybe 100.

Hmmm. But are there other ways to send messages? For the heck of it, I try logging on to Facebook. Then Twitter. No go. Both sites are completely blocked. Inaccessible.

The momentary spark from the Roxi rebellion slips away. No word from the outside. Only the faded angels on the walls know where I am.

From the outside, I hear the sound of a siren making its way down the street.

I learned another thing this morning though. From now on, I'm not going to bother getting my hopes up. I already know no one's going to help. As far as I'm concerned, the cops here are no better than the ones in Farnham.

What the heck, maybe it's time. I reboot the computer and glance at the paper Jeremy handed me. Let's see what the other girls in the other cages are like. Maybe they can tell me what the hell's going on here. What we're all doing here.

Hey. Maybe they can teach me how to survive this place.

CHAPTER TWENTY

ID: iraneus

Screenname: Kamkit

Password: ilc8kr

Kamkit? What the hell kind of name is Kamkit? Are they trying to turn me into a cam-kitty? Grrr, this is so not going to work. I'll need to talk to Jeremy about this.

Kamkit. Hmph. Barbara had a way cooler ID.

I take a deep breath and immediately feel a stab of pain, mixed in with some butterflies. This is it. Stupid screen name or not, it's time to truly enter Barbara's world.

I hold my finger over Enter.

I let it hover there.

Why am I so nervous?

It's not like I don't know what I'll be seeing. Every time I log on I catch glimpses of the world I'm about to enter. Only glimpses, so I'm not discovered. But with good old Kamkit I'm about to be seen by everyone.

Not sure I like that idea much. It's like moving to a new school or being the new kid on the block.

The system setup is easy even without instructions. One click of a button and the show begins.

Do I want to turn the webcam on? I know Jeremy sure would like that a lot, but do I want everyone seeing me before I see them first? Decisions, decisions. I twist at my hair nervously with my index finger.

No. Better to enter first without a face and scope things out.

Finger poised.

Do it.

It's like getting out of bed with broken ribs. Once you swim through the brick, you're fine. Do it.

Okay. I type in my name and password and click.

The screen changes. Up pops my new world.

"GKS: Let the game begin!"

scrolls across the top of the page in the PeoplesCam colors I'm used to. Along with the cams featuring all the girls and their strange names.

I've gotten used to the changes, almost, having logged on as Barbara so many times. Still, I've never taken a good look, trying so hard not to be noticed.

There I am. Kamkit. A blank webcam with my new name underneath it. I am listed as a Girl Next Door, same as Barbara was. Not sure I'm thrilled with that label, but then again there don't seem to be any rooms for royalty.

All the room names are located underneath the GKS banner. I locate the Girl Next Door room and double click. Time to meet the neighbors.

The room has 16 webcams, all of which fit neatly onto the screen. There's no way to scroll down. All the camscreens are live except for one. One guess who that is.

Each cam features a girl around my age. No widowmakers here. Some are smiling, some are yawning. One's reading a book. So many different names: Elektris. Weathervayne. Tomorrowknows. Whoever's in charge of names likes reading comic books.

I scan the IDs of the other girls in the room. Kelaidescope is the girl reading the book. She has red hair cut short and bright blue eyes, hidden behind cool red glasses. They look retro and expensive.

An African-American girl with wild orangey black hair is laughing. Her name is Tangerinewilde. She seems to be all over the place, moving constantly.

To the right is the chat room. Of course, I remember it from the time I saw it as Barbara. This time, it looks a little different. This time, I see:

kamkit has entered the room

Gulp. So they know I'm here. Did Barbara's name show up when I used her name? I never checked for that. Wait, does that mean Jeremy knows I logged on?

I can feel the panic rising. Why hasn't he said anything? Is he that good at keeping secrets?

Hold on, hold on. I force myself to calm down. Breathe. Maybe he doesn't know anything. If he did, why wouldn't he stop me? Of course he doesn't know. It doesn't make sense.

Once my heart stops racing, I scratch at my leg and wonder when the questions will begin. Sure enough, it doesn't take but a few seconds.

TANGERINEWILDE: LOOKS LIKE WE'VE GOT A NEW ONE

WEATHERVAYNE: What?! ;)

ANGELINO18: Kamkit has entered the room

WEATHERVAYNE: NO she hasnt her screens blank!!! ;)

TANGERINEWILDE: WV, UR SO STUPID

VISITOR68: Hello, Kamkit.

VISITOR39: Is your camera working? Turn it on, dammit.

I look down at the keyboard. My fingers are trembling. I'm not sure what to say. Is this a way for the Queen of the Night to act? Queens don't curtsy to the rabble. It figures, the second I'm surrounded by other queens I don't know whether to curtsy or log off and crawl under the bed.

Nope, can't. Crawling under the bed would hurt too much.

Ha! I laugh at my own stupid joke. That makes me braver. One keystroke at a time, I type

KAMKIT: Hey there.

Hardly earth shattering, but it will do.

TANGERINEWILDE: HEY THERE YOURSELF KITTEN

VISITOR39: If she's a kitten, can I pet her?

TANGERINEWILDE: DOWN BOY DOWN DON'T SCARE HER OFF RIGHT AWAY!

WEATHERVAYNE: LOL :)

TANGERINEWILDE: HI KAMKIT

I like Tangerinewilde. I can tell right away she has a certain style that might make her worthy of ruling. She's smiling at the camera and sticking out her tongue. Oh, she has a gold stud on the tip of her tongue. Man, Mom would kill me if I ever did that.

ANGELINO18: Hola, chica.

Automatically, I go through the list of webcams. Angelino18? Oh, okay, there she is. She has dark hair cut shoulder length and full lips with a mole on her left cheek. Her eyes are her best feature—dark and smoldering—definitely bedroom worthy. She's wearing a blue crop top with the camera pulled wide enough to show off her assets. She definitely has big assets.

VISITOR39: Turn the cam on. We want to see you.

ANGELINO18: Yeah what are you a frikkin mystery? Vamanos!

TANGERINEWILDE: SHUT THE HELL UP ANGEL SHE DOESNT HAVE TO IF SHE DOESNT WANT TO

TANGERINEWILDE: NOT EVERYONES A CAMTRAMP LIKE YOU

ANGELINO18: En serio?

WEATHERVAYNE: ROFL

Angelino grins and undoes a button on her shirt.

TANGERINEWILDE: THATS IT SHOW EM WHAT YOU GOT GIRL

TANGERINEWILDE: AGAIN

TANGERINEWILDE: YAWN

VISITOR57: Let's see your face, kamkitten.

VISITOR23: What's your name?

My name. Should I give my real one? I think back to the night I met Barbara. She didn't, not until after our second date. And now that I think of it, how was I able to see her on the PeoplesCam site if the GKS is member-only? How did her webcam show up on both?

Hmmm. It's all beginning to make crazy sense. Maybe some kind of security filter is in place? Maybe that's why this webcam is in real time while I had to wait three seconds for the other one? But who would have done that for her?

No time to worry about that now. A name, dammit!

Well, I could always use Queen of the Night. Maybe it's a good idea to use that one today. No, I'll go with my standby.

KAMKIT: I'm Jeannette.

VISITOR46: How old are you? Where do you come from?

VISITOR57: Show us your face

TANGERINEWILDE: HEY JEANNETTE WELCOME 2 THE DOLLHOUSE

VISITOR15: Only I bet she doesn't look like no wiener dog.

VISITOR38: Only one way to find out.

VISITOR69: Show us.

I place my hand over the mouse. Should I do it?

Maybe it would help me get to know the other girls better. They must have a better idea about what's happening in this place than I do. They might even know what happened to Barbara and why she was killed.

It's worth a try.

KAMKIT: Okay

VISITOR38: Kewl

I start to click the button, but just as I'm about to I hear a soft ping. A gray box appears on my screen.

KELAIDESCOPE: Don't.

Kelaidescope? Oh, okay, the hot librarian with the red hair and cool glasses, reading the book. She doesn't appear to be paying any attention to what's going on, but is sitting there with her nose between the covers. I can't even tell she's typing at all. Guess she's seeing more than she's letting on.

KAMKIT: Why not?

KELAIDESCOPE: Keep yourself mysterious for a while. Sort of like a mystery novel. It'll improve your chances.

Improve my chances? I glance over at the chat room. The screen is filled with visitors and a few of the girls urging me to log on and show them what I look like.

Tangerinewilde is right, this place is a dollhouse and I'm the new doll being taken out to play. But exactly what game do the visitors play with their dolls?

Maybe I should ask my new friend.

KAMKIT: How will that improve my chances?

KELAIDESCOPE: You were friends with GoAskAlice, correct?

Wait. How-?

KAMKIT: How did you know that?

KELAIDESCOPE: I liked her. She was nice. A little cokey, but that's pretty much to be expected around here.

KAMKIT: How did you know I knew her?

I watch Kelaidescope read her book, watch her turn a page, watch her push her red glasses up and half-watch the chatroom screen that continues to babble on about Kamkit showing her face.

And then another soft ping.

KELAIDESCOPE: Will they ever let you out of there?

Okay, that didn't exactly answer anything. But then maybe there's a reason for that.

KAMKIT: I don't know. I hope soon.

KELAIDESCOPE: Good. It'll be nice to talk to you. Then.

How annoying. Clearly, I'm not going to get anything out of her. Is she afraid someone's spying on us? Whatever it is, this reader is choosing her words very carefully.

Another ping.

KELAIDESCOPE: Another piece of advice.

KAMKIT: What's that?

KELAIDESCOPE: Log off soon. Keep the mystery going as long as you can. Don't tell them too much about yourself.

KAMKIT: Why not

KELAIDESCOPE: Do you like to read, Jeannette?

Jeannette. Should I trust her with the truth? It would be nice to have someone to trust in here. I sit up in my chair and the ache in my ribs isn't as bad, not next to her knowing my name. This time I'm the one choosing my words carefully.

KAMKIT: Yeah. I do.

KAMKIT: By the way, my name is Kami.

KELAIDESCOPE: Nice to meet you, Kami. Wish it was under different circumstances.

KELAIDESCOPE: A good book keeps you wanting to turn the pages, right? That's what this place is all about. Think about it like this: it's all one big striptease. Better to take off your clothing, piece by piece. At least, that's what I think. Others disagree. They're morons.

I glance away from Kel and over to the other webcams. The talk about me has faded, replaced by talk about Angelino18 who is busy unbuttoning her final button.

KELAIDESCOPE: See? You want to keep your show going for as long as you can. She's at the end of the chapter if you ask me.Not much left to get through.

Oh. Good. And I'm beginning mine.

CHAPTER TWENTY-ONE

Maybe it's going off the Roxi. And maybe it's happened before and I've been too out of it.

All I know is, one moment I'm sound asleep dreaming about being late for gym class. I've forgotten the combination to my locker so I ask Daphne for help, and she's going on and on and on about her little yellow car. Of course that makes me sad because I don't even have a license much less a little yellow car, so I try to get away. The doors to the gymnasium are locked with huge chains and a padlock. I try to figure out a way to get inside and I spot a huge trampoline . . ..

Before I can bounce I'm yanked out of my dream by the sound of the door to my room being unlocked. Soft footsteps make their way through the living room.

I'm out of my dream right away. My back is flat against the mattress; it's the only way I can sleep without it hurting. I lie perfectly still open-eyed staring up into the darkness of the pitch-black room, clutching my thin orange blanket.

Step step step creak

I want to call out. I want to jump up and hide somewhere.

Step step step

Creak

But how can I? Whoever is there would hear me moving and know I'm awake. I'd lose the element of surprise. I'm still too weak to fight back, and screaming will only make things worse. My best option is to stay right where I am and pretend to sleep. If only there was a razor in the bathroom or a knife in the kitchen. Something.

Step

The footsteps make their way through the outside room. My eyes are blind, useless, busy adjusting to the darkness. What's going to happen? Who is it?

A door opens. Must be to the Black Room. Whoever it is must be checking on what I've been up to. After a few seconds, the footsteps begin again. They're coming closer. Heading to the bedroom.

Step step step

Everything's charged. I can hear myself breathing in, breathing out. My breathing sounds as loud as an oxygen tank. A strand of hair tickles the side of my cheek and my bare feet are uncomfortably warm because they're wrapped too tightly in the blankets.

Creeeeeeeeak

The person's in my bedroom.

I shut my eyes.

Breathe in. Breathe out. Stay quiet, motionless. Pretend to sleep. Breathe in. Breathe out. Keep the rhythm going.

The footsteps stop. They're at the foot of my bed.

It's all I can do to keep my breathing steady.

Is it one of the Ape Twins? Is he going to climb onto the bed, grab my face, place one hand over my mouth, force me to—

No! Stop that. Breathe in. Breathe out.

He's still as a shadow in the darkness. Watching me. I can hear his breathing, soft and low. He's inches away from the bed. Him. Has to be a him. I can tell by the heavy sound of the footsteps, by the smell of his cologne.

Oh.

A chill creeps down my spine as recognition sets in. There it is. That faint familiar scent, slightly sweet but not-too-sweet. Mixed with a hint of cigarette smoke.

Jeremy.

It's Jeremy.

I can't let on I know he's there. I can't. It's one of his surprises, one of his mind games. I can't say a word. I have to keep my eyes closed, maintain the illusion of sleep. I have to.

Jeremy stays silent. He doesn't move an inch, doesn't do anything. He simply stands there. Silent.

He watches me for what seems like half an hour. After a while, I can't stand it any longer and open my eyes a slit.

In the darkness, he blocks the television. I can make out his strong shoulders, his familiar outline. Yes, it's unmistakable. It's Jeremy.

I keep my eyelids at half mast, watching him watching me.

And then, he steps forward. I struggle to stay calm, keep my breathing steady. Did he see me open my eyes? Does he know I'm awake? I can't stand it please help me please Jeremy what the hell are you—

I close my eyes tightly. He's by the little table. He's inches away. I want to scream out, I want to cry. It's too much, way too much. Stop this.

Then his lips touch mine. Softly.

I hear the sound of footsteps walking away.

Step step step creak step

And then the door closes.

The minute it does my eyes spring open. My breathing, freed from the masquerade, comes out ragged and gaspy. I mentally steel myself, then push my body forward into a sitting position. The pain hits immediately. I don't care. The springs creak under me and I hope to hell he's truly gone.

A trace of his cologne lingers in the air like an afterthought.

I still feel the buzz of his lips against mine. Trembling, I bring my hands to touch my lips. Why did he kiss me? Why did he stare at me for so long? I don't know whether to be flattered or frightened.

I sit there, lonely in the darkness. Listening to the quiet night sounds. Praying for the morning to arrive.

CHAPTER TWENTY-TWO

Jeremy's standing at the dresser again. This time the bedroom light is on and I can see him. He's holding a breakfast tray. It's only been a few hours since he was a shadow in my room.

I didn't sleep much after that. Too much going through my head. Plus my ribs were aching something fierce. They were begging me for Roxi. I didn't listen.

The thing is, Jeremy's acting like nothing happened. He's freaking spreading jam on my toast and making jokes about my webcam name. Was the whole thing a dream? Maybe it was someone else. No, no, it was Jeremy; I know it in my gut.

"Here you go, Kamkit," he says, handing me some toast.

If he can pretend nothing happened, so can I. Only I can't control the tips of my ears. They're on fire. Well, maybe it's time to go on the defensive. "Yeah, I wanted to talk to you about that. Who do I complain to about my stupid name?"

He sets down the knife. The sarcastic look on his face says everything. "We don't exactly have a complaint department here. Why don't you like your screen name?"

Funny, he looks hurt. "Jeremy, did you have anything to do with it?"

"Me? Nothing." He shrugs, trying to act all tough. Aha, so he did have a bit to do with my screen name. Artists can be so touchy about their creations. The fact I've bugged him even a bit makes me happy.

I want to dig the knife in deeper. "Can you get it changed?"

"No. Everyone knows you as Kamkit." He hands me a glass of orange juice to wash down my toast but refuses to look at me. Wow, what a baby. He's getting all sulky. If last night wasn't still fresh in my brain, I'd probably find it hilarious.

The OJ is bitter and has pulp in it. I make a face, partly because of being stuck with the name. Still, if he's going to be so sensitive about the whole thing, maybe I need to try and make nice. Don't want Jeremy Hyde coming out to play, after all. "Come on, I was only Kamkit for an hour. Can't you make an announcement? I can be 'the prisoner formerly known as Kamkit.'"

That does the trick. He grins and places the tray on my lap, then takes two Roxicet out of his pocket. "Here."

"Thanks." I pretend to be grateful. I grab the pills and, carefully balancing my food tray, reach over to place them on the nightstand, right next to the lamp. It's nice to see reaching doesn't hurt that much anymore.

"You're still taking the Roxi, right?" He's maintaining eye contact again, but I'm pretty positive he's not convinced. Does he suspect?

"Twice in the morning, twice at night," I lie. "But they make my food taste weird. Do you mind if I wait?"

He doesn't say a word. I stare right back at him and chew slowly on my toast. Go ahead, call me a liar, Jeremy. Come on, say it.

He's the first one to look away. He glances at his phone, apparently bored. I lower my head and smile, pleased with my tiny victory.

He sends someone a text message. What I wouldn't give to read his phone. "Well, listen. You up for a tea party, Kamkit? Today you get to make some new friends. Pick you up around one, okay?"

New friends. Victory gone. I'm going to have to meet the girls face to face, not cam to cam. How will that go? Once again, world turned upside down.

I wonder if "The world of GKS" is the same as PeoplesCam in other ways?

When I was trying to hunt down more about Barbara when she wasn't online, I was able to see her profile. Do any of the Girls Next Door have profiles, too? Might be worth taking a look.

About half an hour has passed since Jeremy left to take my breakfast away and do all those other things he needs to do. Whatever they are. Meanwhile, I'm back in the Black Room using my Kamkit profile in stealth mode. Kel is right, no need to show my face yet, but this doesn't seem like a thing I have to do using Barbara's ID. For this, I can cruise around like a little KamKittie.

I double click into the Girl Next Door room. Sixteen windows automatically pop up, although not all the girls are on at this time of day. Makes sense, because there aren't many visitors hanging around, either.

Kel's camera is dark. She must be reading in bed. That is, if she reads when she's not on camera. Hmm, let's take a look and see if she has any sort of profile, shall we? She seems the type who would. It is kind of like a book cover, after all.

I right click over her name. Yes, there's a profile option. Let's see what it says.

GKS ID: Kelaidescope
Tribe: Girl Next Door
Real Name: Kel. That's all you need to know.
Location: Auschwitz
Age: 19
Gender: Female
Interests: Reading, writing and Nunya business
Writers I have known and loved: Hemingway, Stein, Dickens, Tolstoy, Hugo (and have I dreamed a dream), Oates, Huxley, Flaubert, R.L. Stein. Also like Diary of Anne Frank a lot. I wonder why?
Famous Last Words: Plus ca change, plus ca same old shit. (I stole that. You won't know from where. Damn you, Google!)

Okay. Not as revealing as Barbara's was. I was kind of hoping for some kind of common bond. Like, discovering we had Narnia in common. Instead, all I get is ironic distance. Besides, I don't know many of the authors on her list that well, although I did try to read Tolstoy once (just once). Kel's kept her book cover kind of generic, if you ask me. Maybe that was on purpose.

I click out and glance at the other rows.

Tangerinewilde is on. Well, sort of. Even though her camera's live, she's nowhere to be seen. All I can see is her leather chair, which looks like the one I'm sitting in. Only, her chair has words scratched into the leather, probably made using those long fingernails of hers. The one word I can make out is of the four-letter variety.

I wonder what her profile looks like? I right click and enter.

Interesting. I didn't realize you could use the word "fuck" that many times.

Around one o'clock someone knocks on my door.

The sound scares the crap out of me. I'm not used to anyone knocking. Who could it be?

"It's me."

Wow, why didn't Jeremy enter? Usually I know he's coming in by the rattling of the keys at the door.

Maybe he heard the water running in the sink. I'm in the bathroom trying to make myself look good. It seems strange fussing over myself in the mirror. I haven't done this in a while.

I touch a finger to my left eye and trace the lower lid from the left to right. Oh, dead eyes, dead eyes. The one thing she didn't have was eye liner. I so need to make my blue eyes pop.

This is important. I'm getting out of my room. I'm going to meet Kelaidescope and Tangerinewilde and all the other sassy sad girls with their comic book names.

"Come in," I call out, playing with a curl in my hair one last time. I turn the faucet off, take one last look in the mirror, and go open the door.

It almost feels like a normal life.

He's standing outside looking cool in a leather jacket. He's clutching a blue plastic shopping bag in his hands.

He remembered? Wow. "Is that what I think it is?"

He shoves the bag into my arms and steps into the room. I turned on all the lights before getting ready so it would seem like the afternoon. "I was gonna bring it before. You've got a pair of yoga pants at the bottom, and—"

I look inside the bag. The first thing I see is eyeliner. Eyeliner! I gaze upon its loveliness. "Do I have time to—"

"We need to go, Kami." But he's grinning. He's cool.

I want to see what else is in there. This is like Christmas. "Oh, and lip gloss! Oh, Jeremy, can't I please—"

"Two minutes." He tries to look stern. I think he likes seeing me excited.

I can't help it, I squeeze his arm. "Be ready in a sec." Then I close the bathroom door and dump all the stuff into the sink. Ooh, even some blush! It's not a lot, but it's mine.

Lip gloss. I forgot what it feels like. Eyeliner on the bottom eyelid. Not too thick, keep the hand steady . . .

Being able to feel prettier makes me braver. It's like putting on a mask. My own.

I want to keep my promise, but it's hard not to want to play a bit. To Jeremy's credit, he doesn't knock on the door every five seconds as if he's my big brother and I'm hogging all the bathroom time.

Finally, I'm ready to step out of the bathroom. He's sitting on the crummy green couch playing with his phone, but he stands up the minute I enter. "Nice," he says. It's clear he likes the look. I just know the tips of my ears are burning.

"Are we going outside?" I ask hopefully, glancing at his jacket.

Jeremy gives me a sarcastic thumbs down on that one. "Yeah, right. The field trip's not that far away, Kami."

"Okay." I don't care. At least it's out of my cell. I reach out to open the door.

"No!" He runs over and grabs my arm roughly. "We're going downstairs. One floor down. Don't try anything funny."

"Have I tried anything funny yet?" I try to yank my arm away, but that only makes him hold on more tightly. "Jeremy, that hurts!"

He lets go. I grab hold of my ribs. "Sorry." The look on his face is deadly serious. "But you need to understand."

"Can I ... uh ...." I motion to the door.

He nods. "Follow me." He walks into the hallway and I get my first glimpse of the outside world.

I have to admit, it's not what I was expecting. After all the time locked up I guess my imagination's gone wild. I was imagining a big and overwhelming place, like a mad scientist's lab where they conduct experiments. What I see beyond the door is only your friendly neighborhood tenement slum. I saw a lot of those in New York. It makes sense, I guess.

The hallway is dark and narrow and even scarier than a mad scientist's lab. The first thing I notice is the smell. It's musty, the way most old decaying buildings are, but also has a touch of something rancid in the air, along with a metallic smell, like the pennies in mom's change jar.

My room is at the very end of the hall, although there's one exactly like it across from me. Shoved in the far corner, to my left, is a piece of clothing, covered in dust. Looks like a blouse, crumpled and discarded. It's white, but with dark stains on it. From Barbara? No, it's been there for too long. What's the story behind it? No, I don't want to know. The look of it makes me shiver.

Covering the entire length of the hallway is a wood paneling that goes halfway up, so typical of a lot of tenements. It's covered in nicks and dust. Above the paneling, ugly faded purple wallpaper peeling off the walls. Mostly at the seams, but a few pieces have come off and hang limply against the paneling, and one whole section has been completely ripped off, exposing the white plaster underneath. Someone has taken a magic marker and written the words "Doll Valley" in blood red.

The wooden floorboards are dark and in need of a mop. They might have been nice at one point, but now have dust bunnies everywhere and dark smears in spots. I see footprints in the dust everywhere. I look to my right, to count the doors in the hallway. How many girls inside? One, two—

Jeremy laughs. "Four doors, nosey. Don't worry. We keep everyone separate. You can't knock on the walls in Morse code with your neighbor or anything."

I count only two lights in the hallway, one on each side, located right between the doors, in little white scallop shells attached to the wall. Only one is working, because the other seems to have been smashed. The working one is on the left side. In the center of the hallway, two old-fashioned forced air heaters, one on either side. They appear old and rusty and covered in dust balls. They are clearly not being used, because it's colder in the corridor than it is in my room. Maybe they don't work anymore.

The doors are the only things that look even close to new, which is to be expected, I guess. All four of them look exactly like the one in my apartment: made out of strong mahogany. The better to keep everyone caged up, little girl. Someone has spray painted numbers on all four doors, in bright red. I glance back; I'm number four.

We make our way down the hall. I shiver and hold the sweatshirt I'm wearing more tightly. In front of one door, a long drag mark begins and seems to extend all the way to the stairs at the far end of the hallway.

The floor below seems brighter than this. Then again, anything would have to be. I can't wait to get away.

I get to the end of the hall and grip the rail, a few steps ahead of Jeremy. "Don't go too fast," he warns.

I can see a landing at the end of the stairway. It's a complete revelation, like reaching the end of a dark tunnel.

For one thing, the smell doesn't seem as bad. Also, the landing is bathed in light from the sunshine streaming through the windows. Actual windows! When was the last time I looked through a window? Not since I fell out of one...

The windows seem absurdly large, but maybe that's because I've grown so used to living in the world of artificial light. The ugly purple wallpaper ends abruptly at the stairwell, although the half wood paneling continues downward. Even so, the landing seems brighter, and not just because of the sunlight streaming through. It's as if someone a while back made an effort to try and fix up the area. Maybe when someone actually had dreams for the house. The baby blue paint on the walls and windows seems subdued and tasteful, even with the grimy fingerprints and dust. The window sill is covered in paint chips.

What's going on outside? Would I be able to see? The curtains covering the windows are delicate and gauzy white, with tiny holes running up and down, indiscriminately. Holes? Oh, once upon a time, someone must have had a cat that liked to climb.

Can I catch a glimpse of the outside world? It'll have to be quick and I'll have to be sneaky. Clues, clues . . .

A tinny tweeting interrupts my concentration. It sounds like someone hitting a triangle. I casually glance behind me. I know that sound by heart now, it means Jeremy has a phone call. He grimaces. I've learned by now how much he hates answering his phone, but he always answers. "Yeah?"

He's distracted, so I walk down the rickety stairs to the landing. He may have a call, but the outside world is calling me.

The curtains block most of my view. They're thicker than they seem. From what I can see, it's a sunny day. Looks cold outside though. Frost sticks to the windows, and I can see snow on the windowsill. I want to push the curtains aside, get a better view, get some idea where I've been taken. If only I could force the window open, jump out . . .

I walk to the window. Glance up at Jeremy. He seems distracted, busy arguing with someone. Carefully, I push aside the gauzy curtains.

A glimpse of cars and buildings. It's definitely a city, all gray and industrial and hopeless. A big building is located across the street, some kind of manufacturing place. Looks like it's open for business. Any signs or phone numbers?

The street's a busy one, with lots of parked cars. A sleek blue sports car catches my eye as it pulls into a parking lot next to the building. The car is driven by a man with dark hair and darker sunglasses, talking on a cell phone. He pulls his car next to a big red Ford 4x4. Can I see a license plate on either car? Yes, on the truck. White and blue with red letters.

Illinois. Is that where I am? Big city.

Chicago?

"Shit!"

Jeremy's voice. Is it the call or because I'm looking outside? Whatever, next thing I know, I feel a hand on my shoulder. Time's run out. Before he can get rough I step away from the window. "Let's get going," he says, using his Jeremy Hyde voice, so I know he's not fooling.

Fine. I let him lead me to the tea party.

In Chicago?

CHAPTER TWENTY-THREE

The hallway at the bottom of the stairs is much brighter than the gloomy hallway of horrors I had just left behind. Not surprising, I guess. This hall has one more door at the other end, too. Might be the way out. That door has a window without a curtain, meaning you get a good look at the outside world. That's kind of cruel, if you ask me.

I can see a driveway. Cars outside. I want to be outside, too. An image forms in my head: me kicking Jeremy where it counts, him bent over. Running down the hall. Escape. Yes please.

Jeremy places a hand on my shoulder. His grip is strong. He probably knows what I'm thinking. Maybe I could get in a quick kick? But I don't, instead I walk forward like a puppet as he pushes me to the first door on the left. Shit, what a wimp. Do something. Do. Something. Do—

"Here we go." He pulls a bulky object from his jacket, with a round red medallion that catches my attention. "Cat's eye," it says. And surrounding it, jingling around, a massive amount of keys. His keychain.

The sight of it almost makes me forget about meeting the girls. Almost. His keychain. Freedom. There must be a key for every apartment in the building. They all look the same—silver, with numbers at the top.

Which one's mine? This is good information to have. Might be able to use it someday. I don't get to see his keychain for long, though. Before I know it the door's open and I'm following him inside.

Okay, so this is it.

I wondered how they could fit 16 girls into one tiny apartment. That was the number I expected since I counted 16 screens on the webcam. Turns out I'm not meeting all the Girl Next Door dolls in the dollhouse, though. Only four.

They all look up with bored eyes when we enter, as if I'm a slice of pizza from one of the boxes open on the countertop. Shit! It really does feel like my first day in high school.

The dolls are all placed around a square kitchen table, crammed into the living room. Even with only four, the place seems cramped. It's laid out like my room upstairs, except for the absence of angels. Instead of red angel wallpaper, it's painted a depressing green, sort of the color of the ugly couch in my room. Filthy yellowed enamel covers the floor in the kitchen area, worse than in my apartment.

At the very end, where my bedroom and the Black Room are, this apartment also has two rooms. Both doors are closed. The one that would be my Black Room isn't black at all, but has an old poster of the TV show *The Office* on it. Hmmm, could that possibly be . . . their office?

I notice two boxes of pizza on the counter, wedged between three bottles of soda, a pile of napkins, plates, cups and a booger-yellow glass ashtray piled high with discarded butts. Maybe the pizza boxes have a name of a business on them? A phone number? Address?

The table the girls are sitting around is classic Target. No, worse than that. K-Mart. One of the legs wobbles whenever someone moves or pushes an elbow up against the tabletop. Next to the table is a plastic trashcan desperately in need of emptying.

The small kitchen area has a window by the sink. The shades are pulled down all the way and the bright sunlight makes the shade glow white. Can I get another look outside? Oh, now you're thinking, Sherlock. Between that and the pizza boxes maybe you can figure out where you are, better than a GPS. Elementary.

Can't now, though. A large African-American man is standing by the stove. Someone I've never seen before. He's about twice my size and looks like a bouncer. Not a happy one, either.

But the girls . . . well, I know all of them, it turns out. Even if they don't know me.

Tangerinewilde is sitting closest to me, with her wild orangey black hair. She's wearing a pink jump suit and holding a blue Solo cup. Angelino18 is next to her, amazingly wearing a shirt that doesn't show off her boobs. Kelaidescope's here too, looking bored (as usual) and reading a book. Next to her is another girl, someone I sort of remember. What's her name again?

She's the first to break the silence. "Hi there," she says, sounding like she means it. She has straight blonde hair, green eyes, and puffy, round cheeks. That, along with her high pitched voice, makes her seem a lot younger than the others. She's dressed in jeans and a too-tight T-shirt that shows she's on the heavy side. A gold charm bracelet hangs around her wrist, and it jiggles whenever she raises her arm.

"The new girl," booms out Tangerinewilde, wiping the sides of her mouth with a napkin and staining it with her bright pink lipstick. Yeah, that's me all over. The new girl. "Jeannette, right?"

I nod. The girls all sit there, staring at me. Sizing me up. Oh, right. I guess they want me to speak. Nothing's coming out. I can hardly stand to look at them, much less talk. This is awful.

Maybe Tangerinewilde senses I need a life preserver. "Pull up a chair," she orders, pointing to the only empty one in the room, located between Angelino18 and Kelaidescope. I'm closest to the kitchen counter. Have my back to it.

I hesitate. Tangerinewilde notices. She seems to notice pretty much everything. "Oh, don't be afraid. Angie won't bite. Well, not that much."

In response, Angie—Angelino18—bares her teeth and growls, but in Tangerinewilde's direction, not mine. Everyone laughs and that somehow makes me feel better. Ish.

"I'd rather bite into a big pepperoni," Angie says, clearly meaning something else. She reaches over to grab another slice of pizza. Her arms are covered in bracelets and she has a tattoo on the back of her right arm. Some kind of saying. Looks Spanish.

"Ain't that the truth," mutters Tangerinewilde.

The blonde girl laughs as if that's hysterically funny. Well it isn't, and it's pretty clear she doesn't get it either. When she opens her mouth, you can tell she has crooked teeth. She seems a little off-center. Why?

I can sense someone staring at me. I turn to my right. Kelaidescope is looking up from her book. She winks at me, then goes back to reading.

Angie still has her hand in the box of pizza, but Jeremy grins and slaps that hand away. "Down, girl." He grabs a slice, takes a big bite. Grabs a napkin, wipes his mouth. Then he crumples the napkin into a ball and throws it at Tangerinewilde. "Oh, sorry. Thought you were the trash." You can cut the sarcasm in his voice with a knife.

Oh wow. What's up between Jeremy and Tangerinewilde? It's as if she's getting a special dose of the bad Jeremy all to herself. Even the way he pushed Angie's hand aside was pretty rude. He hasn't been like that with me since my first night here. Is this how he usually acts?

You can tell Tangerinewilde's not happy. Her back stiffens and she throws the crumbled up napkin to the floor. She looks at Jeremy with anger in her eyes, but with a sick smile plastered on her face. She's angry. I kind of think she's scared, too.

"Be a good girl, Lea. Play nice," Jeremy calls out. Sounds more like a taunt. I glance down at Lea's hands, which are tightly clenched. She's muttering under her breath.

Jeremy doesn't like that. "You got a problem, Lea?" And then, even angrier. "Do you?"

Her hands unclench, in slow motion. She doesn't acknowledge him. But she does stop muttering.

Satisfied, he turns to the man at the stove. His tone becomes businesslike. "Got a call. The boss. About tonight's announcement."

Tonight's announcement?

The big guy nods. He's not the most expressive guy on the planet. He seems to specialize in standing there with his big meaty hands in his pockets, looking menacing.

"We can talk about it while we get ready." Get ready? Jeremy's golden gaze turns to everyone at the table. "Keep your hands off the pepperoni, Angie," he says, laughing and patting Bouncer Man on the back. "We'll be back. You all play nice with . . ." He focuses his attention on me. "What was the name you use online? Oh, right. Jeannette. Play nice with Jeannette."

He seems amused. I try not to show I'm surprised he was paying such close attention to what I said online. Is he reading what I'm saying to Kel?

"We'll take good care of her," says Angie, filling in for Lea, who is sullenly picking at the sleeves of her pink jumpsuit and keeping to herself.

Jeremy ignores Angie. He looks straight at Lea. It seems like he enjoys pushing her buttons. "You do that. Make sure she feels right at home. But not too comfortable, ladies, if you know what's good for you."

Footsteps. Then I hear the door lock, same as in my room. The girls are silent after Jeremy leaves.

That only makes things even more awkward. I don't have a clue what to say to break the ice. Maybe my time in isolation has made me weird around other people.

"I hate that asshole," mutters Lea, still picking at the sleeve of her jumpsuit.

"Dios mio," says Angie. "Don't let him get to you."

"Anyway." And then, Lea bangs her hand on the table to shake him off. The whole table wobbles under the pressure. I can't help it, I jump back a bit. "Oh. Sorry about that." And then, like that, Lea's back in charge. I kind of figured she would, having seen her at work online. She likes typing in big capital letters and seems to live her life that way too. "Do you know everyone, Jeannette? Well, I bet you know us, but not by our real names."

"Most of you." I say, finding my voice. "I know you're Lea . . . and you're . . ." I point to Angelino18. "Angelino18, but called Angie."

Angie growls. "Should be Angelina18. Angeli-na, not Angeli-no! They won't change it. Stupid boys."

Well. Instant connection with Angie. "I hate Kamkit, too!"

Tangerinewilde—Lea—rolls her eyes. "Angie's got a lot of names. She's our fucking showgirl." She spreads her fingers as she says showgirl, like her fingers are sparklers and the word is magic. Her pink nails shimmer in the air. Pink must be her thing.

In response, Angie gives Lea the finger. "Doing what I gotta do to stay in the game." Kelaidescope frowns and turns a page in the book she's reading.

"The bookworm's name is Kel," continues Lea and then points to the blonde sitting across the table. "That's Kim. She's a country girl. Got that? The bookworm, the blonde, and the bimbo. I'm the bitch. Easy, right?" She laughs and sticks out her tongue at Angie, showing off her gold stud. Me, I'm thinking about Josh and his dumb blonde jokes and instantly getting homesick.

"I used to be the new one," says Kim whose singsong voice seems out of place. "You got Barbara's old room, right?"

I nod. "I do." They're all being so friendly. A sense of guilt washes over me. Should I tell them my real name, at least? Maybe I can get more out of them if I do. Like, maybe they can even tell me what the hell is going on here?

Decisions, decisions...what are our pizza selections? Making a decision about that might be easier. I've got two choices: pepperoni or veggie with mushrooms. Both look as if they've been sitting out for a while. Well, I am kind of hungry and the pepperoni doesn't look completely nauseating. I stand up to grab my slice of the pizza pie.

"Welcome to the gang!" Kim says with way too much enthusiasm, the minute I get up. I glance over at her. She's smiling wide, showing her uneven teeth. A piece of pizza is stuck to one tooth. Hmm. Yeah, she definitely is marching to the beat of another drummer, all right.

"Like welcome to the club," says Lea, totally valley girl and totally making fun of Kim. "Like after lunch OMG let's go to the mall and then like go paint our toenails, okay?"

Lea laughs at her own joke and Angie and even Kel join in. Kim's smile fades and she folds her arms, looking uncomfortable and scared. She goes back to playing with her bracelet. From where I'm standing, I have a good look at it. It's a charm bracelet, but cheap looking. Like something a kid would wear.

Maybe this is the time to put myself out there. It'll take the heat off of Kim, even if it puts it back on me. "Okay. One thing I should tell you, in case you haven't guessed. My name's Kami. Not Jeannette. That's a fake."

That seems to impress Lea. She raises an eyebrow and takes another look at me, from head to toe. "A fake, huh? I've had a few fake names, too. Where you from?"

"Farnham, Ohio." Wrong response. Lea doesn't seem impressed with my answer. I gravitate to the kitchen area for my pizza. And also, so I can take a look outside.

I grab my slice. But first, I check out the top of the pizza box. Nope, no address or anything. Damn. Then I size up the window, now that Bouncer man is gone. Oh. The shade's not only all the way down but stapled to the window sill. So much for a view. Double damn.

"Where the hell is Farnham, Ohio?" asks Lea, still working through that one.

The way she says it makes me laugh. "I know. No one's ever heard of Farnham. I used to live in New York City, though. You ever hear of that?"

Lea may not get Farnham, but she clearly likes NYC. Her eyes light up and she pushes back in her seat, tapping her pretty pink fingernails against the table. Oh good, I've scored some points. "Son of a bitch, so did I. Love NYC. Lived in Queens. I lived everywhere. Then I was brought here."

Good! An opening. "So where is here, anyway?"

Kel takes a napkin from the table and uses it as a bookmark for her book. "Your guess is as good as ours," she says. "The only thing we know is most of us spent half a day or so in the back of a car to get here."

"So none of you know where we are?"

"These assholes don't like us knowing things like that," says Lea. "Not that I give a shit. They could have taken off my blindfold driving me here, for all I care."

That's weird. For someone so bossy, why wouldn't Lea care? Dammit, I want to peel back that shade and take a look outside. Trying not to be obvious, I take a few more steps toward the sink. "Hey, you think anyone would notice if I pulled the shade back a little? Might help tell me where we are. Could check out a license plate, at least." I try to say it like I'm half joking, which of course I'm not.

Then I notice the look on their faces. Guess that's not a good idea. Lea is all wide-eyed and Angie's shaking her head. Those two are dangerous together. But Kel's not looking that thrilled either. Only Kim doesn't seem to care, but she's clearly been zoned out for our entire conversation.

Lea lowers her voice. "Honey, you may be new, but take my advice. No matter how bad a fix you have for the outside, whatever you do, don't fuck with things like that here. Not if you know what's good for you."

Angie points at Lea and laughs. "Remember the loca puta who tried to break out from that window one time? All the alarms went off and she didn't even get the freaking thing halfway open. That's when they stapled the shade shut, right? What was her name?"

Lea wrinkles her nose. "Bianca. Five dollar name. I think there are still pieces of her near your door, Jeannette." A pause. "I mean, Kami."

My thoughts go to the bloody clothing shoved in the corner of the hallway. Well, so much for that brilliant idea. I turn back to the girls. Take a cup and pour myself some coke. Unlike the pizza, it's warm. Well, if I can't look outside, maybe I can peel back more stuff from the girls.

"How did you all end up here?" I ask.

Lea leans back in her chair and folds her arms. "We all have our own stories." She points to Kel. "Runaway." Angie. "Runaway." Kim. "From another planet. Me? Let's say I like to play with fire and this time I got burnt."

Angie hits Lea on the shoulder and laughs, which only makes Lea give her the dirtiest glare imaginable. "Embuste! Here's another story. How about you like the crack here, especially not having to pay for it."

"Shit." Lea shrugs her broad shoulders and falls back in her chair. It hits the floor with a thud. She gets up to pour herself a drink. "Friggin' better using here than outside, I guess." She frowns and lifts the drink to her lips. "It's warm here. I got a bed. What the hell. Gotta go someday."

Now we're getting somewhere. Finally, they're telling me something. I need more. Maybe if I give them more, I'll get it, too. "My story's different. They broke into my house." I lower my voice in case Jeremy's listening. "Two guys around midnight. I was all alone, watching what happened to Barbara. I tried to get out. Jumped out a window. Broke my ribs."

Slowly, I sit back down in my chair, surprised at how much I said. I look around the table, gauging their reactions. Angie's staring at the floor. Lea is at the counter with her back turned to us. She doesn't seem to care. Kim keeps on eating her pizza. Kel's been staring at me ever since she closed her book. It's like she finds me fascinating. She has spooky eyes. Maybe it's a good thing they are covered by those red glasses.

"So why is my story different?" I ask.

"You're an example," Kel says, as if it's obvious.

An example? "Of what?"

She shakes her head. "No. For what. For Barbara making an outside connection. You're here and she's not because they want to show us what happens if we talk."

Lea takes a deep swig and walks back to the table. She slides right behind me and leans in, so she's inches from my ear. She whispers so only the five of us can hear. "Of course, we all know Barbara shouldn't have been able to talk to the outside world to begin with. Right?"

Kel nods. Her spooky eyes are staring right through me. Is she on my side or isn't she?

"Someone screwed with the system," Kel says.

Lea laughs and walks back to her seat. She throws her plate down, then hits the table so hard it wobbles. "Damn STRAIGHT!"

Kel glances sharply at Lea. "Cool it." She turns to me and places a hand on mine. Her fingers are cool to the touch. "We're not blaming you, Kam." Nervously, she gives a quick look toward the door. Her glasses slump down on her nose as she turns. Oh. Just noticed. Her fancy red frames may look good on screen, but they're broken on the left side. Held together with masking tape. Kel pushes her glasses back up with a finger and opens her book again. She whispers as she reads. "We wish Barbara had been better at it."

"Let me tell you," says Angie in a low voice, leaning in close to me. I can see her hands trembling. "If I had someone to talk to, I'd be wayyyyyyyy smarter. And I'd get the hell outta here. Fast as that." She snaps her fingers, showing off her perfectly manicured nails.

"You're from Ohio? I'm from Iowa," says the girl with dirty blonde hair, out of nowhere. What's her name again? Oh, right. Kim. Should be able to remember that one.

"Yeah, Kim's a real live farm girl," says Lea. "You even milked a cow, didn't you?"

Kim's laugh is high-pitched and childish. I guess she's happy they're not making fun of her. Well, not that much. "I never milked no cow. I lived in a foster home most of the time. After Nan." The minute she says the name, her hands touch her bracelet. Her voice sounds sad, vulnerable. "You know that."

"How did they know where to find me?" I whisper.

Angie leans in. This shit is getting serious. "Chica, you do know you're dealing with something big here, right?"

Big? "What do you mean?"

"What I mean. Big. These people, they can find you anywhere."

"Anywhere," says Lea. "Like—"

Angie cuts her off, not wanting to give up the spotlight. "Like I was walking around in K-Town, you know? And—"

I shake my head, confused. "K-Town?"

Angie waves her hand in the air, as if the location is irrelevant. "It's in Chicago." Oh. Interesting. So, maybe that's not where we are after all. Lea said most of them had a half day dive. Did Angie? "And I'm trying to keep away from this guy that's been giving me crap, see? I knew he was a banger and I didn't want to deal with it no more. Next thing I know, two guys come over, ask me if I want to make some money."

"Didn't want to pay you enough, huh?" sneers Lea.

Angie gives her the finger. "YOU need to stop talkin'. I didn't want money, Lee-ah. I was tired and wanted to sleep so I walked away and next thing you know . . ."

Lea whistles. "Here you are. Eating pizza with me."

"Verdad. And once they have you . . ." Angie makes a fist, deadly serious. "You ain't going back."

I can't stand it anymore. "So what's going on here? All I see you doing is talking on camera to the visitors. Who are they? What's that all about?"

That shuts Angie up. The table becomes completely silent. Even Kim stops humming to herself.

Kel's still focused on me. I wish she'd go back to reading her book. "All of the visitors are Lord High Muckety Mucks. Judges and businessmen and whatever."

"Judges?" I frown. That's weird. "But why are they spending their time talking to you?"

Lea adjusts the sleeves on her jump suit. "They have their reasons, girl. Although you do know, some dudes tell me I'm a fascinating conversationalist."

Angie snorts. "Sure they do."

"No, seriously. What do they want?"

"What do all guys want?" Angie asks, pushing out her chest and grinning. "No mierda. Los hombres solo quieren una cosa."

"Yeah, like we all know what the fuck that means . . ." mutters Lea.

"Jibara! Men are only after one thing. The one who gives it to them the best stays around the longest."

Lea waves that away. "Yeah, yeah, whatever."

Stays around? What does that mean? I want to ask more, but Kel interrupts before I can say anything. "What happens when they get bored with the same old show? With those big tits? What else do you have?" Her words are clearly directed at Angie.

Lea finds that funny even though Angie's eyes narrow and her fingers clench. She's clearly offended. "I've been around longer than all of you. Will still be six months from now too. And it's better than sitting there reading. How far's that gonna get you? I don't know why they keep giving you those stupid libros anyway."

Kel doesn't seem fazed in the slightest. She picks up her book and places it on her lap. "They'll give us whatever we want as long as we're good little girls."

"Nobody reads books no more," says Angie.

"I think I've heard of Farnham," Kim says out of nowhere. Everyone ignores her. She goes back to picking at her pizza.

Interesting. Jeremy said the same exact thing yesterday. "Whatever we want?"

"Abso-freaking-lutely," says Lea. "That's part of the way the game's played. This place is run by little boys, sugar. They don't know squat about what a girl needs. But they'll get you whatever you want if it makes you look good on camera."

Angie nods. "They give me anything."

"True that," mutters Lea.

"You know it is, bitch."

Lea nods and gives Angie a high five. "Yeah, I have gotten some sweet smoke in this place. Phil comes through for me, I'll give him that. Barbara was good at getting what she wanted, too. Of course . . ."

"Not all of us have a Jeremy," says Angie in a singsong voice and sticks her little finger through the long hoop earring in her left ear. In and out, in and out. Lea laughs.

"Jeremy looked after Barbara," explains Kel. As if I need an explanation.

"That's a nice way of putting it. Jeremy was also banging the hell out of Barbara. She had his hands in her pants every chance she could get."

Oh, Jesus. I don't want to think about this. Can we change the subject, please? "I know she said he gave her what she needed." Pause. "I thought it was drugs."

"That too." Lea smirks and glances at the door again. Then she leans over in my direction. "By the way, Angie thinks someone's got a thing for you, too."

"Why do you think . . .?" I stop, realizing how loud that sounds. I whisper, "Why would you think that?"

Angie looks as though she's spread an extra layer of cheese on top of her pizza. "I heard it from a little bird." She sticks out her tongue and starts rolling it around in a dirty way. I glance away, embarrassed. Lea finds that hysterical and that breaks Angie up. Even Kim starts laughing, and this time I think she knows why.

I'm not laughing. In fact I don't know what to say. Do they know about Jeremy's nighttime visits? But does that even matter if—

"So what is this place?" I ask, frustrated, trying to break through what I'm still not getting. Or what they're afraid to say, because someone might hear them. "Who are the visitors? What do you mean about sticking around?" Okay, might as well come out with it. "Do you have sex with these guys? Is that what this is about? I mean, you do, Angie, right?"

The whole table erupts into laughter. Even Kel puts her book down to join in. I can feel the tips of my ears turning red.

"No, we don't have sex with them," says Angie, after the laughter has died down. "Believe me, I wouldn't mind if it was only that. And don't think I haven't tried."

"Then what are we all here for?" I say, way too loudly.

There's that silence again. What are they so afraid to tell me?

Lea raises an eyebrow and places a finger to her lips. It's as if she can't believe what she's hearing. "You mean you really don't know?"

Know? How could I? I shake my head.

"We're here for the game," Kel replies.

Game? "What game?"

Kel looks at me, clearly surprised. I hear Lea muttering under her breath again. "You mean, Barbara didn't even tell you that much?"

No. No she didn't.

"Oh, it's a fun game," says Lea sarcastically. I think she likes that I don't know what's going on. "You're gonna love it. But if the head asshole hasn't said anything to you yet, maybe we shouldn't ruin the surprise. Besides, you'll get to see it all tonight. They always throw us a pizza party right before they let us play!"

The front door opens. Lea stops talking, right away. Angie stands up and helps herself to another slice of pizza.

It's Jeremy, with Bouncer Man behind him. "Lea. We're ready."

Lea gives him a wary look. It's clear she hasn't forgotten what went down before he left. "Do I have to, baby? I was having fun getting to know all about Jenny Jen here."

Jeremy frowns. "Maybe you'll get a chance to talk later on." He motions for her to get up off the chair. "Maybe not."

A look of terror appears on Lea's face—real fear, something I never imagined coming from her. Maybe she's not as strong as she lets on. She stands up, right away. "I hear you. Later, guys."

She walks to the counter and grabs hold of Angie's hand. Angie closes her eyes and makes the sign of the cross. Lea turns to face all of us with tears in her eyes. Tears? "Good luck. All of you."

I look around the room, confused. Is this because of Jeremy freaking out? Why do they all seem so scared? What kind of game is this?

Jeremy clears his throat. Lea squeezes Angie's hand one more time and heads to the door. Jeremy follows her out. As soon as the door is locked I turn to Kel. It's pretty clear we don't have much time. "What's going on?"

"Wait till tonight," she whispers, her face a blank slate. "We'll talk then while the equipment's being moved."

I blink. "Equipment?" Equipment?

"We'll talk," she says and picks up her book. She flips back to the page she was reading. It's clear that's the end of the story for now.

The pizza in my stomach is like a dead weight. This tea party was definitely not what I was expecting. What the hell is going on here? What kind of dollhouse is this?

CHAPTER TWENTY-FOUR

Equipment.

Jeremy opens the door to my room, and it's obvious what Kel's talking about.

So that's why they got us together. It wasn't for a tea party at all. They had other plans in mind. This must have been what Jeremy and the bouncer were up to when they left us alone.

The door to the Black Room is open, giving me a full view to what they've done. I can't look. I turn my head away, shut my mouth, and walk right into my bedroom where a thin wall separates me from it and gives me someplace to hide, even if I'm not so hidden at all.

I want so badly to cry. I throw myself onto the bed and feel the burst of pain and the wind rush out of my lungs. I don't care, don't care at all, because it takes me away from thinking and stops me from feeling dead inside and—

"Kami." Jeremy's outside my bedroom.

"Go away." I can't even look at him.

"I'll be back in three hours," he says.

###

I'm still in bed when the door opens again. The thin orange blanket is wrapped around my face. My safety blanket. I know, it's not going to keep me safe at all.

Footsteps. I hear a voice from the other room. His, of course.

"It's time," he says.

I close my eyes, lower my head. I'm not going to say a word. I decided that a short while ago. He's not gonna get anything out of me. Nothing. No way am I going to help with this.

More footsteps. I twist my head so I can see through a crack in the blankets and look over to the doorway. And then, a second later, he's standing there looking calm and cool.

He's going to ask me to move now, I know it. And even if we haven't discussed it, I don't want to. Even though I still have no real idea what's going on, I've seen the equipment, and I know I can't go into the Black Room. This is no tea party. Not this.

He sees me looking. He points to the Black Room and actually has a smile on his face. Am I really that stupid? "Come on. It's time."

It's like he's trying to make believe I didn't see the equipment when I walked into the room. It's bullshit. The whole thing makes me sick. Through the space in the blanket, I stick out my middle finger at him.

He has the nerve to laugh at that! "Come on, Kami." His voice is calm and even. He's still trying to sweet talk me. Screw you, Jeremy. "I don't like this either, but I can't get you out of it. Look, no way you're going to be . . ." He stops himself. Not quickly enough. "They don't even know you yet."

Nope. Not saying anything. Not going along with this. This is bullshit. I pull the blanket down over my eyes.

I'm like a stubborn eight-year-old not wanting to take a bath. But this is far worse than going to bed without supper.

More footsteps. I know he's standing near my bed. I can hear his breathing, the scent of his sweet cologne. I pretend he's not there. How long will playing statue keep me safe?

"Kami."

Screw you, Jeremy.

"Kami, we don't have much time. I have to get you in that chair by 11:25. I waited to do this as long as I could."

Waited. For what? Was that his idea of doing me a favor?

"Kami, I'm under orders. You have to be in that room and sit in that chair tonight."

Fuck your orders, Jeremy. You can take them and stick them up your—

A hand grabs at the orange blanket from the foot of the bed. I grab back just as tightly from my side. Jeremy's voice is soft but firm. "Get up or I'll make you. That's not going to be good for your ribs."

Okay, maybe the silent treatment isn't going to get me very far. Maybe I need to use my words. He's a reasonable guy, right? Been nice to me, for the most part. "Do I have to?" I ask from under the covers, trying to sound my best like Lea, when she tried to sweet talk him. "I don't want to get up."

He chuckles. "I bet. But you have to. It's time."

Easy. Maintain control. "I'm feeling like shit. The pizza messed my stomach up. Sure I can't—"

"No." A pause. "Sorry."

"But I'm not—"

"You have to!"

"I don't want to, Jeremy!" And yes, it's clear I'm losing my temper with him. The sweet talk is over.

The hand on my blanket grabs it tightly and yanks. I try to struggle but can't hold on. And then I'm lying there on the bed, totally unprotected.

Without a blanket to hide my eyes, I see exactly where he is. He's at the foot of my bed in the same position as last night in the dark.

That's the last straw. My eyes are wet with tears, but I look him in the eye and let him have it. "Do you like coming in here and watching me at night, Jeremy? Do you? Is that how you get your kicks?"

He seems surprised. His cheeks redden. Then he frowns, and I see his hands curl into fists. I see anger growing in his eyes. And at the same time, it dawns on me that maybe I said exactly the wrong thing. What he needs me to say to get him to cross that line. I've let him know I know about his midnight visits. I've exposed his secrets to the light of day.

Jeremy doesn't like that.

Shit no. I try to walk it back, bring back the nice Jeremy. "I didn't mean it. I think I'm going to throw up, I'm—"

Too late. The damage is done.

He lunges forward. Grabs my arms. Jerks me up off the bed. I'm out of breath, my ribs screaming in pain. I struggle pathetically, panting out "no, no, no," whenever I can grab a breath. I try to hit him. Aim for his head. He bats that away, grabs my hands. Lifts me, makes me stand.

"Stop it! Stop it!" I'm screaming as loud as I can, as he drags me forcibly into the Black Room. I try to fight every inch of the way, but I'm too weak, and my ribs hurt too much.

Tough shit. Can't give up. Can't let this happen. Near the doorway, I stamp down on his foot as hard as I can. He cries out and lets go of one of my hands.

Use your advantage, dammit! I push my free hand into his face, grab at his eyes. But before I can, he grabs hold of my wrist. Roughly, he throws me into the soft leather chair.

Before I can get up, he holds me down and bends over to hook me up to the equipment. He doesn't even sound like he's breathing heavy.

The equipment.

He does the whole thing in one fluid motion. Calm and collected. Clinical. Like he's done this a thousand times before. He snaps two steel links around my ankles. The links are connected to two cords that lead to a black box with a blinking red light in the upper red corner. The box feeds into an outlet in the wall. I turn away. I can't stand to look.

I have to get away. Frantically, I try to pull myself up, push the chair out of his grasp. It doesn't even seem to faze him. To keep me from moving Jeremy pushes the chair forward and latches both arms to the front of the desk. Then he grabs my left wrist and snaps a steel link around it. It's attached to the left arm of the chair and also connected to the black box.

He lets go. I'm stuck, so I sit there, panting like a dog. I hear him walking around, behind me. What's he doing?

I hear the sound of a switch being turned on. What's going on? And then, the black box in the corner starts to hum.

The hairs on the back of my neck start to stand on end. What the hell does that black box do?

I stare at the keyboard before me. For some reason, focusing on the keyboard calms me down. Maybe it can help me block out the fear of what's going to happen next. The soft scary sound of that buzzing.

"How am I supposed to type with one hand?" I want to sound angry and defiant. Instead, my voice sounds out of breath and weak.

"You'll figure out a way." His voice is cold.

He reaches down and presses his head against my cheek. I feel a scratchy feeling as his goatee brushes against me. Then I hear the computer starting up, masking the hum from the black box.

"By the way." I can still hear the anger in his voice. "You're on cam tonight. No hiding behind a black screen this time. I don't care what bullshit Kel told you about being like a mystery book."

So, he was paying attention. Fuck you, Jeremy. I sit there in the squishy leather chair, my head lowered. What would he do if I refuse to look at the screen? He can shove me into this chair, turn my computer on, but do I have to play? No fucking way.

The steel link around my left wrist feels cold. I don't like what it's attached to. That little black box is still humming away. What does it do? It's smooth and plastic, about the size of a shoebox. A red light blinks away on the very top, every few seconds.

I clench my fist, jerk my wrist up. One side of the steel link rubs up against my skin. I let it fall, then jerk my arm up again. It's solid. I try to roll the chair back. I can only go so far.

"Stop playing. You can't go anywhere. Log on. I'm not doing it for you."

Fuck you, Jeremy. I'm not gonna do anything. I'm gonna sit here and—

He slams the back of my chair, furiously. "Do it!"

No, no. I can't. I won't.

Another slam to the back of my chair. "Do it!"

My ribs can't take another one of those. Mechanically, I raise my head. Poise my fingers over the keyboard. Enter in my name and password. Mine, not hers. Mine. It's all me tonight.

My late show.

"GKS: Let the game begin!"

"We're here for the game," Kel said at lunch today. Now the words at the top of the page have a whole new meaning.

Everyone's there, of course. Kel. Lea. Angela, wearing...what the hell is she wearing? Looks like the top of a black bathing suit. A practically non-existent top. Kim's there too, with her head lowered. I bet she's playing with the charm bracelet around her wrist. I bet that's what she does when she's scared out of her mind. The way I am now.

And there's the black webcam with my name underneath it.

kamkit has entered the room

VISITOR18: I was wondering if we'd see her tonight.

VISITOR36: But will we see her?

Another hit to the back of my chair. "Turn it on!"

Keep yourself mysterious, Kel told me. Think of it like a story. It looks like a new chapter's starting now.

"Turn it on!"

Before Jeremy can push my chair again or worse, I do what he asks. I click on the webcam. And in an instant, my cam's not black at all, it's live and I'm staring at myself stuck in the box, like all the other girls.

VISITOR18: Well, looks who's here.

VISITOR22: Hello, gorgeous.

Gorgeous? I could hardly look less gorgeous if I tried. All the work I put into getting dolled up for the tea party in the afternoon is still there, but it's been smeared and ruined by being thrown to the bed, by crying, by struggling with Jeremy. I look like hell, and I don't give a shit. I stare at the screen with dull baleful eyes.

"Good girl." Jeremy's voice is calm now. Not the nice Jeremy I know, but more in control. I've done what he wanted me to do. I wish I could spit in his face. Asshole. "All you need to do is to sit there and watch.

Nothing's going to happen to you tonight. Don't try to sign off when I leave. You do, I come back in here. You won't be happy if that happens."

Why doesn't he stay here and watch me, then? But I'm not going to ask, and he probably wouldn't answer, so I listen as he closes the door to the Black Room and walks away. I hear the slam of the door on his way out.

I'm all alone now. The late night show and me.

I look over at the chat room again. All the visitors are going on about finally getting a chance to see what I look like after all this time.

VISITOR32: Feh. This one doesn't look like much of a kitten at all.

VISITOR22: Certainly not the best dressed of the bunch, my dear.

VISITOR18: Can it. I like the way she looks. You can be my little girlie.

I hear a soft ping. Private message. I bet I know who from.

KELAIDESCOPE: I was beginning to think we wouldn't see you.

Her I'll talk to.

KAMKIT: I didn't have a choice.

KELAIDESCOPE: Did he hurt you?

Does it matter? My ribs hurt like hell and the shackle around my left wrist isn't very comfortable either. But other than that—

KAMKIT: I'm okay.

KELAIDESCOPE: It's 11:25. It's time.

Time? Barbara had said the same thing the last night I saw her and Jeremy too, before he slammed me to the chair. Time for what? Maybe the chat room has an answer.

DRUSIUS: Five minutes until this week's GKS finalist will be named! Voting will end in sixty seconds so make certain you've made your selection before it's too late.

Who is Drusius? I scan the cams, but none of the girls have that name.

KAMKIT: Who is Drusius?

KELAIDESCOPE: Interesting question. Sick bastard. He runs the Friday night games. Keeps things moving along.

KAMKIT: Is he the reason we're all here?

KELAIDESCOPE: Don't think so. Pretty sure he knows the higher ups, though. He's a badass. Don't try talking to him, whatever you do.

KAMKIT: What does he mean make a selection?

Right then, at the top of the screen, where it says "Let the games begin," the title changes.

"GKS COUNTDOWN: 60"

That number starts to count down.

The girls all go crazy. The noise is so loud I scramble for the volume and turn it down. Some girls are holding their hands together, pleading at the screen. Some are crying. Kim's one of them. She has her eyes closed, but tears are streaming down her face. Lea is shaking her finger at the screen, saying she's the bitch you want to have around next week. Angie is clearly scared but has a fake smile on her face. She's swaying back and forth as if she's dancing and rubbing her free hand against her boobs. Some other girls are doing similar things. Kel, of course, is the only one reading. Her book covers her entire face.

Meanwhile, the chat room is going crazy. I can hardly keep up with all the comments. All from the visitors, the lord high muckety mucks, all of them rude.

VISITOR11: Think I'll vote for Kelaidescope tonight.

VISITOR32: I kind of have my eye on Stormetrooper.

And every time one of the girls is mentioned by name, her voice becomes louder, more shrill. Even with the sound down, the noise fills up my tiny room.

KAMKIT: WHAT THE HELL IS GOING ON???

KELAIDESCOPE: You'll see soon enough.

DRUSIUS: The voting has ended. In three minutes we'll announce this week's selection. Thank you for supporting GKS.

This week's selection? For what? I scan the cams for a better read on what's going on. Now that the voting has ended, though, all the girls have stopped begging. They're all quiet, not even talking on the chat screen. Even Lea isn't saying much. Angie is still swaying to the music, looking at the camera.

KAMKIT: WHAT THE HELL IS GOING ON???

That doesn't mean the chat room isn't busy. The visitors are busy discussing who should be selected, which one deserves it this week. Making crass jokes I don't even want to look at. I don't get it. If this isn't a sex site, what the hell are they voting on?

KAMKIT: KEL, WTF???

KELAIDESCOPE: Stop it. It's 11:29. Drusius is going to make his big announcement. You'll see soon enough.

DRUSIUS: And the winner is . . ..

DRUSIUS: ***ANGELINO18***

Angie's the winner? Is that a good thing or a bad? From the way she's reacting, it's not a good thing at all.

She's stopped swaying. She looks stunned. All the color has drained from her face. She looks at the camera as if she's been betrayed and starts muttering under her breath. In Spanish. It sounds like a prayer.

DRUSIUS: ***ANGELINO18***

Then her voice rises. She starts to moan. It's clear that she's terrified.

"Please don't do this," she says straight to the camera. "Please don't let this happen. Please don't kill me."

Please don't kill me?

Then she tries to rise from the chair. I catch a glimpse of the handcuff shackled to her left wrist. She's shackled too, the same way I am. The same way we all must be. She tries to yank at it, but it's not going anywhere. She gasps, falls down into her chair. She turns back to the screen, tears streaming down her cheeks.

"No. No. Stop it. Don't do this!"

DRUSIUS: ***ANGELINO18***

Underneath her screams, I hear a humming noise in her room. Same as the one in my room, only this sound is a little higher, a little more intense. She hears it too, because she looks down at the ground, and there's terror in her dark eyes. Her screams grow in intensity. She pulls her body to her right, and it's clear she wants to get as far from the sound as possible.

I glance down at the little black box located near my feet. What do these things do? Why is hers humming so loudly? It's that weird sound, the one I heard the night Barbara died. Which means—

Then the sound changes slightly. It starts to sound crackly, like an egg frying on a grill. Angelina screams out and throws her head back, like she's been stabbed in the back. Her back arches, her arms grow rigid.

The noise ends. She collapses into her chair. Her head slumps down on the desk. Her gasps are audible. Deep breaths. In, out. In, out.

Then the sickening crackling buzzing noise starts again. Softly at first, then growing in intensity. She lifts her head, pushing forward. She whimpers like an animal. "No no no," she cries out and tries to push away from the desk again. She's clearly not as strong as she was before, though. She pushes, strains, tries to push her black chair back.

The noise intensifies. I watch her rise and fall and scream and twist. Rise. Fall. Twist. Back arched. Body rigid. Eyes wild and terrified. Blood around her mouth. Her screams fill the room. I try to understand what she's saying, but it's hard to make out anything anymore. All I hear are screams and slurred words, running together.

I want to look away. This can't be happening. Please make this stop.

The sickening noise stops. Angie slumps over. Falls. Her head hits the table with a dull thud. I can't see her face anymore, her beautiful dark eyes, the mole on her upper lip. Nothing but an outline of her beautiful dark hair at the bottom of the webcam. She's not moving.

She's dead.

They killed her.

The way they killed Barbara.

DRUSIUS: Who will be next week's winner? Your vote holds the key! Digital copies of this week's kill are available on our home page, so you can relive tonight's highlights. And remember, two weeks from now, double kill night! Until next week, this is your humble servant Drusius signing off.

The show is over. The kill is through. And now I know exactly what game they are playing.

KELAIDESCOPE: Kam?

KELAIDESCOPE: Kam, are you there?

I'm sitting at the desk, tears streaming down my face, not wanting to talk, not wanting to move, not wanting to do anything, except be released from this chair and these shackles and the steady stream of messages that keep running through the message board.

VISITOR24: Nice kill.

VISITOR36: I'll kind of miss her shows though.

VISITOR2: I'll kind of miss her jugs.

VISITOR18: One of you girls wanna pick up the slack?

KELAIDESCOPE: Kami, come on!

I can't take my eyes off her window or the image trapped inside. Her figure, her dark hair, slumped over the keyboard.

In some ways, it's worse than Barbara's death. I didn't know what was happening then.

This time is different. This had been instant. This had been live. This had been real time. A steady stream of 24/7 content. And I got to read all the comments and bad jokes, too, and it felt like this was all a game, like one of her sex scenes. To be talked about. To be criticized.

Here we are now. Entertain us.

KELAIDESCOPE: Kam? Kam, are you there?

I wipe my eyes with my one free hand; lift my T-shirt to dry off my cheeks. Then I turn back to the keyboard.

KAMKIT: Yeah

KELAIDESCOPE: Are you okay? I know that was your first time.

KAMKIT: No, it wasn't. I saw Barbara.

KELAIDESCOPE: Are you okay, though?

I take a deep breath.

KAMKIT: No.

A few hours ago, she had been downstairs, alive and laughing. Joking and shoving pizza into her mouth. And now she's a figure slumped over a desk. An hour. Half an hour. Fifteen minutes ago she was sitting there doing her thing. Not knowing her life was about to end. That she was going to be voted out of existence.

I hate them.

I've been around longer than any of you, she said. Will still be six months from now. Not even six hours from now.

Goodbye, Angie.

She wasn't a Queen of the Night after all. She hadn't come close to ruling anything.

Just like me. I'm sitting here same as she had been. Hooked up to equipment. I hadn't been picked because I was too new. Too new . . . at least for right now.

KAMKIT: Angie had a tattoo on the back of her wrist.

KELAIDESCOPE: She did.

KAMKIT: It was in Spanish. Do you know what it said?

KELAIDESCOPE: Vivir para morir. Live to die. Ironic, huh?

KAMKIT: KEL!

KELAIDESCOPE: Well, it is. Or is it? Would that really be the proper use of irony?

KAMKIT: Stop it. We just saw her

I don't want to type the word. Vivir para morir.

KELAIDESCOPE: I'm not surprised. She gave it away too easy and too often. What other resolution was there but to see her fry?

And here's Kelaidescope talking about Angie's death like it's some kind of book review. As if it hadn't meant anything more than what you read between the covers.

KAMKIT: That could have been you, Kel. It could have been any of us.

KELAIDESCOPE: You're not going to act like Tangie are you? All crying and making with the OMGs. Like she's on American Idol and her best friend got booted off.

KAMKIT: I think she did like her.

How can Kel be so dispassionate about the whole thing? The way Lea is acting is real. That was her friend. They were eating and joking a few hours ago, and that will never happen again.

And Kim. She's taking it hard. She'd been so out of it in the kitchen. I think maybe she'd been on heavy medication before she came here. At her foster home. Now she's having trouble sitting up. Her body is rocking back and forth, and she's letting out huge sobs.

The visitors, on the other hand, think the whole thing is hilarious. And that makes sense, I guess. It's all a game to them.

I get it now. This is all a high-tech game of Russian roulette. A game where the GKS members get to decide who lives and who dies. Once a week.

And my overwhelming emotion right now isn't anger, but sadness. Sad that I finally understand what's going on. Sad for everyone involved.

KAMKIT: This afternoon she acted like it didn't matter. Her and Lea joking around. How could they act like they didn't care? If they knew this was going to happen.

KELAIDESCOPE: That's exactly why they act that way.

KAMKIT: What do you mean?

KELAIDESCOPE: We have no control over what goes on here. Talking like that helps them think they have control over something. But you saw how different they acted when they had to go back to their rooms, right?

KAMKIT: Why do the visitors play this game, Kel?

But I know the answer even before she replies. It's clear enough now. They play it because they can. Because it's exciting and secret and nobody knows. Because they are powerful and we are not. To them

Angelino18 and Tangerinewilde and Kamkit are simply faces on a screen. Living to die.

They play it because it's there to play. And there will be another game to play the week after this one and the week after that. An endless stream of content served up fresh by GKS.

And all the sad comic book names, characters that don't live real lives? They will be called one by one week after week. Their time will come for one last Late Night Show.

No way to stop it. Vivir para morir.

Angelino18.

Tangerinewilde.

Weathervayne.

Kelaidescope.

And Kamkit. One of these weeks.

CHAPTER TWENTY-FIVE

He returns as a shadow in the middle of the night.

I haven't been sleeping. I've been expecting him.

This time I don't pretend to sleep. No steady breathing, no pretending I don't know he's there. My eyes are wide open and staring straight at him in the dark.

He shouldn't have the nerve to sneak in again. I should have the nerve to tell him to leave. I don't. I'm too numb. I'm too dead inside, so much so that even if he tried to hurt me more it wouldn't matter. Nothing can touch me. Not now. My heart is made of stone.

We play this game in the darkness for a while. Him watching me, me watching him. Both of us knowing full well what's going on. And then, after what seems like an hour, he walks away.

Something inside doesn't want that to happen. I'm sick of the waiting and wondering and hurting. I need things to move forward, fast forward. And so, before I even think about it, I hear myself say:

"Jeremy."

He stops dead in his tracks.

His shadow makes its way back to the foot of the bed, then even closer.

I sit up in bed, feeling the familiar twinge of pain. "I'm scared."

He lets out a deep breath and sits down on the bed. And then he places his arms around my shoulders.

I need this to be an act of kindness. I need this so badly.

I lower my head to his shoulder. I hear his whispered voice in my ear.

"I'm sorry."

Then it all bursts like a dam and my face falls into his shirt breathing in the scent of cigarettes and cologne. I start crying, deep sobs from the gut. He holds me, pats my back. Whispers that it's okay, and I realize in a strange way this is the first time I've wanted this kind of comfort from someone since Dad died.

That makes me cry all the harder. Jeremy runs his fingers through my hair and makes soft soothing noises. The tears keep coming as he holds me, gently rocking me. "I'm here," he whispers.

After a while I get sleepy. The tears begin to fade. He brushes my hair back and eases me down so the pillow cradles my head.

"I'll be back, okay? I promise." The mattress creaks as he gets up, and his footsteps sound fainter as he tiptoes out of my room.

The door closes. I take a deep breath.

I brace myself against the pain, then reach out my arm. I fumble around, searching for the nightstand.

I can feel a smooth surface. Must be the red lamp. Careful, careful. Don't push it off. An inch at a time, I move my fingers down the surface of the nightstand, to the front side where the drawer is.

Contact.

The handle. There we go. I grasp it and push the drawer open a few inches. I poke my fingers around.

I'm searching for the Roxi tablets hidden inside. My emergency stash.

Found them. They've settled in the right hand corner. I use my fingers to scoop them into the palm of my hand then lift them to my mouth. Without a glass of water, the bitter taste and chalky feel of the pills makes me want to gag. I swallow them down as fast as I can.

A rush of numbness hits me a few minutes later. Sleep begins to cover me like a soft, warm blanket. I welcome the feeling. My eyes grow heavy, and the world starts to slips away. I think about Jeremy holding me, along with the last image I had of Angie's room. Of two guards moving in to unshackle her dead body, lifting her out of the chair she had been chained to.

CHAPTER TWENTY-SIX

DAY SEVEN

Breakfast with Jeremy. This one is different.

I'm still sleeping when he enters. The Roxi worked its magic. Still, as soon as I hear the door opening and his footsteps making their way to me, I know it's time to face another day. And here he is with my breakfast.

"Good morning."

He looks as if he doesn't know how to act around me anymore. Jeremy, looking awkward?

To be honest, I'm not sure how to act around him either. So much happened the night before. I've gone from hating him to really hating him to . . . I don't know.

I know I'm still angry. I'm also ashamed I was weak enough to break down the way I did. In his arms. I still don't know whether I can trust him.

I mean all he did was hold me and say he was sorry, right? For what? For everything that's happened? That Angie died last night? Sorry can mean a whole lot of things when you think about it. Which I did a lot of after he left and before the Roxi kicked in.

What does he want from me? What do I want from him?

"Did they go easy on the grease this morning?" I reach for a lame joke to break the silence.

"Half the grease, twice the fat." He leans over to hand me the tray. There it is. The smell of his cologne and the tiniest hint of his boyish smile. If I weren't dead inside and didn't finally know what the hell is going on, I'd—

"Eggs again," I reply. "What I wouldn't give for a bowl of Chocolate Crunchies."

Jeremy scrunches up his nose. "You like that stuff? I haven't had Crunchies since I was a kid."

I still am, Jeremy. Kinda.

We're silent again. I can't stop thinking about Angie. The silence needs to be here between us after what happened. I lower my head and try to eat, even if I'm not hungry. I poke the fork into my eggs and wonder whether I should bring up what happened in the darkness between the two of us.

No.

"Does it happen every week?" I ask, keeping my eyes on my breakfast plate.

He chews on that before answering. "Does what happen?"

"What happened last night. With Angie."

He licks his lips, brings a hand to his face. I look up into his golden brown eyes. He needs to say something about last night in the light of day. I won't take my eyes off his. He is going to answer. He has to answer.

Finally, reluctantly. "Yes. Every week."

I maintain eye contact. His hand is on his chin absently stroking the fuzz growing there. I'm not sure what to say after that so I say the only thing on my mind. "Seven days from now that could be me, right?"

"Maybe," he mutters. He grabs his phone out of his pocket and starts looking through it. His security blanket, I guess, for when things get awkward. Then, abruptly, he starts heading for the door. "I'll be back. Need a cigarette."

I push the plate aside. I've lost my appetite.

I guess I got my answer.

KELAIDESCOPE: How RU doing?

KELAIDESCOPE: Kami

KELAIDESCOPE: KAMI!!!

KAMKIT: I'm here

KELAIDESCOPE: You're quiet tonight. Sitting there. That's not good for business U know.

KAMKIT: Good for business?

KELAIDESCOPE: The members don't like that.

KAMKIT: You're one to talk. You're always sitting there w/ your nose in a book

KELAIDESCOPE: I beg to differ. In fact I'm rather selective regarding whom I talk to and when I talk to them. But I do talk. That's what keeps me in the game.

KAMKIT: For now.

KELAIDESCOPE: Well, yeah

KELAIDESCOPE: For now. I'm thinking I might need to shake things up. Maybe go insane for a couple and take Angelino's thing over, now that she's gone. Cover your eyes, okay?

KAMKIT: Don't worry.

KELAIDESCOPE: Then I'll go back to reading

KELAIDESCOPE: It'll keep them guessing.

KELAIDESCOPE: Kam?

KELAIDESCOPE: Kam, you there?

KAMKIT: Yep.

KAMKIT: Don't you ever get scared, Kel?

KELAIDESCOPE: Talk to me on Friday.

KAMKIT: Seriously!

KELAIDESCOPE: Yes. Of course. Seriously. But Angie's bought me seven days, Kam, so right now I'm not so scared. I've only got to figure out some way to buy myself another seven.

KELAIDESCOPE: Same as you, Kam.

Kel's right. She's a smart one. That's the way the game needs to be played in the rabbit hole. From now on my life is going to be lived seven days at a time. The countdown began the minute last night's show ended. Seven days. I'd better start playing.

About an hour ago I checked my email under Barbara's old ID. For some reason, I'm still allowed to do that. Doesn't matter to them, I guess since nothing's there. Looks like they've made it impossible for me to send anything inside or out.

So, seven days. Seven days left to buy myself another seven. Stuck here. No hope. One week.

And counting.

CHAPTER TWENTY-SEVEN

DAY SEVEN

"I figured you'd show up."

Once again he's at the foot of my bed. I don't wait half an hour to say anything this time. The minute he's there I break the silence. That is, if it's really him and he's not a monster in disguise. My beauty and the beast.

"I know."

No, it's him. His voice. His delicious scent. It's Jeremy, I know it.

I take a second to think about what to say next. To decide whether I want to or not. Really, though, the decision was made the night before. "You can sit down, you know."

Right away he's beside me. I push myself up to give him room. The twinge in the ribs is present but getting better. The pain is a shadow of what it's been even without the Roxi. I must be healing. I wonder when he'll figure that one out.

Part of me thinks he already has.

I can barely make out his silhouette in the dark. Here he is again. Another midnight visit. It's sort of like . . . oh, that's way too weird. I laugh, nervously.

"What?"

"Nothing! Well, the thing is, your visits sort of remind me of . . ."

"Of?"

"Of my dad."

He clears his throat. Hmm, maybe that's a little weird, even for him.

"No, listen! When I was a kid, Dad and me had this game we'd play. We had this cool bathroom that kind of felt like . . . I don't know, an underground cave I guess. I'd hop into the bathtub in my bathing suit and pretend to be a little mermaid. He'd pretend to be a handsome prince who had come to visit me on the edge of the ocean. We'd talk about our lives. Mine in the ocean, his on land."

"Aha." I think he's more relieved than anything, that it turned out so innocent. "So, how's your life in the ocean, princess?"

"Oh, fine. I collected a fork at breakfast!"

"I know. I gave it to you." And we both laugh and the make-believe is almost enough to transport us from where we actually are. Maybe it's enough to give me some additional courage.

"Why do you come here at night, Jeremy?"

He breathes out a small gust of air as if he's surprised I'm asking.

"Did you ever visit her at night? Barbara?"

Silence. I'm pretty certain he's wishing he'd gone out for a cigarette instead of visiting.

"You don't have to answer. I just wondered if that's the reason you come to visit. I mean, it's dark. You can almost pretend she's lying here."

His voice is strangely soft. "Why would you think that?"

"I don't know. I guess the way she talked about you."

"You never met her."

"I feel like I did. At least, met her through a webcam. What was she like, Jeremy? I always thought she'd be kind of girlish, but not in an annoying way like Kim. More like Drew Barrymore."

He laughs. I can tell he's remembering. The way she acted, a joke she told. "She could get girly sounding. It was funny."

I can see his shoulders in the darkness. His head is slouched over, his hands intertwined. "Does it bother you to talk about it?"

"She had a great laugh. I liked watching her get crazy."

"When she was flying with the angels?"

Silence.

"I wish she hadn't done that so much."

I swear the dark makes me braver, more at ease. Since he can't see me, my usual mask is off. The darkness is my mask. But how much of his mask will he remove?

"Did you ever come to visit her, Jeremy? Like this?"

"No, not like this. Not exactly."

"So you two were—"

"Do we have to talk about it?"

"The thing is . . . I don't understand how you could put those cuffs on her. And then watch her . . ."

He's sitting like a statue. I can hardly hear him breathing. It's as if he's faded away. This has got to hurt. I keep on poking.

"Did you watch? From the other room? Did you see her when it happened? Or did you try to pretend it wasn't?"

His voice is low and raspy. Is it tearing him up inside? "I wasn't in the building that night."

"Oh."

"I don't know what I would have done." He catches himself. He's having trouble getting his words out. "If I had been there. Not that it would have mattered. It still would have happened."

"But you could have—"

His voice is firm. "No, I couldn't. I would have gone ape shit. That was Barbara. I mean, some of the girls, you're almost like, 'Well, that's okay. It doesn't matter.' Barbara was different. Even when she flew with her angels, like you said. When they said they were going to punish her . . ."

He stops. I can smell his cologne so near. I can feel the weight of his body bearing down on the bed, his strong hands gripping the mattress.

"Truth is, they didn't say anything. They texted me. Fucking texted me. And I says to them, 'Well, if that's what you're thinking, I don't want to be anywhere near the place Friday night.'"

"Says." A hint of the street. He's usually so smooth. Am I getting closer to the real Jeremy?

"I came back on Monday. That was when . . ." A pause. Another catch in his voice. "They told me not to come up here."

His voice is rising, growing more intense. It's more than a whisper now. "I was so pissed. I should have quit right there. Quit it all. They knew about us. I mean, I think they knew. Barbara and me. Maybe they were punishing me too."

"Why do you say that?"

"They threatened to switch me with someone else. I didn't want that to happen so I was like I'm cool. I can handle it. They called me soft. Said I wasn't able to keep her in control any more. Thought I might help her escape."

Escape. I have to pretend I didn't hear him say those last few words. Because if I did I might think that maybe . . . well, would he have? And if he would for her, would he—

No. No, don't think about it. "What do you mean soft?"

He lets out a deep breath. "My job's to take care of you girls. Feed you, make sure you're okay. Get you what you want even if it's crazy. The worst I do is on show night. But I never seen what takes place. Not once. They asked me to when I started. I said no, not my job. I don't think I could do my job if I did. Or maybe I'm afraid how I'd do it."

"Do you have a girlfriend, Jeremy?"

He laughs out loud at that. His laughter echoes through the empty rooms. I wonder who can hear it. One of the other girls? Who else is looking after the other dolls in the dollhouse if Jeremy's here with me?

"As if. What am I going to tell her, that I'm a stockbroker?" He shifts and inches closer. "I might be able to get out if I'm smart. My boss says there are opportunities. I can work into a better job if I stay focused and keep my mouth shut."

Jeremy shifts again. We're practically touching.

"Why did you first start working here?"

Silence.

"Well, I mean, I'm only asking. You don't have to tell me if you don't want to."

The words he says are dead. Casual, as if he's said them so many times they don't mean anything anymore. "My first job was in finance, although I was going to school be a teacher. I had this stupid ass idea I wanted to work with kids. I always liked working with kids, you know?" He sighs like he's taking a drag from a cigarette and shifts position in the bed. "Something happened when I was halfway through college."

"Something?"

"I don't want to get into it."

"It was bad."

"Bad enough that I couldn't keep going to school or work in finance."

His voice sounds bitter. I wonder what could have been so bad it wouldn't land him in jail. Maybe it was a first offense. What could be so bad he couldn't work in finance? Wow. Best to let him talk. I can listen.

"I was working at this place called J. Kingsley and Associates. He's a stockbroker. J. Kingsley. But see even though J. Kingsley yammers about how much he gives back to the community he does a lot on the QT. So my boss tells me I'm a good guy and all that, but of course they can't keep me on. Still even after what I did . . . well maybe because of what I did, they said I showed . . . potential."

"Potential?"

He stretches out his legs. I can hear his knees crack. He's closer.

"For another company he has an interest in."

"The GKS?"

"Entertainment Division."

I squirm in the bed and kick my foot against his leg by accident. Entertainment?

"Mr. Kingsley owns GKS?"

Jeremy grabs at my ankle. "Mr. Kingsley is a tiny fish. My boss at Kingsley was even tinier. But they both swim in the same place and because I did this stupid thing I ended up in a different kind of talent pool." He pauses and tightens his grip. "Kind of like how you ended up here."

His hand inches up my leg slowly.

I kick my foot away. His words bother me almost as much as his hand on my calf. "Jeremy, that's not—"

"Don't think of yourself as talent, do you?" He lifts my blankets and reaches over to tickle the bottom of my foot.

I'm not sure if it's what he's saying or the tickle, but the whole thing is bugging the crap out of me. I kick his hand away. He chuckles, sounding pleased. The mattress springs groan as he rises.

"I have to go downstairs. And I've probably said more than I should."

Go? As annoying as he's being, I don't want that. After all the time spent living in the dark, it's nice to finally get a glimpse of what's going on.

"We won't say anything about this tomorrow morning, will we?" Of course. I know the answer to that already.

"I doubt it." And then the scent enfolds me, smothers me. His lips are warm against mine. His lips linger, testing, tasting, probing gently. The funny thing is I don't want it to end.

"Goodnight, princess."

He leaves. My lips are suddenly cold. I touch them. To remember.

My eyes are wide open and I can't see anything. The key scrapes in the lock. He's gone and he left me here in the black void alone. My world is narrower. Emptier. I need Roxi.

I used up my emergency stash the night before. Probably best. I've so much to think about. His story. His bosses being little fish in what appears to be a much bigger sea. What he said about Barbara. How could he say it's okay for some of the girls to die? What the hell kind of sick logic is that?

And I let him kiss me. What's wrong with me?

His kiss. His lips on mine.

Shit! I'm so screwed up. I know I'm going to be extremely tired come the morning. That is, if I can sleep.

CHAPTER TWENTY-EIGHT

DAY SIX

Tap tap
Tap tap
Tap tap
Now that the ribs aren't hurting as much it's time to start learning more about my cage. Hey, it'll give me something to do, in between lying on the bed bored and sitting around on the computer bored talking to Kelaidescope.

This past hour I've tried to figure out the thing that's been bothering me about my bedroom. Actually, the whole apartment, but I'm starting with the bedroom since that's where I first noticed it, the first day I was here.

Why aren't there any windows?

There must have been some at one time. The building doesn't make sense without them. What tenement doesn't have windows? The room where we had the Tea Party had one in in the kitchen. Why doesn't mine?

Only reason I can think of. Escape.

That means there probably are windows, only they're covered up. If that's the case, maybe I can find a way to take those boards down.

Hey, it's not that crazy an idea. Before I moved to Ohio I had a friend in New York City whose parents built an extra room in their apartment by putting a wall in the middle of the kitchen. It was cramped and the wall was kind of flimsy, but it gave them the extra bedroom they wanted. Could this be like that?

Tap tap

I'm tapping in the area behind the headboard, the part of the wall that always looks weird to me because it isn't completely smooth but seems to hollow out in the middle. Right where a window should be.

I'm grabbing on to the white headboard for support and leaning forward. My toes curled up against the blanket. I'm touching the angel wallpaper where the hollow spot seems to be. The wall is cold to the touch and the poor angels must be freezing. I curl my hands into a fist and—

Interesting. When I knock I hear a change in sound. It's not right in the center the way I thought, but a little more to the left. Like there's empty space behind the wallpaper and plaster I'm touching.

Maybe because a window's on the other side?

Tap tap tap.

I follow the hollow sound upwards. It stops sounding that way after about an inch or two. I wonder, how far down does it sound hollow behind my headboard? I need to pull the bed away from the wall and check. Even in such a small room, I should be able to slide it back a few inches.

Tap tap.

Yes, definitely hollow. I tap again against the cold wall scoping out exactly where the opening might be. Are you holding secrets, little red angels? Is there a window behind you?

Maybe it would help if I tore the wallpaper down. The edges by the ceiling and the walls look easy to tear at. Tempting. Let me reach up and grab one of the edges...the curled edge of the wallpaper is so thin and brittle. It'd be so easy to...

"One yank," I whisper. One yank. "Jeremy would love what I've done with the place."

Jeremy. Saying his name brings me to my senses. It's too close to dinner to risk it. He'd be sure to see. There'd be hell to pay.

Still, this wall thing has possibilities. If I could rip off the wallpaper I might be able to dig through the plaster. And if a window's really on the other side, I could lift it and crawl out.

I'll wait until I have more time. Like, when it's dark out. When the lights are all out, I'll pull my bed back, when no one can see what I'm doing. Even if I can't see, I can tap around and rip the wallpaper behind the headboard. Do a little digging and cover it up with the headboard in the morning. Dig my way to freedom, like in a prison escape movie.

That is, if I can find time between Jeremy's visits.

He usually lets a couple of hours pass before he comes in at night. That might give me time, if I sign off from the computer earlier. If they let me. They like me to spend a lot of time there now. Since I'm entertainment and all.

So, what can I do before supper if I can't tear down the walls? Well hmmm, I can always play on the computer.

I stop searching for cracks and windows and sit on my bed to think for the hundredth time about the cracks in the computer.

Barbara found some loophole in the system that allowed her to talk to the outside world. They've fixed things since then. At least, my emails aren't getting to Josh. Elvis isn't leaving the building from what I can see. Or if he is, nothing's coming back.

Maybe there's another way to send messages. Have they blocked everything?

Worth a try. Back to the Black Room.

Back to Barbara's world.

I have the routine down by now. The minute I'm in the room and seated my fingers start typing.

USER ID: Gnostrime

Password: Orknies

The PeoplesCam system pops up. I shut down the webcam and call up a new screen. No need to call attention to my little secret.

Should I try Facebook again? Fine, Facebook it is.

The screen flickers. Then: "Inaccessible."

Figured that. How about Twitter? "Inaccessible."

This is a waste of time. I need other sites, different places. Pinterest? Skype? What else can I try? Can't blog. Mail isn't getting through. Can't use the webcam. What else?

Bored, I look around the folders in Barbara's computer. There's not much there. She was too busy flying.

Hmm, there's a folder called Bananas. What was Barbara bananas about? That might be interesting.

I double click.

There's one document in it. Dontread.

Which of course means I'm going to.

Wow, it's over 100 pages long! What was Barbara working on?

September 25

I'm goin to keep track of the days and mabe also try to use this so I dont end up exploading. Ive already been here for about 5 weeks but stupid me right now I figured out I could keep track of what was going on around here same as I did back when I was around 8 and my mother gave me a red lether diary with a little gold key. I used to write in that evry day.

Her diary. I'm immediately sucked in. I need to read more.

I glance through the pages. I can read the whole thing later on, I've got plenty of time. But one thing I need to see now. Did she write about the two of us?

February 6

She asked me who I trust and I said I didnt know. Why is it so hard to say I trust him? He gave me a way to talk to her right? He gave me a connecsion to the outside world and its nice to talk to someone some other girl almost like Im in school again and we are passing notes.

He gave me this freedom he gave me the drugs he tells me he cares and still I try to cross the line even tho I never do cross it that much He has to see that

So, Jeremy was the one who gave her the way out. Interesting. I scroll down to the end of the document. What were her last words? I'm close. They're dated February 7.

What the-?

Shit. I wasn't expecting this.

Kami if you ever read this and I hope you dont you were asking for a clue not sure this will help but the name is GOASKALICE and the password is orknies I LOVE YOU IM SORY

Wow. This is amazing. Barbara, I can't believe you did this!

But wait. Password for what?

Must be for PeoplesCam. The one she used to talk to me when I first met her as GOASKALICE in the Late Night area.

Wait. Wait wait wait. Barbara never said the ID was shut down. She said I couldn't use it on the night of the finals. So does it still work?

Jeremy would have had to override the system to let her on in the first place, right? Does that mean it's still accessible? Hmm. Worth a shot.

I slide the mouse to the lower left to see if I can call up PeoplesCam . . . well, the other version.

Success. Yes! Barbara, I could kiss you. The cherubs are smiling down on me today.

It asks for my ID and a password. I do as Barbara said.

Next second, I'm back in the world of PeoplesCam. The real one, that is. Not the secret scary evil one.

What a head rush. It's as if I'm sitting back in my old room ignoring my college homework to talk to my friends at GroundUnder. I wonder, are they on? They might be fun to visit.

I check. No, the lights are off in GroundUnder.

I hear a sound outside my door. Is somebody coming? Quickly, I get up and walk into the living room by the ugly green couch. I'm half tempted to sit, but that might look suspicious. Jeremy knows how much I hate this gross couch.

Anyway, the coast is clear.

Still, it's a warning I've got to work fast. And even if the ladies from GroundUnder aren't on, I know one person I can turn to.

Josh McBee. Wirehanger.

Better try it now. I run back to the seat. Type his name in the search bar.

His profile pops up. His photo. His blue eyes staring out at me. Right away it hits home.

Oh, Josh. Why didn't I pay more attention to you? That last drive home it was so clear you were trying to talk about what was going on between us. All I could think about was my note from Barbara. I was so obsessed. So stupid.

His name has a green bar next to it. Is he on-line? Only one way to find out. I send him a private message.

GOASKALICE: Josh, it's Kami.

A second later there's a noise. A response!

WIREHANGER: At school. Where else?

At school? Oh, his away message.

I'm disappointed until it starts to sink in. I got through! He might get this. Maybe, possibly, he can help. At least pass on a message.

Time to send him that message.

GOASKALICE: Josh, its Kami. I'm okay but need help. Please call Mom. Have her call Uncle Dom. He needs to

Footsteps down the hall. I have to move this along. I hit send and log off as fast as my shaking hands let me.

I hear the door open. It has to be Jeremy. I don't turn my head. Don't try to react at all. I sit in front of the screen, pretending everything is right with the world.

"What's going on?" His tone seems guarded, suspicious.

My heart's racing and all I can think of are the words in her diary. "Why is it so hard to say I trust him?"

I know what she means.

"Oh, nothing," I lie. I use the mouse to casually log out. Play this cool, girl. I turn to face him head on. "What's going on, Jeremy?"

The prince returns to visit the mermaid again in the dark of the emerald cave. This time he walks in and sits down next to me.

"Jeremy."

"You were hiding something this afternoon." His voice is low. He's clearly angry.

Time to play innocent. "I was? When?"

"You know when." It sounds like he's barely able to keep it together. Oh great, I've got the angry Jeremy tonight.

"I don't know what you're talking-"

"Bullshit. You were on the computer."

"I'm on the computer a lot, Jeremy. I don't have much else—"

"Jesus!" His reaction is quick, his voice like an explosion. His words shoot through the room, and I can't help it, I cry out and turn from him, push my body as far away as possible.

Then, silence. I hear his slow steady breathing in the dark. When he speaks next his tone is softer. He's in control again. "I hate thinking you're lying to me, Kami. I thought we were making progress. The last few nights."

I struggle to keep my voice calm. It helps that I'm turned away. "We are, Jeremy." Lie, lie, lie.

Well, we were. I can't pretend it isn't nice talking to you. Part of me wants to tell you everything, even when you sound so angry. What we created in the darkness, in our cave, gives me hope. I don't want to see it destroyed. But should I give it all away because of the way you sometimes sound in the darkness?

No. No, I can't.

"What's the weather like outside, Jeremy?" I whisper.

I can hear the springs squeak. Guess he wasn't expecting that one. "What?"

"What's it like? I never get to go out, so I wonder what kind of day it is. Cold?"

"I dunno. Sunny. But, yes, cold. I wore my heavy jacket to work today."

"What a drag, huh?"

He laughs at my sarcasm. "Keep your secrets then. Tell me or don't. I've got time."

He rises from the bed. Is he leaving? "Where are you going?"

"Out for a smoke," he says, sounding as if he's enjoying the panic in my voice. "That okay with you?"

I listen to his footsteps as he exits the room.

I turn over in bed so I'm staring back up at the ceiling. Well, at least I can get some sleep instead of talking and sharing secrets with Jeremy all night. Maybe it's for the best.

Keeping secrets, you said. Well, I have a new secret to keep now, my friend.

It happened when Jeremy left after dinner.

After I was certain he was gone, I went back to the computer for a quick check. To try Barbara's ID one more time.

There was a message. Short and sweet.

From Josh.

"Hold on," he wrote. Hold on.

That message gives me hope, like a crack of sunshine in a dark cold wall that never existed before. So much so I may not bother moving my headboard to search for windows in the dark. Maybe a different kind of window is opening.

And maybe Jeremy doesn't have as much time as he thinks.

CHAPTER TWENTY-NINE

DAY FIVE

VISITOR 24: Hey baby, do you know who I am?

So here I am back to being Queen of the Night. For now.

KAMKIT: Of course. How could I forget? You're Visitor 24.

KELAIDESCOPE: There's something about his name, isn't there? It's so . . . manly. *swoon*

Only this time around, Kel and I are taking turns ruling the kingdom. Tag team this week.

If this works, we're planning to try out other stories. We'll have a huge fight then kiss and make up. The possibilities are endless.

It's like I'm back in the outside world on PeoplesCam and I'm in a really twisted version of GroundUnder. In this world, I'm the NauticalNinja and Kel is JadeMermaid. It would definitely be a primo Late Night offering.

I've even gotten Jeremy to buy me a few things to bring my character to life. Sparkle for my eyes and a yellow hoody. I've asked myself, "What would Daphne do?"

TANGERINEWILDE: YOU 2 ARE KILLING ME

TANGERINEWILDE: LIKE WEATHERVAYNE SAYS LOL

The thing is, Weathervayne isn't saying. In fact, since Friday night, Kim hasn't spoken a word. The guys are getting sick of it. I'm worried about her chances.

Privately, I send her an IM. To check for signs of life.

KAMKIT: Weathervayne, are you okay?

KAMKIT: Kim, I know you're there. I can see you.

KAMKIT: Is everything all right? I'm worried.

No response. Her head is slumped down so her bangs cover her eyes. She seems to be listening to music with a sad, spaced-out look on her face.

KELAIDESCOPE: I think you boys should give yourselves names. More than Visitor insert favorite number here.

KAMKIT: I know! We can call Visitor24 Zayn.

KELAIDESCOPE: We can call Visitor23 Harry.

TANGERINEWILDE: IM GONNA FREAKIN BARF

I look up at the screens to see Lea giving me the finger. I flash my crazy mad smile right back.

Kel's right about playing the game. Hey, it's the middle of the week; we're safe for a few days. We can afford to take chances. And maybe, who knows? If things go my way, I'll be out of the game before Friday comes around.

"Barf all you want, Tangerine," I say looking straight into the camera.

KELAIDESCOPE: Get all Linda Blair on us.

KAMKIT: Hey, how do you keep a blonde busy all day?

Meanwhile, Kel is sending me a steady stream of private messages. She can type super-fast even with her nose in a book.

KELAIDESCOPE: So what is it?

KAMKIT: What is what?

KELAIDESCOPE: The big change. You seemed good last night, but not like THIS.

KAMKIT: IDK

KAMKIT: Kel, can you do me a favor and get in a fight with Lea? I need to leave for five minutes

KELAIDESCOPE: Where are you going?

I lie to her in case big brother's watching.

KAMKIT: To the bathroom.

KAMKIT: BRB

I sign off as Kamkit. Type in the words leading me back to Barbara's world.

GOASKALICE: Josh, are you there?

GOASKALICE: Josh?

WIREHANGER: Kam? Is that you?

Oh my God. Could this day get any better? Josh!

GOASKALICE: YES!!!!!!

GOASKALICE: You did get my message!

WIREHANGER: Yes I did RU OK?

GOASKALICE: I'm fine. I broke two ribs but getting better.

WIREHANGER: Where are you?

GOASKALICE: In a city. Maybe Chicago. I think that's where I am.

GOASKALICE: listen I can't stay on long

GOASKALICE: I mean Im REALLY glad to talk to you but

WIREHANGER: I let your mother know and she had me talk to Mr Torelli

GOASKALICE: Mr. Who?

GOASKALICE: Oh, Uncle Dom

WIREHANGER: Hes doing all he can but having trouble

WIREHANGER: they didn't think it would be hard to trace the address but it's turning out to be

I hear a noise in the hall. Footsteps.

GOASKALICE: GTG Josh

WIREHANGER: Go! Be

I don't wait for the end of it. I shut off PeoplesCam as fast as I can and log off as Barbara.

The footsteps in the hall die down. That makes me unbelievably sad. I could have spoken to Josh longer.

I feel anxious, stifled by these walls. I'm completely caged and wondering what will happen next. What did Josh mean they're having trouble tracing me? Maybe what I said about Chicago might help? Is there anything else I can tell him? Is there anything else I can get out of Jeremy?

Time's up. I need to get back to the game. From what Josh said there's no telling how long it's going to take to figure out where I am. That means Friday might still be on, so I have to be smart about things. That is, if I ever want to play Queen of the Night in my own bedroom again.

My own bedroom. I stop for a minute before I sign back on as Kamkit.

I'm so used to making fun of the little hick town Mom brought us to. Still, right now I'd give anything for a hot summer night in my tiny room, listening to the sounds of crickets chirping outside my screen window.

"I didn't think you'd visit," I say to the shadow of his face.

He twists his body around in the bed. "I'm sorry about last night."

"It's fine." I'm trying to make it sound as if it's nothing. I have to keep things light. Can't afford to let him know what's going on.

"Are you warm enough? It's cold tonight."

"Can you get me another blanket?"

"Of course."

"I'd like one. My feet are like ice."

And then there's a hand on my leg. I jump a bit. Both of his hands slide their way down to my feet. The contact comes as a surprise, but . . . "Mmm. Nice."

"Well, I'm not much of a blanket, but . . . ."

"You'll do."

"I know you sent a message out." The rubbing of my feet stops. He's waiting for a reaction.

As always, I think of Barbara. One of our late night conversations. That bruise on her face. He did this to me.

I tense up. He must sense it because he starts to rub my feet again softly, slowly. His voice is soothing and seductive. "It's okay. You've been using my gift to Barbara, right? I'm not sure how you figured it out, but you did."

He knows. Should I keep pretending?

Flash of webcam. Head being pushed violently.

"You gave her that. As a gift?"

"Wasn't easy. I could have lost . . . well, we both could have lost . . ."

And Barbara did. "Why did you give it to her?"

"She was so lonely. So sad. I thought being able to talk to someone outside, I don't know, might make her happier. This place can break you down. Especially when you're a performer."

Jesus, that word! "Stop calling it that!"

He ignores me. "She was such a free spirit. She had a . . . I'm not sure I can describe it. It was tough to see it die inside her. She promised she'd be good and not use it to get out."

I'm tearing up. "She didn't, Jeremy."

"No, she kind of did. When they found out they went ape shit. And that's when they . . . I blame myself. Of course. I mean, no shit. I gave it to her." His voice is low and gravely and I guess I finally know the answer to my question. Of course he loved her. He did whatever he could to keep her happy. Even if he didn't have the nerve to give her what she truly needed. To set her free.

"Why didn't they punish you, Jeremy?"

He's quiet for a long time. "Someone was punished for the leak. Someone was. Just not me."

"Why wouldn't you be the one to—"

"I wasn't the only one she saw!"

"But you're all she talked about. You're all that I—"

"I'm all you see." He stops rubbing my feet, leans in closer to me. "That's because they changed everything after what happened. I did have her, mostly. There was another guy, though. His name was Phil. Big moron. He had a thing for Barbara, too. I had access to his security code. So . . ."

"So you framed him."

His voice cracks. "I'm not proud of it."

"What happened to him?"

He lets out a short, bitter laugh. "What happens to anyone here when they cross the line?"

"What is the GKS, Jeremy?"

Silence.

"You wouldn't tell me the other night. You said the other place you worked . . . they were little fish."

"Right."

"Who're the big fish?"

My foot massage slows and stops as he grows thoughtful. "I don't know the names of the people way up high. The GKS is like a private club. That's why the people who watch are only called Visitors. The members don't know each other. It's safer that way. That's also why they split all the performers up into different buildings and have the group names. Girl next door." He tickles my foot.

"Stop that!" Okay, that's interesting. So good that I don't even bother fighting him about the word performers. "There are other buildings?"

"Yep. I mean, no shit, right? I don't know where they are. The guys who work here are kept like mushrooms, you know. Kept in the dark, fed shit. Safer that way."

In the dark the way we are now. Is he deliberately keeping me in the dark? Maybe I need to push him a little more. "The other night it sounded . . . like you know . . . more."

He takes the bait, his masculine pride wounded. "I know who pays my check each week. Let me put it like this, I don't think it's a coincidence things look like PeoplesCam. Do you?"

I can't answer. A shiver runs up my spine. I'm thinking about the email I sent to PeoplesCam about Barbara. Maybe Jeremy isn't the only reason she was chosen.

"So maybe I'm here because of your gift," I whisper in the dark.

He lets go of my legs and pushes away from me. "I never meant for you to get wrapped up in this."

"I know."

"Maybe that's why I see you at night. Knowing what I did brought you here." Next thing I know he's leaning toward me near my waist, his hands drifting up my sides. His cologne is stronger. I'm dizzy, my head filled with an overpowering combination of perfume and truth. I inch closer to him, expectant, waiting, wanting . . . more.

"I don't know if I can do this anymore," he says.

I'm like a statue, waiting to hear more.

"I mean, I go home and I don't want to do anything because all I think of is what they do. What I do. I think of what happened to Barbara. I think of Kim and what we do to keep her in line. I think of you. In here. I wish I could find a way out, but I'm stuck here until I screw up again. My days are numbered, too. Like you, only . . ."

He stops speaking. I can hear his breathing, ragged at first and then slowing, steadier. He's getting control back. His head is lowered. In the darkness, he looks as though his head has been swallowed by his shoulders.

And then I reach out and hold his hand.

He grabs it. His grip is so strong. The next thing I know, I'm sitting up. Drawing in closer to him, and he's moving closer to me. Then we're holding each other. My head is on his chest. I breathe in that scent of sweet cologne and stale cigarettes and I whisper, "We can end this."

"End this?" he whispers back. "What do you mean?"

"I mean, get out of here. Bring the GKS down."

He lets out a breath. "I don't think so, Kami."

"Listen! I know people are looking for me."

"People are looking for all of them, sweetheart. "

"But I wasn't a runaway." I take a deep breath before the plunge. "Let me use your phone."

"What?"

"Your phone! Let me use it to call my mother. Or send a message."

I feel his body stiffen. "Kami, you can't use my phone. It's too dangerous."

"Listen! My dad used to be a cop. I was on the phone with his best friend the night Barbara was . . . the night they broke in." I stop. Do I dare keep on going? I've already gone this far. Why not? "I've used your gift to Barbara. I know they're looking for me. If you don't want to use your phone, do something else. Anything. Get me out of here. Take me somewhere safe."

"Kami." I feel his breath on my cheek. His voice is ragged at first and then a deep breath and he's back to being strong and firm. "You can't fight this thing."

"Why not? What choice do I have, Jeremy? I've seen what happens to everyone else. After a while you stop being clever. You make a mistake or you give up and it—"

"Kami!" His hands are now caressing my shoulders. Then, without warning, he stops. What's on his mind? What is he thinking? "Okay." His voice is so low I can hardly hear it. "I'll help. I'll get you out of here."

"You will?" Did he really say that? Did he mean it? I don't know what to say. "You will?"

"Yeah. Somehow." He laughs, but he isn't amused. "We all have to die sometime, right?"

"Jeremy!"

"Let me think about it."

And then he kisses me. And I feel such a wave of relief flooding over me I don't want it to end. I lean into the kiss, lean into him, and let myself go. I don't want to think what it means or what he might think. Right now, this minute, I need to feel close. I need to feel . . . this.

CHAPTER THIRTY

DAY FOUR

Another breakfast. But this morning I'm mixing things up.

Early in the morning, way earlier than when Jeremy usually comes in, I push aside the sheets covering my body. Then, wearing only last night's T-shirt for cover, I rip off the sheets and head into the living room. I'm going to have breakfast with him on the ugly green couch today.

Of course, I'm not going to sit on that disgusting stained thing without protection. No telling what those stains are.

That's why the bedsheets. I'm going to cover the entire couch. I'll ask him to get me a new sheet. Maybe a fluffier pillow, too.

It's hard to tell without an alarm or phone, or even a clock on the wall, what time it is so I have to guess a little. Turns out I've woken up way earlier than I should have.

Now the challenge is staying awake. It's not easy, thanks to last night's super long late night visit. My eyelids droop. I yawn and shift to a spot on the couch with a few less springs poking into my spleen. I jerk awake. Mustn't sleep. And drift away until a line of drool slipping down my shoulder startles me awake again.

I shift in place. Pinch my arm. Stay. Awake!

At long last, I hear his footsteps and deliberately spread out dramatically on the couch, posing like Lady Gaga meets Cleopatra, or as close as I can get in a sheet and T-shirt, and try not to laugh. I love the look on his face when he walks in carrying a tray in one arm.

He's smiling. I wonder if something special is attached to that smile. He's wearing a blue sweater and a pair of black jeans. Ooh, goodbye stubble. Looks like he shaved. Even his goatee! I'm glad. He was looking pretty scruffy.

I rub my eyes and sit up. "Good morning."

He must have left a few hours before. I remember falling asleep in his arms. I also remember opening my eyes later on when he kissed me softly on the cheek before he left. Maybe that's what woke me up so early.

I wonder, how far away does he live? Is his apartment close by? Why can't he take me home with him and let me hide there?

I want to ask. But it's daytime. Day rules apply.

"Tired of breakfast in bed?" He places the tray on the cushion next to me.

"A little." I scan the breakfast tray with half-opened eyes. Then my eyes open wide, realizing what he's brought me. He notices the flash of recognition and squirms back and forth, pleased as a puppy.

"Chocolate Crunchies and coffee." I show off my crazy mad smile. I can't believe he remembered!

"I wasn't sure how you took your coffee."

"That's easy. Lots of sugar."

"Sort of figured you weren't the plain black coffee kind." He reaches into his pocket to take out four white packages. Oh, and two Roxi tablets.

Forget the sugar packets. I immediately grab my spoon and slurp away at my bowl of Chocolate Crunchies. The taste of the cold milk is incredible, even if the cereal is way sweeter than I remember.

It makes me remember how long I've gone without the things I took for granted, like chocolate or a slice of cheesecake at the Fandango Café. It's funny how much you miss the little things once they're no longer part of your life.

Tears form in my eyes.

Jeremy smiles. "I knew you'd be happy."

Calm. Stay calm, girl. He thinks it's because I'm grateful. He can't know it's because I'm so homesick. Not after going out of his way like this.

"Yeah." It's all I'm able to get out.

He's pleased. I shove another spoonful of chocolaty goodness into my mouth to kill the pain. To wash it down. I reach for the coffee cup, which I'm pretty positive isn't going to be half as good as Mom's and is sure to make me miss home even more.

Sure enough.

It was nice of him to try, but maybe the greasy eggs-and-bacon breakfast is better because it doesn't remind me of what I no longer have. I place the coffee down carefully by my side so it won't spill. And I look away from him and over to the kitchen, stifling the memories, putting them back in their boxes, trying to forget.

He frowns. "Are you still tired?"

"Up all night, you know. Clubbing."

He grins his foolish little boy smile. "True dat. Mmmm, your coffee looks good. Mind if I get some for myself?"

"Go for it."

"I'll be back." He heads off.

I watch him leave and think about how he held me last night. I also think about freedom. Will the things he said the night before ever take place in the light of day?

###

GOASKALICE: Josh, it's Kami.

GOASKALICE: I'll try to check later. You okay? Hope you're getting this. Need to hear from U

GOASKALICE: Bye.

It's been my fifth try that day. I thought for sure he'd be around tonight.

###

"Can I still use Barbara's gift?"

With my head on his chest, I feel the slow rise and fall of his rib cage. With that question, the calm rise and fall stops abruptly. And then: "It should be working fine. Why?"

"I tried using it."

His hands play with my hair. "To the same person, right?"

"Right."

"Maybe that person isn't on."

"He's always around at night. Every night. And wouldn't he want to stay in touch?"

"Depends. Maybe he's been told not to say anything more to you. Maybe they're planning to rescue you tonight."

He strokes my hair. It's comforting.

"I doubt it."

"Never know though, do you?"

I close my eyes, even though it's just as dark with my eyes wide open. His tone's light, playful, and starting to annoy me. "Maybe."

He curls a strand of my hair with his fingers. That feels good. "Anyway, it's not going to matter. I've been thinking about what we said last night."

"And?" My annoyance fades away as quickly as a snowball in a microwave. I can barely contain myself, but his voice stays calm. He strokes my hair slowly, steadily, rhythmically.

"I said I'd help you and I will. Soon."

"How soon?"

"Like the next few days soon. Friday's coming up. If you're worried about the gift being discovered then we need to plan now."

"Do you think it has? Gone wrong?"

"No." He stops stroking my hair to scratch at his belly. "I've been keeping an eye on that."

I place my hand on his chest, afraid to ask for specifics, like date and time, afraid it might come across as too greedy. It's too important. "So, Wednesday night or Thursday night?"

He places his hand over mine. Our fingers intertwine. We lie there wrapped in each other's arms. Quiet. Thinking.

"How does tomorrow night sound?"

How? I want to jump out of bed. I want to jump up and down on the bed. I want to hug and kiss him and thank him for being so brave. No, I have to stay quiet. I hug him and whisper, "Do you mean it?"

"I do." He unclasps my hand and starts stroking my hair again. I can hear his heart beating faster. This must be so tough for him. Maybe it's freedom for me, but if anything goes wrong . . .

"How will you do it?"

"Oh, easy. I'm going to walk you through the front door, Barbara, and—"

"What?" I slide my head off his chest and sit up.

"Kami!"

"Barbara?"

"Sorry!" He laughs. That only makes it worse. "I guess I had her on my mind." He squeezes my arm, which does nothing to bridge the distance.

I twist my arm away. Not what I expected. Maybe I'd been right all along. Maybe these nighttime visits are Barbara visits, because in the dark all cats—

"I wish I'd done it sooner." His voice is a whisper that gets lost in the darkness. He sounds so lost.

Earlier, for Barbara. Of course, he should have. But he's doing something now.

"But . . . no. It's going to be way harder than walking through the front door. I was being an ass. Come back, wouldja?" He pats his chest.

Cautiously, I lower my head. "How will you do it?"

"I've got an idea. I know where the fuse box is in the cellar. What I'm thinking is I'll come up here and unlock your door. Let you out. We won't have much time. They have cameras in the hallway. So listen, don't walk out right away. Keep your door open, okay?"

"Okay."

"I'm going to go downstairs, blow the fuse box. That's when you need to move. As soon as the lights go out. You remember how this house is set up, right? I mean, you saw it when I took you downstairs."

"Well, I only saw it once, but . . . yeah."

"You'll see it again tomorrow. I'll be taking you downstairs to visit the girls. Remember this: on the left hand side on this floor, right before you go down the stairs, that's where I stay at night. My bedroom has a window that's not blocked off. I've tested it. The window opens."

"You want me to . . . jump out of it?" I flinch, thinking about my ribs.

"No! I want you to wait there. I'll be able to help get you out of there, Kami. My place is close by."

"What about you, Jeremy?"

He reaches over and hugs me, crushing me to his chest. I wonder if this is all as much a relief to him as it is to me. "I won't be coming back here. Maybe that's a good thing."

"It is." I lie there listening to the beat of his heart.

"Course, once you get out of here, you'll forget about me."

"No!"

He finds that funny. "Yes, you will. I bet you have tons of guys looking to go out with you."

I think about Josh. Sometimes, with his red hair and pale skin, it's easy to think of Jeremy as an older version. If I have to be honest, maybe sometimes in the dark I pretend he is Josh, the same way he pretends I'm Barbara. All cats do look the same in the dark, but I'm not telling Jeremy—or Josh—that.

"Back at school, I'm nothing special. I used to think of myself as a freak the way everyone ignored me. But these past few days, I've decided I wasn't even that much of a freak to them. I was . . . nothing."

"You could never be that."

"I was! I would go to school, then work. I couldn't even figure out how to get my driver's license. I used to wonder if anyone knew I existed, besides Mom and . . ." I stop, not wanting to say Josh's name. "The only time I saw myself as anything special was at night. On camera.

Even then I pretended I was someone else, someone who actually was someone. This dancer from Julliard. Because you know want? That was the only time I felt alive. At least, after--"

I cut my words off, again. I guess the dark makes it so damn easy to—

"After what?" he asks, softly.

"After Dad died." I'm barely able to get the words out.

He leans down, kisses the top of my head. I love having him hold me. Having someone to talk with, say things to I've kept inside for so long.

Slowly I lift my head. Shift my weight so his face, his lips, are close to mine.

"Kami. Are you sure . . . ?"

I nod. And then, he pulls me forward. Kisses me.

I kiss him back fully. There has to be some way to thank him for what he's doing. When he reaches for my waist I close my eyes and dream about escape.

CHAPTER THIRTY-ONE

DAY THREE

Jeremy tells me the tea party is going to be earlier this time around — closer to noon. Since it's not a Friday at least it should be a normal visit . . . I mean, one without an unhappy ending. I'm looking forward to talking to Kel face-to-face.

The space between breakfast and my visit with the girls (I hate that word, but it's the one Jeremy always uses and I guess it's better than being performers) seems to last forever. The few bites of breakfast I managed to eat flop around my stomach like sneakers in a dryer.

It's going to be interesting seeing the girls again. The person they met only a week ago no longer exists. Maybe it's seeing Angie selected or the Queen of the Night games Kel and I play. Maybe it's the nighttime meetings with Jeremy in our cave.

Or that I believe things might turn out okay. That's new.

I want to tell them what's going on tonight. Would that be bad? Getting out of here would help them too. On the other hand, it might freak them out. No, I can't take the risk.

Especially Lea. I mean, I like her, but I know she'd do anything to earn a get out of jail free card, even if it meant burning me to help herself. I wouldn't put it past her to spill the beans if she knew anything. I need to be careful around her. Smart.

This time I barely spend two minutes getting ready for my tea party date. I throw on my clothes, comb through my hair, and brush my teeth. Put on some eyeliner and lip gloss so I'm decent. Then I'm out of the bathroom and back at the computer to talk to Kel. I need to speak with her about—

KELAIDESCOPE: Will we see you at high tea, Madame LaFarge?

KELAIDESCOPE: I'll be wearing my Sunday best. And a wimple.

KELAIDESCOPE: LOL

What can I say? The second I sit down, all my words become frozen. What if this is all being monitored somewhere? Of course, it is. I can't run the risk of ruining everything, especially if being free is only hours away.

Freedom. I whisper the word. Freedom. Saying it makes me shiver. Free dom. FREE!

KAMKIT: I'll be there. With crumpets.

Better not to say too much. We trade small talk until a few minutes before noon when Jeremy knocks on the door. By then Kel's already downstairs.

It's strange how Jeremy unlocks the door and walks in most of the time, except for the tea parties. For these, he always knocks. I wonder why?

I push the mouse aside and make my way to the doorway that leads to freedom.

"You're ready, princess?" he asks and bows. Yes, I am.

I follow down the hall in silence. The walk is different from the last one. Last time I tried to memorize every detail. Every speck on the rusty radiators, every rip in the wallpaper, every doorway in the hallway. This time only one door interests me: the one on the end to the left, with the number one spray-painted in red. I count the number of steps it takes to reach it.

Jeremy stops on the landing with the window. It's as bright and peaceful as it was last time. Even more so, in some ways. He touches the gauzy white drapes and looks over at me with the bright noon sun shining into his golden brown eyes. "Want to look outside?"

Look outside? I hesitate a moment, lingering at the top of the stairs.

"Relax." He motions for me to stand next to him. When I reach him he whispers in my ear, so softly I have to strain to hear it. "You'll be out there soon."

Soon. I want more than anything to kiss him for that. It's the first time he's ever said a word in daylight, and that makes it finally less of a dream. He smiles and all I can do is look at him in wonder.

I stare through the curtains he's opened up and take in the world outside as if it's the first time. It's a gorgeous day, bright and sunny. Not a cloud in the steely blue sky. The thought of being out there sounds wonderful. Maybe it's the brightness of the sun or the thought of freedom, but whatever it is—

Jeremy wipes at my eyes. "It'll happen soon enough," he reassures me before turning away. "Come on. Let's get going."

We walk down the stairs. Outside the tea party entrance is a man I've never seen before, not the big burly African-American dude from last time. This one looks a bit older, like a football coach. Gray hair, steely blue eyes. Kind of a belly. Jeremy nods at him and opens the door.

The gang's all here sitting around the wobbly table, same as last visit. Except for one empty space. Of course. Lea and Kel and Kim. No Angie. No Angie ever again.

Kim's busy slurping from her cup like there's no tomorrow, like it's the last drink she's ever going to have. Kel looks up when I enter and bows her head down courteously. Such a lady.

"Grab yourself a piece of pizza and a seat, Kami," barks out Jeremy, assuming his tough guy attitude. "You've got more room this time around. But listen up, ladies. We're getting a new girl in a few days. Hopefully, y'all will be sticking around for a while."

With that, he walks past us to the door with the Office sign. The other man follows and slams the door shut.

Lea waits until we're alone. "Yeah, that Angie," she calls out so they can hear her in the office. "What was she thinking of going and dying like that?" She pushes out the chair next to her with her legs so I can sit. No fuss and definitely no muss. The quickest—and easiest—way to get things done is Lea's thing. She wouldn't want to raise a sweat.

"Miss her, Lea?" asks Kel.

Lea shrugs. "Bitch had it coming."

Kel turns a page in her book. It's a new one today. *Animal Farm*. "You know you don't mean that."

"Don't I?" Lea glares and pushes back the sleeves of her pink sweatshirt like she's going to hit someone. "You don't know what's on my mind, Kel."

Kel smiles sweetly. Sarcasm, like revenge, is a dish best served cold, she said last night. "Sure I do. Most of the time, not much."

That gets Lea swearing, but I'm too busy getting some pizza and watching Kim. She's been so quiet on camera, and now that we're together she's even worse. Not looking at anyone, not paying any attention to the fight. It's as though she's in another world, sipping her soda and listening to her music, sometimes swaying back and forth to what she's hearing in her head. She has deep bruises under her eyes.

"Kim?" I walk to her and grab her arm to make sure she hears. Wait, her charm bracelet is missing. Where did it go? Did they take it away from her? That must be killing her. It was all she had. Her last connection to her grandmother.

She stops swaying and stares at me. Her blue eyes are unfocused and dulled. She jumps back a bit like she finally knows I'm in the room. "Are you okay?"

Kim blinks her eyes. It's like she's trying to wake up and focus on me. I grab her arm and shake it to break her from her dream. I lean in, speaking louder. "Kim, are you okay?"

Her eyes focus on mine. Contact. Her mouth opens up to speak. Then she shakes her head and pulls her arm away. She's shut down again. She goes back to swaying.

Lea raps on the table to get my attention, a half-smile turning up the corners of her mouth. "You can try knocking, honey, but nobody's home. She's filled with happy juice." Then she turns her attention back to Kel. "Listen, I miss Angie the way I miss Barbara scoring the good stuff. Hell, no, I don't."

I do. And P.S., Lea, you're full of shit. I saw your face the night Angie was taken away. I saw how much you cared. What you're wearing now is a mask.

I try not to glance at the empty chair that's been pushed up against the rusty stove. The room is emptier without Angelina, without her laughter, and her playful banter with Lea. Even their arguments. Come to think of it, I wouldn't mind a good fight right now.

It's as if Kel can read my mind because without warning, she slams her book down onto the table. It looks like Lea's managed to push all her buttons. Finally.

"You're so stupid, Lea," she says, looking more involved than I've ever seen. "All you ever think about is yourself and what's in it for you."

"Damn straight."

"Even if there isn't anything at all."

Lea scrunches her lips up, trying not to laugh. She's not letting Kel faze her at all. "I don't see how Angelina sitting around flashing those big cans of hers ever helped me out."

"That's because you were so busy bickering all the time. Working against each other." Kel's face is turning red. Her eyes seem to be glassy, as if she's about to cry. "What a waste of time. When you get right down to it, we don't have much time here at all, and we only have each other."

"What?" Lea looks disgusted. Her mouth opens wide, and I can clearly see the gold stud on the tip of her tongue. Amazing. I sit down in my seat, shocked. Kel's finally gotten an honest reaction out of her, just by being honest herself. "What ARE you reading this week, girl? 'We only have each other.'" She waves that off in disgust, flips back her wild hair, and rolls her eyes in my direction. "Baby, I like it better when she's quiet. Don't you?"

"Somebody's got to say something," mutters Kel.

Oh. My turn.

"Someone did."

Silence, except for the tinny sounds from Kim's headset. Everyone looks to me, the spotlight focused center stage.

Lea cuts the silence. She doesn't seem disgusted by Kel anymore. Instead, she seems amused, and is looking me over, up and down. "Now this is interesting. No wonder you've been so quiet today, after you wouldn't SHUT UP all week. What are you talking about, girl?"

I keep my voice calm, barely above a whisper. "I said, someone did. Say something." I glance around the table. Even Kim stops sipping.

Kel bookends a page of *Animal Farm* and leans in toward me. "What do you mean?"

So much for keeping my mouth shut. I'm not sure how to say the rest, but the words have already come out. So much for caution. I glance at the door to the office wondering if Jeremy is listening. "I-I've been working on a few things."

Kim places her drink down. "You have?" she asks loudly, over her music. "Like what? Like—"

Lea grabs Kim's arm to silence her. Kim instinctively goes for her bracelet, then realizes it's not there. I turn away and focus on Lea so I don't have to see her reaction. "Like this Friday I'm showing off some things that'd make Angelina loco," she calls out, raising her voice. Then in a lower voice, with a tone like the crack of a whip, she hisses at Kim. "Shut up! What do you have going on, Jeannette?"

I choose my words carefully. "Remember how you said if you had anyone to talk to on the outside, you'd try to get out? Well . . . Barbara's still able to get out."

Lea's eyes narrow. "Barbara's dead."

"I have her password. It still works."

Lea looks shocked, but I see Kel nodding, approving. "So you popped a message out?"

"You've got to promise you won't say a word. If they find out . . .."

Kel places a finger on her lips. Lea looks skeptical but nods her head. I hope I can trust her. I've got no choice now.

"And another thing. About tonight."

I look around the table then at the closed office door. From the sound of it, Jeremy's arguing with the other guard about some dumb football team.

"I've been talking to Jeremy a lot these past few nights," barely able to believe I'm saying anything. "He's sick of it. He's sick of the whole thing. Tonight, he's going to help me break out. I've got a friend . . . my dad's best friend. He's a cop. Once Jeremy gets me to the nearest station, I can—"

I hear laughter. Crazy laughter.

I stop what I'm saying, look around. It's Kim. Laughing so hard it looks as if she's going to fall off the seat. She rocks in her chair back and forth, her blonde curls bobbing up and down. "Oh, God," she says, her body shaking. "Oh, God, you're . . . you're . . ." She shakes her head, tears in her eyes. "Oh, God . . ."

I glance at Lea. She's staring at me as though I have two heads. This isn't good. "What's wrong?"

Lea pushes back her chair, holds up her hands as if she's praying. She turns her attention away from me and stares at Kel.

Kel's voice is soft. Her spooky blue eyes stare into mine with such sadness. It's clear she's choosing her words carefully. "When you say Jeremy, you mean the guy who walked you in here, right?"

A tickle of panic forms in the back of my spine. "Of course. Why?"

Kel closes her eyes. Grabs my hand. "That's not Jeremy."

What?

"He's not Jeremy. His name's Phil."

And then all the blood drains from my face.

"I thought you knew. Barbara's Jeremy was let go—"

Lea snorts. "And we all know what that means . . .."

Kel ignores her. "He got too close to Barbara so they made an example out of him."

Lea hits the table with her fist. She's ready to take over again. Her voice is low, but her words fly through the air like arrows hurtling toward the bullseye. "Which means. They lined him up in front of the others, and—and"

"Lea," Kel warns.

"Pow!"

"After they found out what was going on with Barbara, Phil took over full-time," whispers Kel.

"I don't like Phil," says Lea. "He's a snake. Jeremy was a jerk but treated us with R-E-S-P-E-C-T most of the time. Phil, he don't care about nothing."

I hold on tightly to Kel's hand as my world dissolves like a chalk painting in the rain. All those conversations. All the things he said, the promises he made. And all this time all he was doing was . . . "But if he's not Jeremy, then . . ." Try your best to keep everything together. Try! "What's going to happen tonight?"

Lea rises and walks near Kim who's stopped giggling and swaying and now sits there hunched over with dead eyes. Lea places a hand on her shoulder. "My guess is you won't be seeing your daddy's best friend tonight."

"No!" I try to block her words out, struggle to hear the conversation between the two men inside the office. To Jeremy . . . Phil. Phil. His name is Phil. To make sure they can't hear us. But Phil's still busy arguing. My mind screams out, STOP IT! I shake my head, struggling for control when all I want to do is scream. Deep breath. Calm. "Lea, please don't say anything about this." I'm pleading even though I feel a million miles away.

A smile spreads across her face. "Why would I, KamKit?"

"Lea, please!" I beg, a little too loudly. The voices in the office stop abruptly.

Lea loses the wicked smirk on her face. "I won't say a thing." She turns her back on me to grab some soda from the counter.

"I won't either, Jeannette," says Kim way too loudly.

I nod my thanks and look over to Kel, even if I know the answer without asking. "Kel," I whisper, nervous to say anything now that the argument in the office has stopped. "Are you on the second floor?"

Kel nods.

"Same floor as I am. Which room?"

"The right one before the stairs. Right across from number one. Why?"

The office door opens. I shut my mouth.

"How are things going, girls?" His voice. I look down so he can't see my face. Control. I need to keep control.

"Swell. You got anything harder to drink in here?" asks Lea. Thank you thank you thank you.

"You shouldn't be drinking so early in the day," Phil replies. "Bad for you. You might die early."

Lea sweeps back her crazy wild hair, and her earrings shimmer. "I plan on living for a long, long time," she says defiantly.

So did Angie.

Phil's all business. "Five more minutes, girls." Then he turns around and closes the door.

"I'm glad you're near," I whisper to Kel.

"Knock on my door if you get out, Kami," she whispers back. "I've been saving a little gift for a rainy day."

CHAPTER THIRTY-TWO

DAY THREE

GOASKALICE: Josh RU there?

GOASKALICE: Josh it's me. Barbara. Are you there are you there are you there

GOASKALICE: Where are you?

Josh, were you ever there at all?

Somehow, I managed to keep it together through dinner. After he took away my half-eaten meal, I ran to the computer and logged on as Barbara, something I resisted doing all afternoon. Now here I am trying to get through to Josh and watching the minutes tick away.

Dinner was weird. Half-eaten chicken and potatoes and half a conversation with Jeremy who is not Jeremy, putting on an act that everything's swell.

"You're excited about tonight, aren't you?"

Every time he spoke, I could feel my ears burning. When he said that, I felt like throwing the tray at him. It was all I could do to stay calm. "I can't believe it's happening," I managed to say.

"You should eat more," Not-Jeremy said.

"I'm not hungry." And that at least was true.

Then he started going on about all the things we'd do once we got out. He didn't seem to care any more about who might be listening. All the time he was pouring on the charm. I wonder how many lies he's gotten away with because of how sweet he looks when he's smiling? It's so easy to want to believe him when he smiles that angelic smile.

No more. Now I know what's behind the smile.

He left me alone after supper. To get things ready, he said. To check on the other girls. Good. That gave me time to run to the computer and try to find a way to talk with Josh. Before I can't.

It also gave me time to think.

How could he lie to me all this time? How could he hate me so much he could sit there all those nights pretending to be someone he's not? And then carry that lie one step further? Give me hope, get me to reveal my secrets, make me believe I have . . .

A chance.

That's why. He's been dangling hope in front of me all this time, hoping I would play along. I was stupid enough to take the bait. Well, there's the real late show. All this time he played his game like a pro. Tonight, a new game's about to begin.

I hear a noise at the door. I swing the chair around to see what's up. The door's been opened. Barely.

I wait for him to make the next move.

Nothing comes. No instructions on what to do next. Just an open door. An invitation. And footsteps walking down the hall. If what he said is true the lights will go out soon enough.

There won't be much time after that. Once the juice stops flowing, all the electricity goes off in the building, and all the webcams will be down. They won't stand for that. They need their entertainment.

So it's show time. With an effort I rise and walk hesitantly to the doorway. Fingers trembling, I push back the door a crack and gaze down an empty corridor.

I need to know how far away Kel's door is before things go dark. Knock on my door, she said, when it's time. Knock on my door. I've been saving a little gift for a rainy day.

The hallway's empty. It feels spooky, as if there are ghosts in the shadows waiting to pop out. The blouse covered in dried blood is still shoved in the corner.

The smell seems even worse tonight. I can't stand the thought of that, either. I have to get away and fast.

Same floor as I am, she said. Last door to the right, before you get to the stairs. I should be able to walk down and—

And then the world is plunged into darkness.

I let out a cry, even though I know it's coming. Stupid girl, you can't afford to make a sound. Not now.

Sound downstairs. Footsteps. Somebody stumbling around. Are they coming up? Before I lose my nerve, I pull the door open all the way, push myself out.

The entire world is an inky void. I tiptoe forward as quiet as I can. Please, please, don't let the floorboards squeak. I make my way forward until I feel something solid in front of me. The scratchy touch of wallpaper. The cold hard feel of the half paneling. I'm on the other side of the hallway.

A second to catch my breath. Then I start walking down the hall. Kel's door, I have to find Kel's door before the lights go back on. But what will Kel have once I get there? Her room's locked. She can't help. I should be hiding—this is crazy—

Stop. Keep going.

Using the wall as my guide, I walk forward. Feel a cold metal surface. My fingers must be on one of the radiators. Good thing they're not being used. I hit one door, stumble past it. My fingers graze its smooth surface, then wallpaper again that feels like the skin of a dried orange. I continue forward until I reach the area where the wallpaper is starting to peel off. I stop. Carefully, I cross back to the other side of the hallway. Okay, keep walking until—

The doorframe bumps against my right hand. Kel's. Should I knock? Would Jeremy hear that? I mean, Phil. Where is he, anyway?

I have to send a message. I curl my fingers into a fist, tap against the door. Kel must be waiting to hear from me now that everything's dark. She's got to be waiting on the other side. Oh, please . . .

Another knock. "Kel," I whisper urgently and then stop, knowing the price I'm paying. "Kel, I—"

I hear a tap on the other side of the door. Relieved, I press my fingers near the source of the sound. I repeat the sound on my side. And then I hear the tapping again, moving down . . . down . . . down . . .

I follow the taps all the way to the floor. There's a soft push. She's slid her gift forward, through the crack underneath. I reach out for whatever Kel's sending my way.

Kel's gift scrapes against my knuckles. I pull back a bit. Reaching forward, I slide it out from under the door. I know what it is.

Something for a rainy day. Thank you, Kel.

I want to whisper to her, say thanks, but there's no time. He might hear. I've got to focus on what's ahead.

The house is eerily quiet, everything completely still. Where is he? He must be waiting somewhere. Why isn't there more noise? Why aren't the other guys scrambling around trying to get the lights back on?

Kel's gift makes me braver. I hold it close to my chest and push myself up using the door for support. With one hand touching the wall, I walk forward knowing even the smallest sound will give me away.

My eyes are starting to adjust to the darkness. I can make out shapes, somewhat. I can see what looks like a large black hole right across from Kel's room. I go forward, although every step seems like quicksand sucking at me.

A few steps later and I'm at the room he wants me to enter. My fingers hover at the edge of the doorframe. And I stop dead still, unsure. This is it, this is the room. Is he waiting inside?

A sound. Small, indistinct. Movement from the bedroom. A creak. Someone's in there. Waiting.

Him.

Did he hear me whispering to Kel? Sure he did. He knows I'm near. That means he's waiting for me to enter the black hole so he can spring his trap, so he can end this game with a quick leap forward and a—

No.

Moving forward is playing his game. That's what he expects. I think back to my conversations with Kel and smile. The trick is to make the game your own.

I back track, one hand tracing a line against the wall. Moving into that black hole is too much of an unknown, moving downstairs too risky. But if I go back, wait in the bedroom until he plays his hand . . .

With soft tentative steps, I tip-toe toward my bedroom. Creeping backward, inch by inch, and—

Suddenly, the floorboards make themselves known with a loud squeak. The sound echoes through the empty building. I stop where I am, paralyzed.

He must have heard. I look across the hallway, straining my eyes in the darkness. Where am I? Yes, I'm at my room. Another open black hole, but one I know. I tiptoe across the hallway as fast as I can. Past the radiator. Back to my room.

I hear movement at the far end. Cautious steps into the hallway. He's grown tired of waiting.

Where should I hide? The bathroom? No, that's too enclosed, he could trap me in there. I can try the kitchen area. Yes, the spot where the refrigerator used to be. I can hide in there until he—

Footsteps down the hall.

"Kami?" His voice breaks the silence, trying to sound friendly. "You there?" His footsteps are closer to my bedroom. "Where are you? It's Jeremy."

My belly tightens. I'm so sick of that name.

"We don't have much time!" He's by the door now, inches from where I'm standing. I hold my breath. This is it. I know it. Any moment now and the trap will spring.

"Kami?" He's right near me. I can hear the pleasure in his voice, the thrill of the chase. "I know you're there."

And then, softly: "I think you figured out my surprise, didn't you?" The tone in his voice has changed. It's darker. I think he likes it that way.

I'm so close to him I can smell his cologne. He chuckles. It makes my skin crawl. "Come on, Kamkitty." He makes his way farther into the room. Is he by the couch? "Let's get this over with. You can't hide forever, can you?"

I hold Kel's gift behind my back, hold on for dear life. Maybe I can make a break for it, run past him . . .

Wait. The door. It automatically locks from the inside. If he's far enough in, maybe I can run out, close it. He'd be locked in, and I can run down the hall, open the window, and head for freedom.

Can I do it? I've no choice. Carefully, I place Kel's gift in my back pocket, close my eyes for a few seconds. And then: 1 . . . 2 . . . 3 . . .

"What's that?"

I'm making a run for it. But then there's a quick fumble and a crash and the sound of footsteps following. I try to stay focused, grope for the door, swing it closed. If I can shut it, then . . .

A hand grabs a hold of my shoulder.

"Gotcha!" He yanks me toward him.

I bite my lip. He's not going to get the satisfaction of hearing me scream. He laughs anyway. "Little bitch. Trying to lock me in, were you?" His face is next to mine, his hands rough, possessive, holding my arms tightly.

He turns me around, pushes me forward through the darkness, through the room. I'm finding it hard to breath. My ribs are killing me. He pushes me into the bedroom.

"Looks like you lost again." He shoves me onto the bed. I feel a sharp stab in my left leg. It hurts like hell, and I cry out, try to push away from the mattress.

I hear him undoing his belt. "That was fun, wasn't it? Kept things interesting, pretending to be Barbara and Jeremy. Don't you think? You may not like the next game as much."

The back of my leg feels sticky and wet. The pain's worse than ever. What? Oh. Kel's gift.

The knife. And he doesn't know I have it.

I hear his pants drop to the floor. Instinctively, I draw the knife out of my back pocket and place it in front of me. It's clear what's going to happen next.

He grabs my hair. Pulls me to him.

With a cry, I push the knife forward. I can feel it make contact, dig into him. The cut is surprisingly easy. A bit of resistance, then in like a hot knife through cold butter. I wasn't expecting that. He pushes himself away, screaming. I hear a fumble, then a crash. He must have hit the nightstand and smashed the red ball lamp.

Screw the red ball. I scramble off the bed. Push the knife forward again. And again.

"Fuck!" His screams are louder. He's yelling at the top of his lungs. He lurches forward, shouting obscenities. His hands grab for my arms my shoulders. Then they're around my neck, gripping tighter and tighter. "Bitch!"

His tight grasp makes it hard to breathe. I slash with the knife. He yowls. His hands are off my neck. I can breathe. Fresh air. It feels good. I take another drag of air.

No use. His hands are everywhere. They're on the knife. We struggle for control.

The knife's pointing my way.

Frantically, I twist my body. He's too strong. Pain slices deep in my right side. I'm screaming now. My hands slip off the knife. I crash to the bed. It hurts so bad so bad—

He makes a soft grunting noise. My breath is quick and shallow, little gasps of pain. "You bitch." The air changes, He's moving forward.

The knife.

It's the only way to stop him. Make it fast. I lift my leg and kick out. Every ounce of fear and rage goes tight between his legs.

He grunts, air whooshing out of him.

I climb off the bed, but he grabs my shoulders and pushes me against the bureau. He shoves me back against it. His body presses down upon mine.

I grab for the knife. Have to get it. Everything's so wet so slippery. So much pain. His hands slip in the blood. He can't get a grip.

The knife shifts. Crash! We're on the floor.

"Bitch!" The air is full of BITCHES, isn't it, Phil? On the floor as we struggle his face is next to mine. My eardrums thunder with his curses.

Can't listen.

He's on top of me, crushing me. My ribs creak. He hits me again. I gasp and let go. No, no!

I need the knife. The knife or I'll lose everything. Without the knife I'm—

A sharp jab to my stomach. Hard. Solid. Then wet and warm. I feel a wet warm spot in my middle, sticky, oozy stuff running through clothes. The knife. Slashing me as we fall.

I close my eyes. Dizzy. So weak.

He's so heavy, pressing me into the carpet. He thrashes about, hits me in the face. Flopping like a fish out of water. Is this what dying is like?

It's so hard to breathe. No air no air.

I pull together the last rags of energy and raise my hands, reaching up to touch—

Whatever is up against me is smooth. The pain in my belly is nothing to the fire in my side.

Wait. That's not the blade.

It's the handle.

It hurts. It presses between us. Stiff, hard, unyielding. I bet it hurts him more. He got the point end.

It's in deep. He flops and squeals. No more bitch. No more curses. Just please and pleas and begging for help.

Who's the bitch now, Jeremy?

The begging turns to whimpers that fade into the darkness with the hard end between us. And then . . .

Silence.

I lie there in the darkness, his body on mine. Air scrapes down my throat. The hard end of the knife is still hurting me. I need to get up. I need to crawl away from the pain.

The room feels empty. Still.

He's not moving. Is he dead?

The only breathing is the air that rasps up and down my throat. His chest doesn't rise and fall against mine the way it did all those nights when we shared secrets.

Is he . . . ?

Did I . . . ?

He's dead. He must be.

I have to get out of here. Fast. But how? He's so heavy.

The angels on the wall press closer, tighter. I'm trapped. Weighed down. I have to get away.

I can't stay. Have to get away. Can't stay. Nonononononono. I push against his weight. He won't move. I push again. Beat at him with my fists. He doesn't move.

No!

With all my strength I push with my hands, jackknife my knees. Then his body tips, shifts, slides to the floor.

I stifle the scream. Hold back the tears.

With tears trailing down my cheeks, a wailing cry creeps out between my lips. Someone's downstairs. We're never alone. Someone must have heard Jeremy (Not-Jeremy) scream. Heard the scramble, the crash to the floor. They must have. How could they not?

Using the bed, I push myself up. I twist and squirm my legs from beneath him. I'm free.

Blindly, I push forward. Over his body. I'm on top of him, and it's so slippery. There's so much blood. Can't stop. Have to push forward.

I climb over his body. My leg gives out and I fall down onto his chest, feel a hard jab to my upper thigh. I muffle the scream building up inside me. It's the handle of the knife. I scramble across the floor beyond the spreading darkness.

I stop, panting. Wait. Keys. He has the keys to every room in the place. The silver keys on the Cat's eye keychain. I need them.

Breathing in shallow gasps, I reach down, force myself to search along the floor. He took off his pants. Where are they? Oh, here we go. Pockets.

Success. Oh, and his phone, too.

I grab both, scramble to my feet. Make my way through the room, reeling drunkenly. I have to get out. Get away while I still can.

I stumble through the living room past the kitchenette toward the door. Moving forward, arms out, no longer worrying about the noise. Somehow my fingers scrape wood, and I'm out in the hall. Down the corridor, fingers brushing the walls, I touch doorways, counting. Kel's room.

In my head the cherubs whisper. They've been watching it all. "You killed him. Murderer. He's dead, he's dead. You'll never get to heaven that way."

I have to get out of here fast.

I'm at Kel's room. I want to call out, knock on her door let her know what's happened. Set her free with the keys. Get away. No time.

I push away across the hallway enter the black hole.

Jeremy (Not-Jeremy) said he has a window in the bedroom. Can I open it? Climb out? Doesn't matter how high. All that matters is getting out to the street, away from this place.

Inside the black hole my teeth chatter. It's cold. Must be the window. It's open. Freedom.

I need to keep moving. I bang into a cabinet. The pain doesn't reach me. I don't care about the pain. Not the blood from my leg or the squeaks on the floorboards or the noise. Have to keep going forward. Move! Move!

Seconds later, my hands sink into softness. It has to be a bed. He said the place is like my room. I climb up, searching around for a window. Must be there, must be. Where?

The surface is flat and smooth. Where's the window? It's all flat all flat nothing no ridges no curtains no window nothing. Why does this remind me of my last night at Mom's house climbing out the window hurting my ribs? Can't stop, but there's no window here no exit.

No window. No exit.

He lied. Again. Lied totally.

No choice. Have to go downstairs. I'll face whoever's down there, but I don't have the knife. What can I do? What hope is there? Oh, God, I'm so scared but I have to keep moving have to keep going

Wait, I have the keys. I can open Kel's door. Set her free. We'd have power in numbers. More power than being all alone.

And then the lights snap on.

I blink, eyes streaming, adjusting to the light. I stare down at my clothing. Blood covers my pants my shirt my hands. Oh God, my hands are so red. Blood. His blood all over me. Covering me, his blood . . .

Shouts. Footsteps banging up the stairs. Down the hall.

But the blood. Blood on my hands. On my body.

More shouting. I fall to my knees. What's going to happen next.

I have to use his phone. Call someone. Call for help.

I drop the keys and fumble with the phone. My hands are slick with blood. Have to do this quick, have to do this quick. Oh thank God, no password.

The phone slips out of my hand. Dammit! I reach down and—

I hear a commotion in the hallway. Outside this room.

Lights glare at me. Voices shouting. Curses, then . . . .

Blackness.

CHAPTER THIRTY-THREE

DAY TWO

There's a red smear on the floor.

I'm back in the bedroom. The one where I stabbed Jeremy. I mean, Phil. Phil. I have to get used to saying that. Jeremy is someone I never knew.

I never knew Phil either. Everything with him was made up, every second, every single nighttime conversation. It was all a game. For him, at least.

I didn't black out for too long, I don't think. I know I was awake when they found me, barely. I heard voices over me. Two men.

"Christ, that's a lot of blood."

"In the hall, too. What a mess."

"Should we-"

"Leave her here. Let's see how he's doing."

"She has his phone. What the hell was he thinking?"

A dirty laugh. "Not this."

"Crazy bastard had this idea about taping a live kill. Thought he might get noticed that way."

"He got noticed, all right. The members are freaking out. I wouldn't want to be Phil."

I wouldn't want to be Phil either.

Air around me, arms around me, then floating like the angels, and a soft landing. A bed under me. It was a short flight. Must be Jeremy, no, Phil's bed. That is, if this really was his room. Who knows if he was even telling the truth about that?

"Damn! Look at my arms. I don't get paid enough for this."

More laughter, then the door closes. Silence.

No one came back for what felt like hours. I'd hear movement in the hall. Angels flying up and down the corridor? One time, I heard two men yelling at each other.

The yelling woke me. I opened my eyes and tried to get my sense of bearing. They left the lights on. I looked down, at my body, at the bed. They were right. Damn, that's a lot of blood.

The white bed sheets dyed red like an old tie-dyed shirt. Old blood. New blood. My blood?

I gingerly felt around. The cut in my left side was bleeding. A fleeting touch and PAIN. No more touching. I sat there, shivering, head throbbing, wondering what next. I'd give anything for some Roxi.

I needed to know how bad things were, so I pushed up the left side of my T-shirt. Some of the blood had dried, sticking the cloth to my skin. I inched it away from the old blood. A sticking tearing sound followed. It hurt. Like a bandage being ripped. Clenching my teeth, I yanked. It was like ripping off a layer of skin.

I stared at my side. The cut crossed the bruises along my ribs. It looked raw, about an inch across. I fingered the area around the cut. Blood seeped up over my fingers. Definitely still bleeding.

I limped to the bathroom. I needed a washcloth. Good, towels. I grabbed one and ran it under the faucet until the water steamed, holding onto the sink for support. I wrung it out as much as I could and placed the towel against my side. It stung like hell. After a while the white towel was red.

So I dropped the towel and grabbed a dry one. A hand towel. I pressed it to my side, ignoring the pain, and limped back to bed.

I lay gently down and drifted into the darkness and out again, grasping at the threads of sleep. My head throbbed in time with the blood pulsing out of the cut in my side. I was dozing when the door opened again.

For a second I thought it was Jeremy coming for his nighttime visit. When I opened my eyes, I recognized bouncer man. He stood by the bed, arms folded. He didn't look happy.

"Get up."

I struggled up.

He frowned. "You stained the bed."

Stained the bed. Yeah, I guess so.

"Get out of those clothes," he ordered.

I stumbled up from the bed then hesitated for a moment as he stood there. Pain and modesty made me brave. "Aren't you going to leave?"

"Do it!"

As carefully as I could, I lifted my shirt. Good thing I had taken care of the cut earlier. It was easier this time. I removed my shirt and unbuttoned my pants and stepped out of them. The towel fell to the ground.

"Phil cut you," he said.

I stood there in my underwear, teeth chattering. I nodded.

"You'll need new clothes. And a box of bandages. That's the best I can do."

He walked to the hallway. Obediently, I followed him. He grabbed my arm as soon as I reached the door. As if I had enough energy to jump him and beat him to the ground. As if.

He led me back to my room. Barbara's room. It had never been anyone else's.

I wasn't sure what I was going to see, but I refused to close my eyes. The bedroom was trashed. Someone had tried to clean things up. The sheets and pillow cases had been changed. My thin orange blanket was now a thin blue one. The red ball lamp was gone. Figured. Goodbye, eighties. The TV was gone, too. Again. That crashed to the floor when we hit the bureau.

And now I'm here looking down at the red smear on the floor. Not dried blood. Just a faint stain. Something to remind me. Like an old coffee stain or a drink from a party. Memories written in the carpet.

Is Phil dead? No one's said. What will they do with his body? Will he end up unnamed and unremembered, like Jeremy? Like Angelina? Like Barbara? Like whoever it was the week before that and whoever it will be in the weeks to come?

Like me, soon enough?

Soon enough.

The bed is uncomfortable and I feel like shit. My side gnaws and throbs. Better take care of that. Carefully as I can, I get out and limp to the bathroom.

The bandages haven't arrived yet. Will they ever? Dammit, bouncer man promised and everything. Oh well, at least the bathroom has a small towel, like the one in Jeremy's room. I mean Phil's. It'll do.

I grab it and walk back to the bed, drop down on top of the new, clean sheets and start to fade. Within minutes, I'm fast asleep, even with the lights on.

When I wake up, it's the next morning. Or at least it feels like morning. The lights are still on.

Something seems off. Maybe because I'm half-expecting someone to unlock the door and serve me breakfast. Trade small talk. That world's gone.

And another thing. It seems later than usual. Not early morning. More like noon?

I climb out of bed. I glance over toward the bureau to make certain last night happened. It did. The red smear on the floor reminds me.

More blood on the white sheets. Am I still bleeding? Have to peel the towel off to find out. I wince as it catches, but it falls away. Yep, still bleeding, but not as much as last night.

Gotta pee. I head for the bathroom. Oh look, the lights are still on in the living room. And the bathroom. Good, there are clean clothes on the sink. Bandages, too. Bouncer man may not say much, but he's a man of his word.

It's weird waking up on my own. Jeremy . . . Phil . . . always arrived bright and early. Where's breakfast?

I yawn loudly and try to stretch out my arms, but stop when a branding iron sears my left side. Guess I'll need to take a better look at the damage again.

I slip out of my underwear and drop the towel. I step into the shower, twist the knob. A cold burst of water spits out. Old building, old pipes. Hot water takes a while.

The cold water is good against my body. It almost makes me feel alive, for a moment. While I wait for some heat, I examine my body, black and blue and yellow and streaked with blood.

His blood's there. I want his blood off me. Last night I couldn't care less, but now I can't stand it any longer. My skin itches.

When the water steams, I scrub and I scrub and I scrub until my skin is raw. My ribs mutter with pain, but the blood is gone. Down the drain with the rest of Phil.

When I'm done, I dry off and grab the box of bandages. It takes at least half a dozen to cover the wound. From the looks of it, they won't stay on for long. Exhausted, I wrap the last clean towel around my body and exit the bathroom. I only make it to the green couch before my legs fail me. I don't even care if it's gross or if the blanket has slipped mostly to the floor. I collapse onto the rusty cushions, adding a little fresh rust, wondering whether someone will ever pay a visit.

###

Hours pass. No one comes.

I check my side. The blood has soaked through the bandages. I clamp my hand to my side and walk back to the bathroom to get some more. I pull the bandages off and drop them into the trash. Grab fresh bandages from the box. Cover the cut. Not enough. Already, I'm running low.

To pass the time I dress. Comb my hair. Brush my teeth. Try to find some normal. I'm so far from normal it's pathetic.

I go to the computer. Log on. Kel IM's me right away.

KELAIDESCOPE: RU all right???

KAMKIT: Yeah. I don't think Phil is

KAMKIT: Did you have breakfast today?

KELAIDESCOPE: Of course. Not from Phil.

KAMKIT: How about lunch?

KELAIDESCOPE: Yes.

I want to ask her about the knife, but I don't dare. If they read our IMs that would be bad for her. Right now, Kel can't be blamed for anything. Better keep it that way.

I hang around the computer until around three. That's when I can't stand it any longer. I run to the bathroom and turn on the tap. I keep it running until it's super cold, then place my mouth underneath the faucet and take a long drink. God, I'm so thirsty.

It looks as though my deluxe hotel accommodations have been cut off. But for how long?

February 5

Help me. I said Help me. How stupid can you get?

With nothing to do except stare at the same old walls, the only thing to do is use the computer. I'm logged on as Barbara to see if I still can. Since Phil was the one checking on me, it now makes sense that Barbara's ID still works. He didn't know I knew. Jeremy did.

I'm reading Barbara's diary. I never looked through all of it after I discovered it. And yet I'm probably the only person who will ever read about her life.

Im not sure why I said it either. Jeremy says he can take care of me that theres nothing to wory about when it comes to being chosen. He says Kel and Angeleena and Tori might go - will go - but that I have nothin to worry about. I want to believe him I DO but why cant he take me out of here if he cares about me the way he says he does???

My stomach rumbles. The lack of food is starting to get to me. Maybe it's also not knowing what's going to happen next. I'm feeling shakier than someone on their eighth cup of coffee.

February 7

Why did I have to do it? He gave me a gift a gift no one else here has because he said I'm special I meant a lot to him And I have to be stuipid about the whole thing stupid and go talking to her. Who the hell is she and no I didnt start talking to her she started talking to me. Christ I hate her

No I dont I dont even know what Im saying.

But why did I start this thing with Kami? Why didnt I ignor her I SHOULD HAVE KNOWN SHE WOULD TRY TO GET HELP Maybe I wanted her to I dunno only now Phil knows and even Jeremys mad and scared because they know its me and how could I be so stupid damn damn damn

Phil hit me He flew in the room and I could see the look in his eyes It scared me He screamed out my name and hit me He walkd right up and grabbed me started to shake me. I tried to push him away Of course that made everything worse

Jeremy saved me. He ran in, looking like a crazy man. I thought the two of them were going to kill each other Guess I was also hoping Jeremy would win and maybe get me out of here

Jeremy and Phil were sepparated and taken out of the room.

The point is Jeremy saved me

Saved her. So Jeremy had been trustworthy, after all. It was Phil, not Jeremy, who hit her. He may not have had the strength to find a way out, but clearly, in his own way . . .

He said he loved me LOVED ME! After all the trouble Ive been to him after I betrayed him like that He says he loves me and I love you too Jeremy and I wish I hadnt screwed up and done this stupid thing. I'd take that hit ten times over if only I could stop this whole thing

He says hes going to work it out. He says I dont have to worry about this Friday. He said its all going to be okay God I love him, and I just wish

But Ive got to talk to Kami I have to see if she talkd to someone. what she said

I did talk to someone, Barbara. And I'm so, so sorry.

But you were wrong. You didn't screw up. You were only human. Phil had no right to hit you. They had no right, none of them, to treat you the way they did. The way they treat all of us. You shouldn't have blamed yourself for telling me. I wish you'd told me more. Maybe if you had none of this . . . well, maybe I could have found another way to help.

I wipe away the tears and scroll down.

February 7

Ive lived here for almost six months. Six months! In some ways its like six years. I hardly remember what its like to be outside this room. To be on the outside with other people.

I hardly remember what my mother looks like either or the little room we used to live in with the front door that never closed

It gets harder and harder to remember my mom. Especially when I take stuf. Jeremy just gave me some It gets harder to rember and probly pretty soon I wont want to write any more. But I do now. Because I think this may be the last time I right anything in here, dear diary

I think tonight its my time. I think Jeremy does too, even though he wont say that to me.

I can see it in his eyes. Those beautiful green eyes. I love to look into them I love to kiss him I love to stare at him. I couid stare at him for hours. He gives me hope. He makes me fly even more than the angels do

More than anything, I wish I could say goodbye to Mom one last time. She wasnt the best person in the world and had problems. Problems I picked up from her. But I do know she loved me and I dont like to think of her wondring where I went

That gets me thinking about my own mom. I didn't know before she left that night I'd never see her again. I'd been too distracted. Thinking about Barbara. I hardly said goodbye. Where is she now? What has she been going through?

I remember warm summer nights, reading under my sheets while mom lay next to me. I remember the flashlight and the nightgown and the ript copy of Lion Witch Wardrobe I would read. I rember mom tickling me and teasing me and calling me a bookworm

It was the 2 of us Always the 2 of us

I wish things had turned out difrently

My heart is breaking. I wish things had turned out differently, too.

I love U mom. And Im so so sorry.

I love you too, Mom. I wish I had the chance to tell you how strong you were after Dad died. I didn't tell you even once. I should have. You kept things together. You worked so hard.
I wish I had been better I wish we had spent more time together. Movies and Chocolate Silk. I wish I knew what I had when I still had it.

And I love you Jeremy. And whatever happens tonight . . .

Whatever happens.

Ill get through it. Im scared to death. But whatever happens you never need to doubt my love Never

That's the end of her diary. Well, except for the note to me. She must have typed those words right before they turned on the equipment.
She knew she was going to die that night. That she was going to be chosen. She didn't seem to even want to put up a fight. Maybe all those months of living alone had kicked the fight out of her. Killed her hope.
I wipe the tears from my eyes. I'm not ready to give up like that. I don't want to go down, not ever. I don't want to end my days as part of this sick, twisted game.
There has to be a way out. A way I haven't considered yet. I have to get these walls to fall down, to break free.
The walls! The wall behind my bed. This is the time to try and tear down that wallpaper. No one's going to care. And even if they do, better try now while I still have the chance.
Before I do, might be worth it to try one other thing. Back to PeoplesCam to log in as Barbara, the way I've done so many times the past few days.

GOASKALICE: Josh?

GOASKALICE: Josh, are you there? I need you so bad.

I glance over at her friend's list. Wirehanger isn't on at all even though he's been added. But wait a minute . . . looking at the list . . . what the hell?

NIGHTQUEEN22: Babyfish??

Someone's logged on . . . as me?

CHAPTER THIRTY-FOUR

DAY ONE

Now I'm flying with Barbara's angels.

I'm on the floor staring at the red wallpaper, at the tiny cherubs with the little wings and puckered lips. Sometimes I reach up and touch the wallpaper and let my fingers drift down caressing their tiny smiles. I wish they could whisper secrets to me. After all, they've seen enough of ours.

They finally fed me around noon after a day and a half of starvation. It happened right after I had pushed back my bed and was starting to pull back the wallpaper.

I heard footsteps in the living room. Cautiously, like they were afraid I might attack. It made me smile. I didn't have a knife any more. What could I do?

As soon as they left, I went to see what there was to see. I found a tray resting on the counter in the kitchenette. My stomach rumbled, and without thinking I rushed over and began shoving food in my mouth. They wouldn't poison me, right? After all, they needed me for tonight. For the entertainment. I was talent after all.

It was chicken and rice and a bottle of coke. The chicken tasted chalky so I washed it down with a lot of soda.

I think there was something in the chicken. Maybe they sprinkled in some Roxi, maybe something worse. All I know is when I finished eating I headed for my room to go back to tearing down the wallpaper, and before I could get there, I felt the room turn upside down. Pretty soon everything was spinning and it was hard to stand. I fell to the floor and tried crawling to my bed. All I wanted was to lie down. I wasn't able to make it that far, though. I ended up collapsing on the floor, right next to the red smear.

Now I'm awake on the floor and staring at angels. The taste in my mouth is awful. It burns slightly and my head is swimming.

I hear sounds in the other room. Is that what woke me? What's going on?

I lean with my hand against the bed for balance. Steady, steady. I shove hair out of my eyes then raise myself. The earth is spinning, spinning world. The minute I'm up I want to sit down as a wave of nausea washes over me.

The sounds are louder in the other room. Someone is heading to the bedroom. To me. I want to find a way to protect myself, but I'm so dizzy so dizzy.

Someone drags me up, holds me. The side with the cut rips apart, but whoever's lifting me doesn't care. The pain forces my eyes open and when I look up it's someone I've never seen before. A man with a shaved head and a big thick moustache. He looks stronger than Phil. Is this my new keeper? My new Phil?

He carries me like a rag doll. His touch feels strange. I look down; he's wearing black gloves. I try to get my bearings, to fight back, struggling in his arms. I'm too weak.

"Where you taking me?" My voice sounds like an echo of an echo.

He leads me to the Black Room. Sits me down in the chair. And then the echoes and the chalk don't matter anymore. I remember what day it is, what time it has to be.

Time. It must be time.

I see the red blinking light on the floor by the chair. The box.

"No, come on." Weakly I batter at him, push him away, grab at his face.

He grabs me back. He grips my hand and pushes it down and then grabs me by the chin. "Stop it." He reaches down and pushes my legs apart to strap me in.

"Please don't do this," I beg, blinking back tears.

It doesn't matter. He doesn't want to talk or play games the way Phil did. He snaps my left wrist to the chair. And like that it's seven days earlier and I'm chained to the seat and there's no way to stop what's going to happen next.

I'm trapped. Like Angelina. Like Barbara. I know they're going to pick me tonight.

I am shaking all over. "Please don't do this."

"Already done." He walks behind me so I can't see him directly, only his image in the computer screen over the rows of live PeoplesCams. "You've caused a lot of trouble. Phil's not going to be easy to replace."

This man sounds different. He sounds almost official, not like Phil at all. I must be talking to somebody higher up. A boss. "Phil shouldn't have been playing games."

"No, he shouldn't have."

On the screen, I see him playing with the edge of one of his gloves. His voice is smooth. Corporate. I wonder if he has a wife. Or children. I wonder if they know what he does for a living, where all his money comes from.

"Then again, Jeremy shouldn't have taken up with your friend. That's where this whole thing began. It ends tonight."

"Why do you do this?" My words are slurred. "Just tell me why."

"Why should you care about that?" He doesn't have a trace of emotion in his voice.

"I do! How can you . . . do this?"

"Do what? I think we're extremely generous. You girls get a place to stay. You get fed. Clothing. You get to play on the Internet all day long. Most teenagers would kill for all that."

Kill. I hear the striking of a match. What's he doing? Then, the stench of a strong cigar. Smoking? "So what if a few wards of the state get taken away once a week? That's the price of admission, young lady."

I raise my left hand, struggling against the steel link. I want him gone. I don't want to hear his words any more. I don't want to smell his cigar. I want him out of here.

But he continues on. "Do you know what GKS stands for, young lady?"

I shake my head. No. I don't care, either.

He takes a puff of his cigar. It smells like burnt paper and tobacco. The smell is way too strong for this tiny little room, and I think he likes it that way. "Of course you don't. We don't talk about those things with the performers. Each client is sworn to secrecy and they know the consequences if they speak, even to one of our employees."

Another puff. I think he likes having a captive audience. "GKS stands for the Gold Key Society, young lady. Do you know what a gold key is?"

My thoughts go to the key chain that Phil carried with him everywhere. But no, those keys were silver. This is bigger than that.

"People like to think it's a Christian symbol, although of course, like so many things, we stole it from the Romans." Oh great, a history lesson. Old white guys. How fitting. I stare dully at his reflection in the screen as he puffs at his cigar. "Perhaps that's too harsh. Borrowed is perhaps a better word. Influenced? No matter. Do you know who Saint Peter is?"

No. Can you please shut up and leave?

"He's known as the Gatekeeper of Heaven. Holds the keys to the Kingdom. One key is gold, and it opens the gates. The other one is iron. You can guess what that one does. Right?"

Another puff. "All we do is to open the kingdom of heaven to one lucky girl each week. A ticket to freedom from this land of pain and sorrow and our base needs and wants. Our clients have the privilege of voting on who that fortunate soul shall be. At least, that's our sales pitch."

I hear a squeak on the floorboard. He's moving away. "We do this because there's a market for it," he says. "Enjoy the show."

The door to the Black Room closes with a soft click. Cigar smoke lingers in the air.

I don't even wait to make sure he's gone. I push my chair forward and reach down as far as I can to turn off the computer. I'm logging on as Barbara one last time.

As the computer shuts down, a message pops up. Probably Kel. I glance over at the clock. It's late. I slept away most of the day. What time is it?

11:12. Eighteen minutes until a decision. Not much time. Why did they wait so long to wake me up?

It won't take them long to figure out I've logged off. They need me for this show. I don't have much time.

It isn't easy moving around with one hand. "You'll find a way," Phil had said to me sarcastically the night Angie died. I'm finding a way, now.

GOASKALICE: Josh, you there?

And then. The blissful sound of a leopard purr.

NIGHTQUEEN22: Kami.

NIGHTQUEEN22: I've been waiting here all night.

It was smart of Josh to figure out that Phil blocked all outside IDs to make sure I didn't talk to anyone. But Phil of course didn't bother blocking the one person Barbara spent so many nights talking to in the first place. Me.

Of course that had been when I was on the outside looking in. Now I'm in Barbara's place and Josh is in mine. Alice and the Black Queen are talking to each other again, even if the names behind the names have changed.

GOASKALICE: Josh I can't talk for long

NIGHTQUEEN22: Where have you been all day?

GOASKALICE: I've been out of it. Long story

GOASKALICE: Where's Uncle Dom?

NIGHTQUEEN22: I spoke to your mom and they're close he wants me to tell you he's close

GOASKALICE: Hope he's close. I don't have much time

GOASKALICE: Call my mom, Josh. Please tell her

GOASKALICE: I love her.

GOASKALICE: I love you, too Josh

GOASKALICE: That kiss.

GOASKALICE: What did you mean by that kiss?

NIGHTQUEEN22: I meant I wanted to be more than friends, Kami. I have for a long time.

NIGHTQUEEN22: Maybe that's why it never worked out with anyone else. I only wanted to be with you

NIGHTQUEEN22: And I'm going to. I'm going to kiss you again, Kami. You'll get help. I promise

GOASKALICE: I don't know things are going to happen soon.

GOASKALICE: Josh, do me a favor, would you?

NIGHTQUEEN22: Anything

GOASKALICE: Its going to sound weird

GOASKALICE: But

GOASKALICE: Can you tell me a blonde joke?

NIGHTQUEEN22: What???

GOASKALICE: I want

GOASKALICE: I want more than anything

Tears sting at my eyes.

GOASKALICE: I want to pretend life is normal again. The way it used to be. You and me in the prop room eating lunch and joking

GOASKALICE: Tell me the one about the two blondes in heaven.

NIGHTQUEEN22: There were these two blondes waiting at the gates of heaven and they start talking to each other

NIGHTQUEEN22: And the first blonde says "How did you die?" And the second blonde says "I froze to death"

NIGHTQUEEN22: So the first blonde says

NIGHTQUEEN22: Kami

NIGHTQUEEN22: Kami, I can't don't this

NIGHTQUEEN22: I'm too sad. It's too

NIGHTQUEEN22: I'm too

GOASKALICE: It's okay, Josh. I understand.

GOASKALICE: I have 2 go anyway. Tell my mom. Please?

NIGHTQUEEN22: I will

NIGHTQUEEN22: Kami

NIGHTQUEEN22: I love you too

Josh, why couldn't you have said that sooner? Why couldn't we have had this talk face to face? Instead you gave me a kiss and ran off. Why do we have to say these words this way, when it would have been so much different, if only—?

At least we finally got to say it.

GOASKALICE: Bye, Josh.

I sign off because I have to switch back. Time's up. The clock says 11:20. Time's going by way too fast and no way will Uncle Dom ever get here in time even if the police do figure out where we're at. No way I won't be named tonight, either.

I log back on as Kamkit. To the purple and blue PeoplesCam colors and the row upon row of webcam screens.

What was that stupid slogan? "PeoplesCam—Connecting you to the rest of the universe."

Hello, universe. Here I am.

"GKS: Let the game begin!"

They're all there: Kel and Lea and Kim, and all the other performers waiting for the day their number gets called. Probably most are happy it's my turn this time around.

Do they even know? From the looks on their faces they're all sweating it out with no idea that I'll be taking one for the team. Makes it more entertaining that way I guess. Here we are now. Let us entertain you.

I look at the faces of the girls I've gotten to know, all trapped in their little boxes. Lea, with her wild hair and bad attitude trying to hide that she's scared to death. Kim with her iPod on, swaying to her music pretending she's somewhere else. That it's not going to happen again.

And Kel. Kel with her books. Kel the smartest of all of us lost girls. She starts sending messages right away.

KELAIDESCOPE: Kami! I saw you on a few minutes ago, but I didn't know what happened.

KELAIDESCOPE: You weren't on last night.

KELAIDESCOPE: After all the moving I was worried.

KAMKIT: Nothing to worry about Kel. Not last night

KAMKIT: Tonight's a different story

KAMKIT: The fireworks are starting soon.

11:25. I glance over at the chat window. The host is on tonight keeping the action moving.

DRUSIUS: Five minutes until this week's GKS finalist will be named! Voting will end in sixty seconds so make certain you've made your selection before it's too late.

The chat room goes crazy with all the girls making last minute appeals and the visitors filling the space with not-so-empty threats.

TANGERINEWILDE: 1 MORE WEEK GUYS WAIT TILL YOU SEE WHAT I GOT NEXT WEEK

VISITOR68: I want to vote for Weathervayne.

VISITOR39: Yes! Great idea.

Of course that has its desired effect. Even in her medicated trance she reacts, crying out, tears streaming down her face.

"Not me," she begs. It's nice to hear her voice again, even if I found it so annoying the first time we met. "Please, please. Not me, please. Not me."

In some ways, I still feel like I'm on the outside looking in. It must be whatever they gave me still burning its way through my system. Or maybe all the blood I've lost or the cut on my side. Whatever. Maybe it's better this way.

So this is how the Queen of the Night ends her reign.

One night. One vote.

KELAIDESCOPE: You don't know that it's going to be you.

KELAIDESCOPE: What Phil did was stupid. They can't blame you for that.

The steel link hurts my wrist. I tug at it hoping I can find a way to break free. But even if I could there's still the link around my leg connected to the red blinking light. That's not going anywhere.

Behind my shoulder I feel a presence. The hair stands up on the back of my neck. I feel electric tingles down my back. Have the angels finally come down to play? Is Barbara waiting and watching the same way I watched her? Waiting to guide me . . .

KELAIDESCOPE: Don't worry, Kam. This might work out for you.

11:27

DRUSIUS: The voting has ended. In three minutes we'll announce this week's selection. Thank you for supporting GKS.

I stare at myself in the webcam barely noticing the endless stream of babble in the chat room. Not from Kel, not from the announcer.

I look awful. I look wild and spaced out and gross, the ghost of the person I once was. Who wouldn't vote me off? I look as if I'm dead already.

Uncle Dom, I wish you could have gotten here in time. Maybe when my time runs up you'll be able to find this place. Find out what the GKS is all about. Maybe that will mean hope for Kel and the others even if it's too late for me.

KAMKIT: Don't worry Kel. This might work out for YOU

11:29.

DRUSIUS: And the winner is . . ..

Despite all the lies I've told myself, I'm sitting on the edge of my seat my eyes glued to the screen. Part of me is still hoping someone else's name will be chosen. That even after everything I'll live to see another seven days. Because maybe then . . . maybe then . . .

DRUSIUS: ***KAMKIT***

It's me. Of course it is. But then there wasn't any question I was going to be chosen for the Late Night Show tonight, was there?

I brace myself for the next few minutes. Strap 'em in, it's going to be a bumpy ride . . . oh, look. I'm already strapped.

DRUSIUS: ***KAMKIT***

In the hallway, it sounds like a party's getting started. I hear a loud banging, and shouts.

DRUSIUS: ***KAMKIT***

I close my eyes and wait for the next moment. I pray and I prepare for what's coming. Knowing what's coming. After all I've seen it before with Barbara . . . with Angelina . . .

Oh, Barbara.

I hear the hum of the machine coming to life. It'll hit me like a fork in a toaster because I've seen it frame after frame and now I'm going to—

There's a spark and a crash. Something's burning. And my fingers tingle and I—

I hear voices all around me. Voices all talking at once. I have no idea what they're saying. It's so loud, so confusing. Then someone grabs me, shoves me. The chair's moving. It's wrenched backward. I hear a crash. I feel a wave of vertigo, but more than that, a shock in my legs running up my spine and a huge jolt of pain. I stiffen up—I scream—I open my eyes, but I can't see anything. Why can't I see anything? It's all blank and the pain is unbearable—the pain is—

I feel that presence over my shoulder again. Fluttering like the wings of a moth. Someone's in the room.

Somebody's waiting.

EPILOGUE

And now somehow I'm back in the bedroom and the teenage bed has been pushed all the way up against the bureau and my ribs and my side are no longer hurting at all, and I've got all the time I need to rip away at the cherub wallpaper to find out what's on the other side.

For some reason the cherubs are alive and watching me. Pointing and smiling. Flapping their little wings. One keeps winking at me and pointing upwards.

Rip. Rip. Riiiiiiip.

R.I.P.

And each time I rip off another strip of paper? The most amazing thing happens. I don't see plaster on the other side, just a view of clear blue sky. Free and open and inviting. Not cold at all.

When I've ripped off enough pieces of cherub from the wall to form a big wide hole of blue, I take the next step. I'm not even scared, either. I take a deep breath because I can do that now without it hurting. And I jump.

Now I'm falling through thin air.

Like oxygen, like oxygen.

The cherubs wave good-bye. And now I'm behind the wheel at last taking a spin in Daphne's fast little car, zooming down the highway at ninety miles an hour. The roof is down and the wind whips my hair around my face.

I've got my license to drive at last. I'm free.

The bright blue sky darkens in the blink of an eye. It's nighttime, but the darkness seems like a painting. The night canvas is a dark blue and the twinkling stars in the sky sparkle like diamonds. The road in front of me is one long ribbon up a mountain. I'm free from the tenement. From Phil. From everything.

The wind against my skin is flat and warm and two-dimensional. And there's music in the night, a dull throbbing bass line punctuated by a jazzy drumbeat.

Someone's sitting in the passenger's seat. I look over at Barbara next to me. She's wearing the tight black halter top she had on the night she was chosen, the night I was taken away from my world and transplanted into hers.

It's as if she's actually sitting there, no longer an image on a screen or a shadow over my shoulder. No longer a lonely whispering memory in a locked room.

"Barbara . . ." I don't know the right words.

She touches my hand. I can feel her touch, her soft fingers intertwined with mine, her fingertips brushing up against my palm. I look into her brown eyes. She seems so sad. Instinctively, I take my hand from hers, press it against her pale white face.

"Barbara, what's wrong?"

She shakes her head and smiles and glides closer to me until her lips hover near my ear. "Thank you." I feel a chill because she's next to me saying those words. The sincerity in her voice. It moves me to tears.

With her free hand, she points to the rocky, barren terrain. Oh right, I'm driving a car. At last. Somehow I've been freed. The road arcs upward getting steeper and steeper with each passing moment.

"Kami."

Next thing I know it's not nighttime at all. The sky's no longer dark blue; the stars have disappeared. All that's left is blinding white. The light's too strong. I want to cover my eyes, but I can't lift up my hands to do so.

Barbara?

No, no, it's someone behind me. I want to turn around, but the road's too twisty. I need to concentrate. Is it Josh? Is it Jeremy? There's no way of telling, although I can see Barbara looking into the back seat and smiling. Maybe it's Jeremy . . . the real one?

"Kami."

But I can't look back. The car veers off the road, spinning in the gravel. I'm losing control and then there's a jump and I cry out and—

I wake up.

I close my eyes. The room I'm in is way too bright. Practically blinding.

But I have to know where I am. Am I in heaven? Is this it? I open my eyes a crack to look around. Are there any angels flying around?

Interesting. It's definitely not the room I've lived in for weeks. Where have they taken me?

This room is too bright. This room has windows; it's a bright sunny day beyond the glass, the window glass.

Is it my bedroom? Am I back home? No, the sheets covering my body are white and the room is white and empty, the walls bare, the smell antiseptic. This is nothing like my messy bedroom filled with stuffed kitties and monkey pillows.

Oh, and a tube is sticking out of my arm. A tube? I follow the plastic serpentine trail that leads up to a plastic bag filled with clear liquid. Okay, an IV. Along with a plastic tag around my wrist with my name and my date of birth on it.

Oh. I must be in a hospital.

I hear someone stirring to my right. I'm not alone.

I turn my head. A man stands in front of a door. He's tall with wiry black hair and a salt and pepper beard. Gray sweater and dark pants and a gun attached to his belt.

I blink my eyes. A gun?

It's been so long since I've seen anyone besides the girls and Phil I'm completely disoriented. He looks familiar. Without the beard, he would look exactly like . . . wait . . .

I really am waking up from a dream.

"Uncle Dom?"

Yes. He grins and walks to the bed. "Kami."

I made it. It's impossible, but somehow I made it out alive. How?

"Where's Mom?" I'm free, this is crazy. I raise my head pushing myself up and shifting around.

Uncle Dom places a reassuring hand on my shoulder. "Relax. You need to take it easy. Your mother's downstairs getting something to eat. We didn't expect you'd wake up so soon."

"Were you . . . ?" I catch my breath, so relieved, practically babbling. "Were you the one in the room that . . ."

"No." His hand on my shoulder is soothing me, grounding me. "I wasn't in the building at all. I wish I had been." He sits down on the side of my bed. "From what I've heard, you've suffered quite a shock. Lost a lot of blood, too. You were lucky they got there when they did."

"I don't remember them at all. All I remember is a sound behind me, before they . . ."

"You were so out of it when they found you," Uncle Dom says softly.

"Who found me?"

Uncle Dom pats my hair. I know he's trying to be nice, but I wish he wouldn't. All I can think is how disgusting I must look. "You've had a lot of people searching for you. You were rescued by some of Chicago's finest."

"Chicago?" Well, look at that. I grin, pleased with my detective work.

"Joliet, which is on the outskirts." He looks down at me, his gaze deadly serious. "It's nice to have you back with us. That night you called me ..." He turns away. "Your mother was beside herself. It reminded me too much of ... well, I did everything I could to help."

"Mom said you'd always be there." I pat his rough hands. "I'm glad you were able to find me ..." I stop as realization sets in. "Us! Uncle Dom, what happened to the others?"

His hands twitch underneath mine. He tightens his grip and looks me straight in the eyes. "What do you mean?"

Mean? What does he mean? "What happened to the other girls? The ones in the rooms. Kel and Kim and Lea."

He clears his throat. It takes him a while to answer me. "Kami, you're going to be asked to speak to an officer in a while about what you saw in the—"

I know that. Of course I will. What is it he's holding back?

"What happened to the others, Uncle Dom?"

He lowers his voice. "There were no others, Kami."

"Were no ...?"

"It's the damnedest thing," he says. "Aside from your room and your computer, the place was completely abandoned. Stripped clean. We couldn't find a trace of anyone anywhere."

"That doesn't make sense." I want to sit up now and yank the IV out of my arm. "Kel had a room right down the hall from me! We used to meet downstairs, in the ..."

And then it all makes sense. "In the kitchen."

That's what they had been so busy with after they found me, after they returned me to the bedroom. That's what Kel meant when she asked if I was okay after all the moving. They were closing up shop, moving the other girls to another place. Disposing of the evidence.

Why hadn't they disposed of me?

The words of the bald man with the cold eyes: "We do it because there's a market for it."

They took their chances. Figured they could get one last show out of me. They got spooked because of Phil's death and decided to relocate the game. No sense relocating me. Not if I was going to be the one chosen that night. They could dispose of me afterwards.

Kel. Lea. Kim.

They're still stuck in the game. They're all out there somewhere waiting for their week to come. My being chosen only gave them seven more days.

Or did it?

The GKS and all the visitors have to know what happened to me. They would have seen it all online. Maybe Kel and the others would be safe. For a while at least. Maybe the GKS would decide to lay low, stop the late night show.

Maybe there was a way to bring them down after all. This isn't even close to being over. My computer's been recovered, after all. Barbara's diary is on it; that should prove I wasn't all alone. Maybe some of the data on the hard drive can help.

And then, there's me.

"I'll do whatever I can, Uncle Dom." I grip his hands as tightly as he grips mine.

"They'll want to talk to you then. Soon." He releases his grip and bends down to kiss my forehead. "Why don't I go get your mother? I know how bad she wants to see you."

I nod. "Yeah."

He walks to the door. Opens it, then turns back to me. His smile's returned. "Oh, and by the way. Someone else does, too."

I hardly hear him. I'm too wrapped up in thoughts of the girls. About what happens next. This isn't going to disappear without a trace, like the GKS sneaking into my house in the dead of night. Barbara's death is going to have meaning. This isn't over, even if-

"Hey."

That's when I notice Uncle Dom's gone and someone else is at the door.

Someone's there all right. Someone with a shock of red hair and too many freckles and a big wide smile . . . .

"Hello, babyfish."

My eyes grow wide. The next thing I know he's moving closer and I start to shiver. Then he's by my side and craning his head, moving down, so his face hovers over mine. I look into his eyes.

This time, Josh McBee doesn't settle for kissing my nose.

About T.J. Alexian

T.J. Alexian has been writing since the first grade, ever since his father tucked him to bed with stories about Nancy Drew's younger brother and the Lone Ranger and Tonto. And T.J.'s first thought: "I don't want these stories to ever end."

As a result, the stories kept going. The author of four novels and twelve plays, T.J. lives in a recently-purchased and greatly-rehabilitated stately green Victorian in Attleboro, Massachusetts, along with seven ghosts and his long-time (and long-suffering) partner. He also has three kids and one spiritual kid, and their stories and their spirit form the heart and soul of everything he does.

T.J. continues to write and create and currently has more novels in the works. Keep an eye out for *Confessions of a Diva Rotundo*, coming soon to an eReader near you.

Connect with T.J. Alexian

Finally, thank YOU for reading this book. I hope you enjoyed it. (and if you did, would you consider taking a moment to leave me a review?) If you like what you've read, I'm around and I'd love to hear from you. If you want to read more, you can follow me at:

Facebook: http://facebook.com/ted.mitchell.18

Subscribe to my blog:

http:// http://snapshotsfromeldredge.blogspot.com/

Made in the USA
Middletown, DE
28 March 2018